# Dance of Desire

Waltz music floated from the ballroom. He swung her into a gentle dance in the corner of the garden. Everything was proper, even the distance he maintained between them, but the movement wove a spell that affected her as never before. Her heart pounded in time with the music, and lightheadedness weakened her knees as magic filled the air.

Devall was stunned. He had not intended to waltz with her. He had not even intended to speak with her. His sole reason for slipping in without an invitation was to pass along information that would spread the gossip he desired. Or so he had thought.

And he certainly should not be keeping her here in the dark or leading her into a provocative dance that fed temptation. How long had it been since he had danced with a lady? How long since he had touched even the fingertips of a respectable female?

Without volition, his arms tightened. Stepping farther off the path, he caressed her lips with his own. . . .

# Devall's Angel

## by

## Allison Lane

A SIGNET BOOK

SIGNET
Published by the Penguin Group
Penguin Putnam Inc., 375 Hudson Street,
New York, New York, 10014, U.S.A.
Penguin Books Ltd, 27 Wrights Lane,
London W8 5TZ, England
Penguin Books Australia Ltd, Ringwood
Victoria, Australia
Penguin Books Canada Ltd, 10 Alcorn Avenue,
Toronto, Ontario, Canada M4V 3B2
Penguin Books (N.Z.) Ltd, 182-190 Wairau Road,
Auckland 10, New Zealand

Penguin Books Ltd, Registered Offices:
Harmondsworth, Middlesex, England

First published by Signet, an imprint of Dutton NAL,
a member of Penguin Putnam Inc.

First Printing, August, 1998
10  9  8  7  6  5  4  3  2  1

# Chapter One

"How can my own daughter be so foolish?" sobbed Lady Forley as their carriage pulled away from Hartleigh House. "You should have demanded Andrew's support. He could hardly have ignored both of us. You will never attract a husband without a proper come-out. Skimping on clothes and entertaining only lowers our credit."

She wrung her hands in exasperation when she received no response. "Why won't you listen to me? I was a respected London hostess for years before Andrew forced me away from town. How could my own son be so cruel? Or so stupid! If only your father were here! *He* would have sponsored a come-out ball. *He* would have provided a suitable wardrobe." She dabbed at her eyes with a lacy handkerchief. "And he would have escorted us to Lord Cavendish's masquerade, too."

Angela Warren sighed. Already exhausted from last-minute planning for the ball she was to share with Lady Sylvia, Lord Hartleigh's sister, she was in no mood for another confrontation—not that silence ever stifled her mother. Nor did logic, pleading, or cold, hard facts.

Lady Forley had already spent the afternoon arguing fiercely over every detail, determined to squander a fortune by staging the most lavish come-out London had ever seen. It had taken the combined efforts of Lady Hartleigh, Lady Sylvia, and herself to squelch her—not that any of them had heard the last of it. The woman continued her complaints long after they served any purpose. Lord Cavendish's masquerade was an example: It was over.

"Attending that ball would indeed have been foolish," Angela said wearily. "I was not out until the Queen's drawing room yesterday, and you know that none of Lord Cavendish's entertainments are suitable for green girls—especially his masquerades."

"Fustian. Your father always took me."

"But you were married. I am not. My reputation would never recover."

"Nonsense! You may brag about your intelligence, but you are remarkably ignorant of London customs. You even admit it, so why do you persist in ignoring my advice? Your father and I never missed a Season."

"You have forgotten the strictures on innocents." Angela sighed again. If only her mother possessed even the tiniest bit of sense. But Lady Forley was so excited over her return to London after a six-year absence, she often forgot that bringing out a daughter restricted them to Marriage Mart events. "Think, Mother! Would your parents have allowed you to grace one of his parties before your marriage? Grandmama Hollister was as high in the instep as Mrs. Drummond-Burrell. I doubt she approved that acquaintance even after you were wed. And you have forgotten the patronesses. Had we attended, Lady Sefton would have revoked my voucher so fast, your head would spin."

Lady Forley snorted, but the words obviously struck home. She tugged on her hat to change its angle, twisting to glimpse herself in the coach window. Preening had always been her way of dropping a subject without admitting fault.

"Just look at the muddle you and Andrew have made," she charged once the hat had been adjusted to her satisfaction. "Cruel fate, to leave me under the thumb of so ungrateful a son. His pinch-penny ways will ruin us. Our consequence is already reduced after skipping five Seasons. How are we to recover if he insists on pretending penury? I will never forgive him for selling Forley House. Upper Brook Street was a perfect location, commanding respect and even envy from our guests. Society's elite ran tame in my drawing room. And the balls! Such crushes! You can never make a noteworthy come-out from Clifford Street. Who will dare visit us? Half the neighbors are cits; there is barely room for morning callers and none for entertaining. But refusing to sponsor a come-out ball is beyond enough. His miserly ways will condemn you to spinsterhood."

Their coach rocked to a halt behind a tradesman's dray that

had broken a wheel. Carts and carriages jammed the street, their horses stamping and snorting. Shouts from drivers and pedestrians added to the pandemonium.

Angela sighed *again* at the delay, resigned to hearing another diatribe. The subject of their rented house resounded a dozen times a day—its small rooms, its worn furnishings, its unassuming location in a mixed neighborhood. "We have discussed this too often already, Mother. Andrew *had* to sell the house."

"Fustian! In a fit of pique, he deliberately cast away our consequence and reduced our credit. Oh, that your father were here! He always insisted we go first class."

"You wrong him," she snapped. The woman refused to believe even truths that stared her in the face—which was why Angela was nearly prostrate from nerves after only a fortnight in town. "*You* insisted on first class. It is *you* who have brought us to this pass. Papa was a scholar who preferred to remain in his study, but he denied you nothing, nearly bankrupting the estate. Had he not died, we would have lost everything. Thank God for Andrew's good sense. Selling a house he could not afford saved us even worse indignities. Without the money it brought, he would have lost every last acre of unentailed land, requiring fifty years instead of five to dig us out of the River Tick."

"You exaggerate, as usual. And display a vulgarity that belies your breeding. Proper ladies care nothing about money. Making a good impression is far more important. How can you find a husband without holding a fashionable ball? You will never attract a wealthy, titled gentleman if you hide in the shadows and claim poverty."

"I cannot imagine that our ball will be unfashionable." But her protest covered another surge of uncertainty. Oh, God! What if her mother was right? She *had* to marry this Season. Was she really destroying her chances by sharing a ball? Sylvia swore not, but what did a seventeen-year-old know? Yet she had no choice. The Forleys could not afford to host a ball. Surely they were not the only family with a limited budget!

Grasping at her frayed nerves, she forced control over her voice. "Hart and Cassie have enormous credit, so this ball will attract all the best people." The earl would never approve something that might harm his favorite sister.

"But it isn't yours!" screamed Lady Forley. "Can't you understand so simple a truth? I swear all that reading has turned your brain to mush! No one of consequence would *dream* of forgoing her own ball. No one—"

Angela closed her ears. Why did she even try to make her mother see reason? The task was hopeless. Thirty years earlier, Lady Forley had married a fashionable viscount, believing that his charm and elegant wardrobe denoted fabulous wealth. Nothing had changed her convictions, not even the last six years of scrimping to rescue Andrew's inheritance from debt. Now that the woman had returned to town, she was determined to regain her position as a respected London hostess—in her eyes only the most extravagant entertainment was worthy of respect.

But Andrew lacked the means. Lady Jersey's annual income surpassed the value of Forley Court and all its contents. Others were equally wealthy. Thus Lady Forley had no hope of competing, and her refusal to admit this basic truth placed a huge burden on Angela's shoulders. Despite inexperience and uncertainty, she not only had to plan her own come-out, but must constantly recheck all arrangements to prevent her mother from making changes behind her back.

As had happened two days ago. What a fiasco! Though Lady Forley had already overspent her clothing allowance, she had ordered four expensive gowns from the very exclusive Madame Florentine. Andrew had had no choice but to confront the modiste, cancel the order, and announce that he would no longer honor his mother's debts. Such news hurt them all, but Lady Forley refused to accept responsibility for precipitating the crisis.

A cheer announced that the dray no longer blocked the street. Their carriage moved forward. Only another six blocks . . .

Lady Forley's litany of complaints shifted to her daughter's vulgar ideas and unladylike behavior.

Angela stared out the window, determined to control her temper. Admittedly, her social training was inadequate. She had never learned to flirt—and didn't want to—but she could surely find a congenial husband anyway. She wasn't looking for love. There simply wasn't time.

She must return to Forley Court in June to prepare for Andrew's wedding, which added yet another burden to her load.

Several burdens, actually. Once Andrew returned from his brief wedding journey, Sylvia would take over running Forley Court—a position Angela had held for years. Despite their growing friendship, she could not stay while another woman stepped into her place—especially a girl fully five years younger than she, who had little experience in household management. Nor could she face moving into the dower house with her whining mother. Thus she had to marry, and with her brother's wedding so close, she had only two months in which to arrange it.

"I will choose which entertainments to attend," Lady Forley was saying. "You have already done too much to lower our consequence. We cannot afford any more mistakes. Balls, routs, picnics, theater parties. Those are acceptable—but only if they are sponsored by reputable hostesses. You must avoid soirees, lectures, and similar gatherings that would label you as a bluestocking. The slightest hint of your faults will destroy your credit. It is bad enough that we must associate with Lady Sylvia."

Angela grimaced at this old argument. She hated to think that every member of society despised education, but even Sylvia had admitted that the matrons who controlled the Marriage Mart looked askance at bookishness. Sylvia had the freedom to disclose her interests only because she was already betrothed.

She glanced out the window as the carriage rounded a corner, grimacing over the challenge she faced. Hiding her edu—

"*Stop!*" she suddenly shouted at their driver. Without waiting for a response, she jumped to the pavement. Roberts cursed, jerking the team to a halt and tossing Lady Forley onto the floor.

Angela ignored her mother's outrage. "What is the meaning of this?" she demanded, pushing through a crowd to accost a burly man who was shaking a small child.

"Stay out if it, ma'am," he snarled. "'E's a thief."

Murmurs of agreement swept the crowd.

"A thief? What did he steal?" The boy held nothing in his hands, and only a wrinkled, half-rotten apple lay on the ground.

A backhanded slap snapped the boy's head around and raised a red welt on his left cheek.

"'E stole one of me apples, the snivelin' brat. A man cain't make a honest livin' these days."

A street vendor. She glared, grabbing his arm as he raised it to strike again. "Honest? For shame! If that apple represents your wares, then you are a knave. And vicious as well. Can't you see that he's naught but a baby? How dare you turn the full weight of a grown man on a starving child? Why not direct your anger toward his parents where it might do some good?" She turned to the crowd. "Does anyone know where the boy lives?"

Several onlookers had stepped back, and some now slithered away, loathe to be involved. Shouts and curses rose from drivers furious to find the street blocked by those watching the altercation. A saturnine gentleman leaned against a building, taking in every word.

She ignored them. "Well? Does no one know the child?"

" 'E ain't got no 'ome," muttered a woman.

"Showed up 'round 'ere 'bout a month back," mumbled another.

"Is this true?" she asked the boy.

He nodded, his terror sending a dagger deep into her heart.

" 'E's got a 'ome now," hissed the vendor. " 'Tis off to the workhouse for you, me lad."

*"No!"* Astonished eyes stared at her. She pulled a coin from her reticule and pushed it into the vendor's hand. "For the apple and for your trouble."

"Don't interfere, ma'am," he growled. "Go back to yer fancy 'ouse an' forget it. The boy's nothin' but trouble. If ye lets him get away with this, 'e'll just take encouragement."

"No, he won't," she swore. "He doesn't belong on the streets. He needs shelter and food. But not the workhouse. I know just the place for him. He will never bother you again.

Murmurs greeted this pronouncement. Ignoring them, she crouched before the orphan, heedless that her skirts were dragging in filth. "Come with me, child. We will find you something better to eat than that horrid apple." She gently grasped one arm, glaring at the vendor until he reluctantly released his grip on the other. In a trance, the lad followed her to the carriage and let her help him inside.

"Mercy!" screeched Lady Forley. "What have you done now? Becoming an *on-dit* in fashionable drawing rooms will destroy you. We will be cut. I know we will. And he is undoubtedly crawling with fleas, or worse. Why are you determined to throw away your reputation?"

"Enough! Who would ever know?" A raised hand prohibited a response. "But even if word gets out, it matters not. If society can countenance such treatment for children, then I care not for society."

Lady Forley gasped for nearly a minute, giving Angela a chance to settle the boy comfortably on a seat.

"Who would know?" she squeaked as the carriage again crept forward. "Who would know? Did you not see that gentleman leaning against the wall? That was Lord Blackthorn—the Black Marquess. The tale will be on every tongue by dinner, for he despises sentimental gestures and cares nothing for female sensibilities."

"Nonsense. He doesn't even know who I am. Why would he bother?"

"Because he is the blackest blackguard ever spawned by the devil." Fumbling through her reticule, she produced a vinaigrette. "After destroying so many others, he would think nothing of pillorying you. He is a heartless libertine who has ruined countless women, a confirmed gamester who has squandered a fortune at cards. But those are the least of his crimes. He publicly jilted his own betrothed, blackening her character so thoroughly that she fled town and hasn't been seen since. His father died of the shock. Grief drove hers to the bottle. I witnessed the whole thing, for it happened in Lady Jersey's ballroom scarcely a sennight before they were to wed. He denounced her as a fallen woman, though she was one of the sweetest girls in town that Season. Shocked by his unwarranted tirade, she lashed back, revealing his cruelty and debauchery."

"You exaggerate," she murmured, trying to soothe her mother's temper. "No one behaves so recklessly."

"You are naïve! That man is a demon the likes of which you cannot imagine. We had heard hints of his misdeeds for years, though he had successfully hidden the details. But no more. When Miss Quincy sobbed out the truth, he merely laughed, offering no explanation and no apology." The vinaigrette waved fretfully. "And he has made no effort to hide his crimes since. Two years later, he eloped with Lady Cloverdale, abandoning her overseas. They say he was as calm on his return as if he had merely misplaced a pocket handkerchief. Lord Cloverdale was heartbroken. But when he realized that she would not—or could not—come home, he had no choice but to bring a divorce suit against her, citing Blackthorn for criminal conversation. It was the most sensational crim-con trial in history, resulting in an enormous penalty. And I have heard other tales too awful to discuss in polite company."

Angela shook her head, unwilling to believe her mother's harsh judgment, though she could not deny the Black Marquess's impact. Recalling his face still robbed her of breath. It was long and thin with dramatic planes and heavy peaked brows above dark eyes.

She shivered.

This was not the first time she had seen him. Just yesterday she had spotted him on Piccadilly, talking to the three ragged soldiers who customarily begged there. Each had clutched a banknote in his hand. At the time she had thought little of it, for many gentlemen tossed alms to London's ubiquitous beggars. But now that she knew his identity, their murmured exchange took on a terrifying new meaning.

"Tonight," he'd ordered, staring at one of the soldiers.

The man had nodded briskly. "We'll be there, guv."

"Remember to keep my name out of it. You'll regret it if anyone learns I'm involved."

"As you wish."

Angela again shivered. Blackthorn's voice had held a very real threat. What had he hired those men to do? He had been opening his mouth to say more when his eyes clashed with hers, then stuck, impaling her. Something akin to fear had flashed in his, but it disappeared before she could fully identify it, replaced by a piercing stare that banished further thought. She had no idea how long he'd kept her pinned, but when he turned to stride away, the soldiers were gone.

And that harsh face wasn't all that had stuck in her mind. He wasn't a man one forgot. Tall. Angular. Broad-shouldered. A man whose very appearance announced his disregard for convention. His black hair was long, curling over his ears and covering the nape of his neck. His coat fit loosely across his breadth, and his pantaloons were black instead of the light colors most men favored. Yet the stark appearance suited him—even more so now that she knew his identity.

Another shiver tickled her spine, this one leaving heat in its wake. Appalled that she could feel even a flash of attraction for so depraved a man, she focused all her attention on her mother.

". . . which is why he would relish exposing your folly to the world." Lady Forley was sobbing as she reached the end of her recital. "The blackguard delights in hurting people."

She had missed hearing the full extent of his crimes, but their severity mattered not. No matter how black the marquess's character was, he posed no real threat. "Who would believe a man of his reputation? Surely he must be ostracized himself, so who could he tell?"

"Again you show your ignorance! His title is too lofty to ignore. While it is true that he is unwelcome in drawing rooms, he visits all the clubs, so his words will be repeated everywhere. You have ruined your Season." She burst into fresh tears, dropping her vinaigrette as both hands covered her eyes. "What could you be thinking? Inviting a street urchin into our coach! He will rob us blind. I know he will."

Angela retrieved the vinaigrette. Would this ride never end? She turned back to the window, only to find the Black Marquess's eyes again clashing with hers, much closer than before. They were mesmerizing—dark, dark gray glittering with silver highlights in the afternoon sunlight. Piercing. Penetrating clear to her soul while revealing none of his own thoughts. Was he plotting a crime or some other nefarious scheme?

Not until the coach moved past, breaking the contact, could she breathe. He was dangerous. Yet she still did not fear exposure. Glancing back, she watched him cross the street and disappear around a corner.

Why did she trust him? Pondering the question carried her all the way to Clifford Street. Her reaction lacked logic and sense, though they were her most consistent virtues. Or did it?

Her mother dramatized everything, making the woman's claims suspect. After all, Blackthorn was still received in his clubs. But that was not why she trusted him. Those eyes had promised silence. She didn't know why, but he would not reveal her actions.

*Idiot!*

She was not reading his mind. Such a feat was impossible. Flustered by an impression unsupported by any fact, she concentrated on logic. His intentions or lack of them counted for nothing. He could not know her identity, for their coach had no crest—another of Lady Forley's complaints; Andrew was entitled to one. Thus she was safe. Even if he mentioned the incident, no one could connect it to her. Describing her appearance might make her momentarily uncomfortable, but she was not the only red-haired lady in town.

The carriage rocked to a halt. A footman helped the sobbing Lady Forley down.

Having convinced herself that she remained anonymous, Angela turned to the orphan. "Come with me. We will find food, and then we must talk."

Warily setting his hand in hers, he allowed her to lead him into the house.

Devall Sherbrooke, ninth Marquess of Blackthorn, scowled as the carriage moved past. The chit threatened his peace of mind—which was a ridiculous thought to have on a sunny afternoon. Nothing could disturb him. Certainly not so unconventional a hoyden!

He had seen her twice before, once on Bond Street—the memory momentarily distracted him, for it was the fact that she had not cut him that had drawn his attention to her, which only proved that she did not know his identity—and more recently on Piccadilly, where she had sneaked up on him.

He nodded. That second meeting explained his discomfort. His well-honed sense of danger always protected him when he was conducting business. So why had it failed? More importantly, how much had she heard?

That last concern had focused his eyes on her. She had still not known him. Why else had she held his gaze so long?

He usually had no interest in society misses—scheming opportunists, every one, with more hair than wit. Their only interests were gossip and parties. He'd known many of them in the years before his betrothal, and had approved none of them. Society hadn't changed since those days.

So why did he have to work so hard to drape the image around this newest arrival? Even yesterday it hadn't quite fit. That auburn curl escaping her bonnet had hinted at a passionate nature. As did the sparkle in her moss-green eyes. Yet he had never expected this!

Good God! She had jumped from a moving carriage into a crowded street. She could easily have broken a leg, been kicked by a horse, or been knocked down by a wagon. And she'd risked a worse danger than injury.

She might have been seen.

He shook his head. The only explanation was that she'd recognized the boy. He was a thief—hardly surprising in London. Perhaps he had accosted her as she exited a shop, stealing her reticule or a package. Most girls kept a footman at hand to prevent such an occurrence, but her behavior today proved that she was inadequately supervised. The lad's appearance was distinctive enough that his victims would remember him. Yet she had not turned him over to a constable. How naïve!

Was she stupid enough to think she could reform a London thief? She wouldn't be the first, but turning him into a page would be a big mistake. The boy would rob her blind. He probably lived in a flash house, where continued food and shelter depended on bringing in his daily quota of goods. For his master to move him into Mayfair, he had to be experienced. Should he warn her?

He snorted. Even this unconventional chit would never believe him.

Pain stabbed his chest. It was so unexpected that it took a moment to realize that the admission hurt. Why should he care? Granted, she was different from most people—and not just because she had a soft spot for supposedly helpless orphans—but her opinions meant nothing. Yet he could not get those differences out of his mind.

Again she had not cut him. Her eyes had bored into his as if she could see into his tortured soul. Yet they had held no censure. She'd recognized him—after yesterday, that was inevitable; someone would have warned her who he was—so why did she not despise him? She was not bad looking, either. A whole tangle of auburn curls had peeped out today, framing her heart-shaped face. A truly unique and delectable maiden.

Damnation!

He strode rapidly around a corner, resisting an urge to look over his shoulder. Were her eyes really boring into his back? Thinking about her was dangerous. Despite her odd behavior, she was obviously a lady, which widened the gulf between them. He had repudiated the hypocrisy of society six years ago, along with its cheerful backstabbing and double standards. Thus respectable women were off limits. Aside from sex—which he could easily get without attached strings—he had no use for females. Especially for naïve girls like this one. Even if she did indeed prove to be different, he could not pursue her. The slightest attention from him would ruin her.

Again that delectable face distracted his thoughts, diverting his attention from business. She was older than most new arrivals, which only added to her attraction. Her eyes danced with intelligence. What had kept her from town earlier? Had her family suffered a series of deaths? He rarely spent much of the Season in London, but he surely would have noticed her if she had been here before.

*Devil take it!*

He was doing it again. He had more pressing problems than one intriguing hoyden. Banishing the incident from his mind, he concentrated on business.

Despite his lurid reputation, he took his position as head of the Sherbrooke family seriously. He did not tolerate misbehavior, even from those related only by marriage. Gabriel's transgression demanded satisfaction, but he had no interest in hearing his family's private affairs bruited about clubs and drawing rooms. Thus he needed another pretext. What insult would provoke Gabriel into issuing a challenge? And how soon could he complete this chore? He much preferred Wyndhaven to the noise and filth of London.

Thoughts of his estate raised a lump in his throat that nearly choked him. He had renovated the house and grounds when he'd acceded to the marquessate, erasing everything that reminded him of his childhood. It was now his refuge from the world, his sanctuary, the one place where he could be himself.

The town house never let him relax, he realized, again distracted from business. It still reflected his father. He must do something about that. Family affairs and private interests were bringing him to London with increasing frequency. As long as he was already here, he might as well order its refurbishing. Cost was irrelevant. For all the man's faults, his father had made wise investments, expanding a comfortable inheritance into a fortune. It was a knack he had inherited, increasing his worth three-fold since gaining the title. Not that he cared.

*Enough!*

How was he to initiate the necessary confrontation? Where? When? His reputation barred him from society gatherings, so he would have to study Gabriel's habits. Once he knew where to find him, inciting a response should be easy. Gabriel was too accustomed to adoration to tolerate contempt.

"Lord Hartleigh," announced Paynes, stepping aside so the earl could enter the drawing room.

Angela sighed in relief. Andrew was out. Her mother's complaints had given way to strong hysterics once they'd arrived home. Convincing the woman to rest before an evening excursion to the opera had drained her last reserves of energy.

The orphan had remained silent, allowing as his name was Jimmy but refusing to answer further questions. So she had sent for Hartleigh, who owned the estate next to Forley Court. He would take care of the boy.

"Hart." She smiled as Paynes closed the door. "I was afraid you might have gone out, but Cassie was so tired when we left that I hesitated to disturb her by returning in person."

"Thank you. What happened?"

She sighed. "I realize I am not supposed to know this, but Cassie once mentioned your orphanage."

He raised his brows but said nothing.

"I found a child this afternoon. A vendor was beating him for stealing an apple."

"Poor boy," he murmured under his breath. "Where is he?"

"In the kitchen. I can have Paynes fetch him."

"No. He will be more at ease if we go to him. What do you know about him?" He followed her downstairs and through the door leading down to the servants' hall.

"Nothing, except that the bystanders claimed he is an orphan who moved into the neighborhood about a month ago. His name is Jimmy. Beyond that, he refuses to talk. I would estimate his age at around five, and it is obvious that he has not had enough food for some time."

Hart shook his head. "It couldn't be," he murmured, but gasped when they entered the kitchen.

Jimmy sat at the table, still eating, his thin body so frail it was a wonder he was alive. Even heavy grime had not muted his blazing red hair, but washing now revealed a blanket of freckles covering nose and cheeks. His growing bruises revived Angela's anger.

"Jimmy," she murmured soothingly. "This is Lord Hartleigh. He has a house full of boys where you can stay."

Fear coursed through the blue eyes.

Hart dropped onto a low stool, bringing his eyes to Jimmy's level. "It's not a flash house," he assured the lad, pausing to examine his face more closely. "Is your name McFarrell?"

Angela gasped.

Jimmy finally nodded.

"I thought so." Relief threaded the words. "Your brother Harry had been frantic about you."

"You know 'arry?" Tears sprang to the boy's eyes.

"Yes, I know him." Hart rested his large hand atop Jimmy's small one. "A month ago I rescued him from a beating. He was unconscious for nearly a day, but his first words on awakening were to ask where you were. I've been looking for you ever since."

"I was scared when 'arry didn't come 'ome," he sobbed. "Then I 'eard 'bout a body nosin' 'round, askin' questions, so I ran."

Hart pulled the boy into his arms, letting him cry out his fear and loneliness against the superfine wool of his jacket. "It's all right, Jimmy. You needn't ever live on the streets again. Harry is waiting for you at a house in the country. As soon as you recover your strength, I will see that you both go to school."

"I can't believe you know him," said Angela, shaking her head. "Who is he?"

"The McFarrells were a poor but respectable family that fell on hard times," he answered, still patting Jimmy's back. "The father was a dock worker, but seven years ago—shortly after Jimmy's birth—he suffered an injury that left him incapable of lifting heavy loads. Without employment, they had to move into two rooms on a mean street. He did odd jobs until he died two years later. The mother found work with a seamstress, though they had to give up one of their rooms. But her eyes steadily weakened until she was no longer able to sew. Ten-year-old Harry tried to provide for the family, but soon fell into the clutches of one of the more reprehensible thief-masters, and the pittance he was paid barely kept the family in food. Mrs. McFarrell died three months ago. Harry kept things going for a time, but his master was dissatisfied with the goods he brought in and set on him as an example to the other boys. That was when I found him. If only he had been conscious, I might have recovered Jimmy then. This month must have been brutal for him."

"From his looks, he is near starvation."

Hart nodded. "Come, Jimmy." He swept the boy into his arms. "Let's go home. You can sleep in a soft bed, and we'll find you some clothes. Then tomorrow, I will take you to Harry."

"Thank you, Hart." Angela smiled damply.

Returning to the drawing room, she stared at the uninspired furnishings. Thief-masters and Almack's patronesses. London contrasts were even starker than she had imagined.

The city had seemed magical when she had first spotted it in the distance, its skyline dotted with church spires and dominated by the dome of St. Paul's and the bulk of Westminster Abbey. Yet her first close view was of mean streets, derelict buildings, and poorly dressed people. Disappointment had been settling over her when the streets suddenly widened into the opulent glory that was Mayfair.

Yet even here, contrasts were everywhere—well-dressed lords and ragged beggars, haughty matrons and cowering shop girls, nanny-tended children in the park and boys like Jimmy on the streets. Even her own class contained contrasts. Lisping fops minced about clad in outlandish costumes; intimidating dandies wielded pretentious quizzing glasses; boisterous Corinthians endlessly relived the latest mill or race. They were joined by sober clubmen, starchy hostesses, pushy matchmakers, giggling girls fresh from the schoolroom . . .

Where did she fit into this mosaic?

And the emotional extremes were nearly as bad—terror over appearing at the Queen's drawing room; relief when she survived the ordeal; mortification at Lady Forley's insistence on vulgar extravagance; nervousness that tied her tongue in knots whenever the *ton*'s highest sticklers appeared; fear that she might say something to alienate them; anger at Jimmy's treatment; painful sympathy for his story; trepidation about her upcoming ball . . . Where in this muddle was pleasure? Or even contentment? So far, her London Season bore no resemblance to the glittering tales Lady Forley had spun since Lord Forley's death.

Blackthorn's face again hovered before her own. Now there was a man who wasted no time agonizing over what society thought. How much simpler life was for gentlemen. They could break any number of rules and still be welcomed at their clubs. Ladies did not have that freedom. Only through rigid compliance to every expectation could she expect to find a husband during her brief stay in town. Failure was unthinkable—and not only because she was losing her place at the Court. Andrew had made many sacrifices to provide this opportunity for her. How could she waste it?

*I must marry!*

She sighed. Conformity must become her watchword. Society's matrons had already made that clear. They had watched her like hawks when she first entered their drawing rooms, relaxing only when she proved to be quiet and deferential. But their attention was never far away. Any mistake could ruin her.

It would be difficult. She had so many faults—an unladylike education, questionable manners, an unfashionable concern for the lower classes. Revealing any of them would lead to failure.

Again she sighed. Why couldn't she just be herself?

# Chapter Two

*Dear Lord! This is going to be a disaster!*

Angela stood in the receiving line, a false smile pasted firmly on her face. What was she doing here? Her mother was right that sharing a ball would harm her. She was an interloper, a mushroom, an upstart who did not belong in this illustrious company.

When Sylvia had offered to share her come-out ball, their difference in station hadn't seemed to matter. After all, they were only one rank apart, and Sylvia was happily marrying down. By the time Angela met society for herself, it was too late to change the plans.

Why had she never realized the enormous gap that separated the upper and lower aristocracy? It was a difference she would have learned at school had she attended one. But beyond even that natural separation, Lord Hartleigh's credit was high, guaranteeing that the ball would be a squeeze. Not that it would do her any good. The friends of a wealthy, powerful earl would hardly be interested in the barely dowered bluestocking sister of a viscount. And how could she become acquainted with anyone in this frenzied atmosphere?

"You will be ruined," Lady Forley had moaned as their carriage approached Hartleigh House. "How can we hold our heads up after making a public admission of penury by bringing you out as an afterthought to someone else's ball? We might as well place an ad in the *Times* announcing that you are unmarriageable."

"Hardly." She had still been insisting that all would be well. Admitting her own fears would make it impossible to survive the evening. "Sylvia and I will be sisters in only two months. Cassie sees nothing wrong with it."

"How would she know? She's hardly older than you, with no experience in entertaining. She shouldn't even be here. Appearing in public when she is increasing is outside enough!" The ubiquitous vinaigrette waved beneath her nose.

Angela bit back a sigh at the memory and smiled at the latest arrival. It was too late to rectify any mistakes. If only her mother had kept quiet just this once! That diatribe had done little to settle nerves already stretched to the breaking point.

For six years Angela had listened to tales about the magic of the London Season—the parties, the people, the clothes and jewels, the sparkling conversation. All exaggerated.

London intimidated her in ways she had never experienced at home. There, she entertained the neighbors with confidence. Whatever duties she had faced—and they were many, for Lady Forley refused to run the house or see after the tenants, devoting her time to endless complaints over her absence from London—she had handled with calm confidence.

Yet here she could never relax, especially around the Almack's patronesses and gossips like Lady Beatrice. The sparkling conversation was only endless repetition of the latest scandals interspersed with acid condemnation of anyone not present. The other girls were giddy, giggling pea-brains interested only in clothes and flirting. She had nothing in common with them. How could she relate to people who accepted social facades as reality, dreamed only of jewels and gowns, and spoke nothing but regurgitated *on-dits*? They ignored her, content with the friendships they had formed at schools she had never attended.

The gentlemen were worse. Corinthians. Dandies. Fops. All were alien beings in their formal clothes and impeccable manners, intimidating her with their self-possession while flustering her with insincere compliments and meaningless flirtation. Framing a reply that did not sound hopelessly conceited was impossible.

"Lord Atwater," she murmured as that gentleman was introduced. "So nice of you to come." She had discovered that if she avoided looking into people's faces, she could utter greetings without stammering.

"At last, a beauty worthy of notice," he said warmly, touching his lips to her gloved hand. "Your face is a blazing light shining into the darkest corners. Such exquisite loveliness casts all others into shadow." His words were so pat on her thoughts that she nearly choked. Tongue-tied, she ignored him and turned to the next arrival.

London was not her milieu. She hated its shallowness and the way intelligent people changed when they entered its portals. Even Hart and Andrew sounded brainless here, though both were reasonable men. And that disturbed her. If everyone donned masks in public, how was she to see past the surface? Unlike most girls, she did not view marriage as either a duty or a business arrangement. She wanted a partnership with her husband. And friendship. Love was unlikely, of course—she banished a spurt of envy for the love Andrew and Sylvia shared—but she could not compromise beyond friendship. Yet discovering a kindred spirit meant she had to know the real character of any suitors.

Her mother's jostling reminded her that she was supposed to greet all arrivals. "Mr. Garwood."

If only she could set aside her fears and doubts—at least for tonight. She had been wrong to think that anyone attending Hart's illustrious gathering would be interested in her. Yet even that realization failed to relax her, for new fears now joined the old. She had not previously grasped the size of the *ton*. Hundreds of people already thronged the ballroom, with more arriving every minute. Not all were eligible gentlemen, of course, though dozens might be. And dozens more would skip this ball. How could she find the best one for her in only two months?

"Mr. Brummell." Her voice quavered, her composure threatening to disintegrate as the dandy made his way along the receiving line. He was another who terrified her. The dark jacket he had popularized set off his coloring to perfection. As usual, the dreaded quizzing glass hung close to hand. Lady Forley had already overwhelmed her with warnings of what his approval would mean. *He can make or break your Season with a single lift of his brow,* she had moaned yet again as their carriage pulled up to Hartleigh House. *You must make a good impression. He sets fashion, so his regard is vital. Flatter him. Amuse him. Flirt if you can manage it—though why you are so inept at such an essential skill I will never know. Do you want to fail?*

She shuddered now as he looked her up and down. At least her clothes were all right. Once Jeanette had delivered the ball gown, even Lady Forley had ceased harping about patronizing such an inexpensive modiste. But who knew how Brummell would react?

At close quarters, he was daunting, his legendary disdain obvious in the eyes she forced herself to meet. Somehow she managed an exchange of comments, though she had no idea what she said. But it must have been all right, for he actually smiled before sauntering toward the ballroom. Her shoulders sagged in relief. With luck she need never speak to him again. He didn't dance.

Encountering the Beau and his ilk was yet another aspect of sharing this ball that she had not considered until it was too late. Hart was a powerful figure in both social and government circles. Thus his guest list encompassed the highest in the land— every Almack's patroness; most dukes and marquesses; the heir to nearly every title in the upper aristocracy; many government leaders. And the Prince Regent.

Her knees tried to buckle. *Pull yourself together!* Somehow she responded to Lady Jersey without making a cake of herself. How did other girls cope with the stress? Or did they enjoy socializing so much that they suffered no stress?

Few of them shared her problems. At two-and-twenty, she was much older than other new arrivals. Cassie had often sworn that age would give her the poise to enjoy the Season.

*Hah!*

All it gave her was the experience to know how many disasters lurked in the wings. The constant fear sapped her vitality, leaving her aloof and utterly colorless, reducing her chances of success. God knew she didn't expect to become a diamond, but acquiring a reputation for insipidity boded ill for the future.

"It is time to begin the dancing," announced Cassie.

Andrew reluctantly tore his eyes from Sylvia—beside whom he had stood for the past hour—to place Angela on his arm. The action was so obviously a duty that she laughed—and relaxed.

"You'll get your chance soon," she reminded him. Hart was leading Sylvia out for the opening set.

"I know, Angie." His eyes had already returned to Sylvia. "But why could we not have wed at Christmas? This waiting is driving me crazy. Five months before he would allow a betrothal and another five until the wedding."

"You are nearly there." She squeezed his arm to force his attention back to her. "Don't drool so publicly or God knows what rumors will start."

"You're right, but somehow I'll make Hart pay for putting me through this. He certainly called a different tune with his own bride. They married just two days after their betrothal."

"Three. But can you blame him?" They stepped into the first pattern. "Cassie had been out for five years and was in mourning. Sylvia is only seventeen and deserves a Season before settling down."

"I just wish it was over."

She laughed. "In the meantime, you can concentrate on seeing me off your hands. And then we must consider how to move Mother to the dower house so you can have the privacy you so obviously crave."

He actually blushed.

Hart and Andrew exchanged partners for the next set.

"You are beautiful tonight, Angela," he said as he led her into a cotillion.

She sighed. "I hope that is not Spanish coin, for I am nearly falling apart with nerves." Admitting that to a man she had known all her life was easy.

"They do not show, so you needn't worry. Nerves are expected at one's first London ball, but you will manage admirably."

"Did you have to invite the Regent?" The words burst out without warning, and she stiffened.

He laughed. "I did indeed, but you needn't worry there, either. He will undoubtedly dance with you, but the set will be short, and if you can keep from giggling at how he creaks, you will do fine."

A chuckle escaped. "You did that on purpose, didn't you?" It had worked. Her fluid grace returned as they moved into the figure.

"Of course." He grinned. "Not one of these people is perfect, Angie. If you feel intimidated, simply list your partner's flaws and you will relax. Sylvia is just as terrified as you are."

"Really? She has been so confident since we arrived."

"Cassie is also very nervous."

"Now that I don't believe! This is her sixth Season. How can she have any fears?"

"It may be her sixth Season, but it is her first as a matron in charge of planning entertainments and being responsible for bringing out another young lady. The fact that she is increasing makes it worse, for she feels conspicuous and tires far too easily."

"Oh, Hart, I had no idea," she exclaimed in chagrin. "And I have been hanging on her arm for support and advice."

They finished the figure and moved into the next change. "You have done no harm, for she honestly enjoys your company. I merely want you to realize that you are not the only one with anxieties. I have plenty of my own, if you must know, for Cassie cannot stay in town for the entire Season. She will try, of course, but at some point I will have to put my foot down and take her home."

"What will happen to Sylvia?" Concern for her friends had nearly banished her own fears—which was undoubtedly why he was baring his personal problems. Perhaps he recognized how Lady Forley's complaints had affected her.

"My sister Barbara will arrive in about a month, and my step-mother a fortnight later. Sylvia will stay with one of them. Cassie understands. And she will have more than enough to do preparing for the wedding."

By the time the set concluded, Angela was actually enjoying herself. Lady Forley had also relaxed and was sparkling now that her old friends were complimenting the arrangements. If anything, hanging on Hart's impressive coattails had improved their consequence.

"Lord Atwater has requested the next dance." Lady Forley's excitement contrasted sharply with the *ennui* displayed by most other guests.

Angela smiled and accepted his arm, though she had only the haziest recollection of his arrival. How could she have missed so handsome a gentleman? His light blue coat fit tightly to show off his athleticism. Blond hair curled around his face, brightening his deep blue eyes.

She had heard his name often during morning calls and had the impression that he was about thirty. But his face belied that age, retaining the innocence and wonder of youth, a knee-weakening dimple appearing whenever he smiled.

Her tension returned ten-fold. He was society's darling, inciting worshipful adoration from even the highest sticklers. How was she to converse with a paragon? Concentrating on people's faults only worked if you could identify them. But she knew nothing about London gentlemen beyond surface impressions. Lord Atwater's surface made her nervous. So much was riding on this Season. Only success would lead to a home and family of her own.

"How truly blessed I am to escort the most beautiful angel to grace London in many Seasons," he declared as they joined a set.

"You exaggerate, my lord."

"Fustian! You are too modest." He bestowed a heated gaze that silenced her. "I like that," he added seductively.

She grimaced. Fault number one: insincerity.

He quizzed her on her family and other connections whenever the movements of the country dance brought them together, but that was expected. Perhaps he sought a wife, just as she was looking for a husband. She didn't enjoy feeling like a mare at a horse auction, but she shrugged the irritation aside. How else could one get acquainted in so short a time? And why did she care, anyway? An earl who held society in the palm of his hand would reach up the social scale for his wife, not down.

Feeling gauche, rustic, and inadequate, she retreated behind a cloak of shy dignity. The change increased the warmth of his adoring glances. His compliments grew more effusive. Only then did she suspect a different motive for his interest. Did he think to pursue some other arrangement with her? Perhaps he was a libertine instead of a suitor. She shivered.

His dimple immediately flashed, deepening when she again shivered. Surely he didn't think she was encouraging him!

Perhaps he felt her trepidation, for he abruptly abandoned personal remarks, though his tone still implied intimacy. "The most extraordinary event occurred in the park yesterday."

"Really?" Which of the half-dozen park stories was he about to repeat?

"Indeed." He chuckled suddenly, his smile one he must have

used to great effect on other girls. "I never thought to see such a sight. You may know that Lord Shelford is one of the best horsemen in the *ton*, a member of the Four-in-Hand Club and rider *extraordinaire*."

She nodded silently, resigned to playing her part, though the tale was humorous enough. She had laughed the first time she'd heard it, but a dozen repetitions during today's calls and last night's rout had stripped it of its charm.

"Never did I expect anything to fluster him. But at the height of the fashionable hour, his eyes lit on a newcomer to London, a veritable vision of beauty—though not so lovely as you, my dear—delicate face, blond curls, pouting rosebud mouth. His jaw dropped into his cravat. Jerking his mount to a halt, he froze in amazement. Such a stupor! And this from a gentleman who has long declared he would never wed."

She raised her brows to show the expected surprise.

"Exactly. Never have I witnessed a man so suddenly besotted. It was obvious that he had forgotten all else, for when a passing horse jostled his own, it unseated him."

"How embarrassing."

"Too true. But the cream of the jest is that the young lady is already betrothed—to Shelford's cousin."

She gasped, hating herself for reacting like a pea-brained widgeon, but he expected a response, and she could think of no other.

"Yes. His very own cousin. He will be the butt of jokes at family gatherings for years."

She refused to giggle, though most girls did at this point. Fortunately the dance separated them so she did not have to come up with an alternate response.

Atwater was treating her like an idiot. Everyone had heard this tale by now, so why did he expect her to behave as if it were news? Yet in all fairness, she couldn't blame only him. Half the dancers were chuckling over the same tale, just as they had done during both previous sets.

*The Black Marquess would never indulge in such inanity.*

She stumbled. How could she guess the behavior of a man with whom she had exchanged not one word? And why would she assume that he was so different? He had frequented society gatherings for several years before becoming an outcast, so logically, his conversation would be just as insipid as Atwater's.

*No, it's not. That man would* never *be insipid.*

She quickly stifled that inner voice, refusing to argue the subject. But banishing the image of dark, brooding eyes proved more difficult. She had glimpsed him again that very morning, though his back had been turned so he had not seen her. Why could she not forget his face? It had intruded on her dreams more than once in the past week.

Suppressing further thought, she flashed a false smile as the dance brought her back to Atwater's side. Calling attention to her wandering mind could only cause trouble.

Sir Alan Kenwood led her out for the next set, immediately announcing that he needed a wife. Despite his businesslike tone, she found him quite amiable. And his presence proved that her earlier fears were unfounded. The guest list included numerous gentlemen at and even below her own station. She should have known that Hart would remember her.

Subsequent sets were equally entertaining—a pulse-fluttering reel with Captain Harrington; a light-hearted country set with Lord Rathbone; a minuet with Lord Hartford, whose own retelling of Shelford's embarrassment was genuinely funny; and the dreaded set with the Regent.

Yet even that went better than she had feared. The prince was light on his feet for someone of his girth, though Hart was right about the creaking. His corsets occasionally drowned out conversation. But he smiled as he concluded their abbreviated set. Even Brummell smiled at her this night. And she had not a single set free, though she had to sit out the two waltzes.

Mr. Garwood partnered her for one of those. He was the first gentleman she had met in two weeks who seemed genuine. His evening clothes were loose enough to don without assistance. His appearance was average. And he spared her from insincere flattery. They joined several other couples who were likewise barred from dancing.

"I can't believe Lord Atwater is already looking for a second wife," exclaimed Miss Sanderson, watching the earl twirl a partner around the floor. "His first is barely in her grave."

"What tale is this?" asked Angela. "I had not heard of the

lady's demise." Actually, she had not heard that he had been married, though losing a wife was all too common.

"He married Miss Sherbrooke last Season, putting on a great show of eternal love and devotion, though if true, I cannot see how he could be here. She died of a miscarriage barely six weeks ago."

"But one can hardly blame him," protested Mr. Harley. "He must produce a son as soon as possible. His current heir is the most odious man I have ever met and unscrupulous enough to scheme for an inheritance. But you are mistaken about his emotional attachment. Though he liked her well enough, I saw no evidence of anything stronger."

"You can be sure that no one will censure him for appearing in town so soon," added Garwood. "The gossips all dote on him, treating him like a favorite nephew and ignoring any wrongdoing. He nearly came to blows with Oaksford last Season when the man corrected one of his misstatements, but Lady Debenham just shook her head, tut-tutting as though he had dropped a biscuit rather than nearly precipitated a brawl in her drawing room."

"Very true," agreed Harley. "Lady Beatrice is the same. It will be interesting to see whom he chooses this time."

Garwood nodded, then turned to Angela. "Are you enjoying the Season?"

"So far, though I do miss the country."

"Both are enjoyable," he said lightly. "The country stales after a time, yet town frivolity cannot sustain the spirit forever. Balancing both keeps life intriguing."

"You sound a wise man." She made no attempt to sound flirtatious.

"Shall we stroll until this set is ended?" He offered his arm.

They chatted contentedly, comparing his estate to Forley Court. She encouraged him to do much of the talking, heartened to find that she agreed with most of his statements. He was the most relaxing partner of the evening.

The remnants of her nervousness disappeared during the next set. Unlike the intimidating gentlemen who might be seeking a wife, her new partner, Mr. Crawford, was barely down from school and appeared even more nervous than she had been. In trying to set him at his ease, she forgot her own problems. But it was not an easy task, for he had little head for wine. The punch he had already consumed left him rather boisterous. Midway through a pattern, he stepped on her hem, tearing her gown.

"Devil take me! I am so sorry." Horror filled his eyes as a red stain crept across his face.

"It is nothing, Mr. Crawford," she said soothingly. The rip was barely an inch long. "But it would be best if I repair it at once. The set is nearly over."

It took only a moment to explain the problem to Lady Forley and seek out the retiring room where a maid waited to cope with just such emergencies.

"Are you serious?" an elderly dowager was exclaiming as Angela entered. "Blackthorn actually had the nerve to return to town?" She examined her hair in the looking glass, anchoring a diamond-studded flower more firmly into her silver locks.

"Well, it will avail him naught, for I certainly will not include him on any of my guest lists," said another.

"That blackguard should have been driven from the country," said a matron in her late twenties. "How can he hold his head up after that horrid scene at Lady Jersey's ball? Miss Quincy had done nothing to deserve such venom—his charges were lies from top to bottom. The poor girl disappeared that very night. Even her father has received no word in six years. Lady Beringford believes she must have done away with herself."

"Another reason Blackthorn should avoid town," said the dowager.

"Perhaps he only wishes to rebuild his fortune," suggested the second lady, smoothing her gown's rich purple folds over an ample figure. "After all, he has made no attempt to call on any of us, and his gaming is notorious. Of course, he loses more often than not."

"Can you have forgotten the way he fleeced poor Graceford last year? That fortune should keep even the most disgraceful gamester in funds."

"Graceford's luck certainly turned that night," said a middle-aged matron suggestively. She had not joined the earlier speculation.

"You don't mean to imply something underhanded, do you?"

"Of course not." Her tone belied the words. "But Graceford's winning streak was legendary, as was Blackthorn's penchant for losing. Strange that both should experience a change of fortune at the same time."

"Even more reason for him to avoid town. Who would dare play with the man after that?"

"They say Graceford fled to Italy, though how he supports himself I have no idea."

"Had you not heard?" The dowager sounded triumphant. "He died just after Christmas. His heir refuses to discuss it, but Lady Haliston believes he killed himself in a fit of despondency."

"Oh my!"

"The poor man!"

"How can Blackthorn live with himself?"

Repairs finished, Angela quickly checked her own hair and slipped from the room, leaving the gossips to their task of dissecting Lord Blackthorn's character. He had left quite a trail of bodies in his wake—his father, Miss Quincy, Lady Cloverdale, Lord Graceford—at least according to gossip. Apparently her mother had not exaggerated the man's reputation. Yet her own impressions had also been correct. In the week since Jimmy's rescue, no hint of her unconventional behavior had surfaced.

Lady Forley was chatting with a silver-haired gentleman. "This is Lord Styles, Angela."

They murmured greetings. He was one of the late arrivals who had not passed through the receiving line.

"I have not seen Lord Styles since my own come-out," Lady Forley continued. "Regrettably, his wife passed away last year, leaving him to bring out his youngest daughter alone. What a cumbersome task you have ahead," she added, simpering.

Angela cringed.

"I have help." He shrugged. "My eldest daughter and her husband, Lord Hervey, are chaperoning Grace. I am merely escorting them. And here comes my girl now."

Lord Atwater approached with a vapid blonde whose curly locks framed a face notable only for China-blue eyes. An older replica appeared at Lord Styles's elbow, and Angela recognized the young matron from the retiring room. Both proved to be empty-headed and giggly.

But she held her tongue. Protesting their silliness would

merely reveal her bluestocking tendencies. Atwater had reserved her next set, so they excused themselves.

Angela closed her eyes as the carriage pulled away from Hartleigh House. She was exhausted. Even after a fortnight in town, she had not adjusted to society's late hours.

"You did very well," said Lady Forley, for once without complaint.

"It did go well."

"You must be very careful with Lord Atwater. He will make the perfect husband. The earldom is ancient and includes at least five estates, guaranteeing that his income will continue. Tomorrow will allow you to set his interest." He had arranged to take her driving the following afternoon.

"It is a little early to assume that he is considering marriage," she reminded her mother. "After all, the man's wife is hardly cold. And even if he is shopping, there is no reason to believe that he would choose me. He gave equal attention to several other girls, including a well-dowered duke's daughter. And at least three other gentlemen seemed interested in me, including Mr. Garwood, who is also driving me in the park this week."

"Nonsense. It is up to you to choose which one you want, for your behavior will determine whether each man continues the pursuit or turns his eyes elsewhere. Garwood will never do. He is a younger son with no hope of achieving the title—which is only a barony anyway—and though he owns an estate, he has limited funds. This is the first Season he has spent in town and will undoubtedly be the last, for he will retire to the country as soon as he weds."

"You are wrong." Something goaded her into defending him. "He spends a portion of every year here and has done so since leaving school five years ago. He maintains rooms at Albany, which requires a considerable income. Why would he change habits now?"

"I will look into that, but Lady Stafford was sure he had not been here previously."

"Perhaps she meant he had not been searching for a wife until this year."

"Perhaps."

"Or maybe he has avoided the insipid Marriage Mart gatherings that Lady Stafford favors."

Lady Forley bristled. "You should not waste time on him in any case. Albany is less expensive than supporting a town house. An underfinanced husband is a disaster you must avoid. If you marry where there is little money, you will find yourself tucked away in the country and forgotten. Such a fate is worse than death. So concentrate on Atwater. He is wealthy enough to shower you with clothes and jewels, and he will certainly bring you to London to enjoy the society that represents the only reason for living."

Angela sighed, but refused to argue her mother's skewed priorities. After an enjoyable evening, the last thing she needed was another lecture. All she wanted to do was sleep. But when had her preferences ever mattered?

The only gentleman she had learned anything about was Garwood, and even their conversation had been superficial. Atwater had uttered *on-dits* and ridiculous flattery, saying nothing of himself. She would not even know that he was in mourning if she hadn't heard it elsewhere, and her expression of sympathy during their second set had drawn only a cold *thank you* and an immediate change of subject. Sir Alan and Captain Harrington had been pleasant but uninformative. Rathbone was witty and charming, but like Crawford, he was just down from Oxford. So she was in no position to narrow her choices. But declaring that aloud would start an argument, despite this being only her first society ball.

"You must be sure to encourage him," Lady Forley ordered. "Compliment his dress, his manners, his ideas. Show him that he is the most wonderful man in existence. Never contradict him. And above all, do not allow him to suspect that you read all those horrid books, Should he discover your faults, he will flee."

"Yes, Mother," she replied automatically, not caring who they discussed.

"Your Season will be a failure unless you find a wealthy, titled husband to care for you in the future."

"Yes, Mother."

"Ignore anyone below your own rank. Marrying down will destroy you."

"Yes, Mother."

"What a glorious return to town! Imagine seeing dear Henry again! Lord Styles," she corrected herself when Angela raised a quizzical brow. "He was one of my most persistent suitors, though ineligible at the time, for he was merely a younger son. His brother died about ten years ago, having sired six daughters but no heir. You will like him, I know, for I always found him delightfully entertaining. I expect his daughters will become your closest friends."

Letting the voice wash over her, Angela stifled another sigh. Lady Forley had never understood her. She had barely exchanged two words with Lord Styles, so could hardly judge him, but the daughters were two of the most feather-brained idiots she had ever encountered. Expecting them to become bosom bows was ludicrous. The only less likely event would be falling top over tail in love with the infamous Lord Blackthorn.

She shivered.

# Chapter Three

Angela perched nervously on the high seat of Atwater's phaeton as they swayed around the corner and into Hyde Park. He seemed an adequate whip, but his was the least stable variety of carriage, and it was all she could do to remain calm. At least his dappled grays did not appear to be high-strung.

Unclenching her hands, she forced them to lie quietly in her lap. Unclenching her teeth was more difficult. He had been dumping the butter boat over her head since arriving at Clifford Street. Ignoring his excess did nothing to slow him down.

But he finally ceased his overblown compliments, allowing her to relax. How could he utter such fustian with a straight face? Surely he didn't expect her to believe it! Praise for attributes she neither possessed nor admired was yet another cross she had to bear.

London was far different from her expectations, demanding contradictory behavior at every turn. Truth was prized, yet gentlemen uttered false flattery that ladies had to accept. Honesty was lauded, yet even men hid educations behind fatuous facades. Women were allowed no independent thought.

She suppressed a sigh, pasting a smile on her face. Society expected her to be untutored, and she had promised to follow convention. Since she was hiding her education, she could hardly complain that Atwater treated her like a widgeon. But if she preferred an empty-headed wife, then he would never do as a husband. So how was she to discover what he truly prized? Even as she groped for words that would begin an honest discussion without branding her as a bluestocking, the opportunity slipped away.

Obviously Atwater did not expect this drive to improve their acquaintance. Once they passed the gates, he all but ignored her. He was immensely popular. Every lady stopped to chat with him, from the venerable Lady Beatrice to newly presented misses. Most flirted shamelessly. But he was not merely a lady's man. Gentlemen hailed him as well.

She soon gave up trying to talk to him, turning her attention to the view. It was her first afternoon visit to Hyde Park. During her early morning rides, the place offered the solitude and spaciousness that eased her longing for home. Now crowds stripped it of familiarity, creating as big a squeeze as last night's ball.

The fashionable hour was at its peak. Elegant equipage clogged the road, from tiny vis-à-vis to handsome landaus, from flashy phaetons to dashing curricles. Gentlemen atop showy horses snaked between them. Others paraded on foot.

Park conversation proved to be simple—ritualized greetings followed by repetition of the day's *on-dits*. But her own contributions were negligible. Carriages stopped on Atwater's side of the phaeton, and he invariably answered for her, not allowing her to get a word in edgewise.

So she turned her attention to the horsemen and pedestrians who approached on her side. These included several gentlemen who had danced with her at her ball. Most had adhered to custom by sending round nosegays that morning. Chatting with her in the park was probably another custom. She bit back a sigh at the realization that even here, everyone's behavior followed a ritual as formal and meaningless as the advance and retreat of a cotillion.

Perhaps her mother was right to criticize her training—though it was the woman's own fault that she'd never had a governess. Sharing Andrew's tutors had opened her mind to ideas entertained only by men. When Andrew had left for school at the very advanced age of sixteen, she had continued studying on her own, using their father's library as her teacher. Lady Forley had visited the Court as rarely as possible, ignoring her children even when she was there. But such a background left Angela feeling out of place in the world of the *ton*. No matter how she tried to conform, she was different. Thus her criteria for choosing a husband were also different. She had to dig beneath gentlemen's facades if she was to find a man she could live with.

Garwood arrived while Atwater was flirting with Lady Jersey. "Lady Seaton seems strained," he noted after the ritual greeting.

"She has reason to be."

The lady was laughing with a pair of officers, but the lines around her eyes did not denote gaiety, and she sat her horse like a wooden statue.

Angela's maid had been bursting with the tale that morning. Lord Seaton was a well-known rake who had carelessly been discovered *en flagrante* by his current inamorata's husband. A duel was inevitable. Lady Seaton must have heard the news.

Garwood shook his head. "She knew his reputation when she married him, so she can hardly complain."

"Perhaps she thought to reform him."

He laughed. "More fool she. He is incorrigible—not that any gentleman is likely to change his habits for a wife. If she wanted fidelity, she should have chosen a husband who believed in it."

She nodded, but made no further comment.

Atwater bade Lady Jersey farewell, glanced coolly at Garwood, and moved the phaeton forward. He started to speak, but was interrupted by Lord Styles, followed by the Bradbury sisters, then Lady Delaney and her daughter.

Angela tired of the repetitious conversation long before they completed their circuit of the park. The voices kept changing, but the same words echoed from all sides.

"Lady Chesbrooke and Lady Fullerton had another falling out last night . . ."

". . . and then Delaney upset the table—accidentally, of course—but poor Williamson spilled wine all over his . . ."

"Shelford is thinking of trying his grays against the London-to-Dover record . . ."

"If Mr. Conelaugh thinks he can slip into the garden with . . ."

"Mademoiselle Jeanette is the best modiste you have ever found?"

"I cannot believe Lord Seaton . . ."

". . . Lady Jenkins lost a hundred guineas at loo, of all things . . ."

The fashionable hour was merely an extension of the drawing room—the same faces, the same gossip. Only the addition of horses and carriages made it different. As Atwater turned toward the gates, she exchanged one last nod with another departing lady.

"Devil take it, didn't your mother teach you anything?" He glared. "That was Lady Shelby."

"Who is she?"

"A person to be cut."

"Why?"

He shook his head. "Such innocence. You needn't bother your pretty head over it. But ignore her from now on." His condescension irritated her, but she could not find the words to express herself. How was she to gain a man's respect if revealing intelligence would ruin her?

She sighed. Perhaps she was not as smart as she thought. Otherwise, she surely could sound out her escort's mind without revealing her own. But the words wouldn't come.

Devall ignored the cuts as he strode down Bond Street, his face twisted into a formidable frown. One look at him prompted most to give him a wide berth. Two weeks had passed since his return to London. Two weeks. Yet he had made no progress.

Gabriel's only regular activities were morning calls and attendance at Marriage Mart events. He didn't spar, shoot, or fence. He didn't patronize Tattersall's. He visited his clubs sporadically, favoring none.

For the first time in years, he cursed his reputation. The only place he could be sure to catch the fellow was in a ballroom, but society had long barred its doors against him. Somehow he must garner some invitations.

*Devil take it!*

He hated the insipid conformity of the polite world. But abandoning this quest was impossible. Heaving a resigned sigh, he mulled the list of London hostesses. How far must he humble himself to gain a hearing? And who might give him a chance? Pride had kept him quiet for six years, allowing the popular misconceptions to stand. Pride and the freedom that ostracism provided. But perhaps it was time to press for his rights.

Few names passed his scrutiny. The sticklers were out, of course. They all wished him to Hades and would never reconsider. Since he felt the same way about them, he would continue to ignore them. The intellectuals? Lady Chartley might do. As would Mrs. Barnthorpe. But Gabriel disdained intellectuals, ignoring any event that attracted them. Joining the intelligentsia would get him no closer to his goal—unless the exposure garnered invitations to social affairs. But such a roundabout course would take time, and more patience than he possessed.

He hated delays, especially when they postponed achieving his goals or kept him away from Wyndhaven. So who else might help?

Approaching other social outcasts would only generate new tales to blot his reputation. He routinely received invitations from people on the fringes of society, but accepting them would diminish his consequence even further. The few gentlemen who might champion him lacked the clout to wangle him invitations from respected hostesses.

So he must start with the intellectuals. Lady Chartley did not care a whit for him, but she did enjoy shocking society.

He was crossing Piccadilly when he spotted Gabriel emerging from Hatchard's, barely fifteen feet away. Perfect. And when he had least expected it, too. Perhaps he could avoid groveling to Lady Chartley.

Carefully maintaining his ground-devouring stride, he lowered his head as though deep in thought, then stumbled, lurching sideways to knock Atwater into one of the small-paned bow windows that flanked the entrance.

"Clumsy oaf!" Devall glared at the impeccably dressed earl. "Disguised already, Gabriel? Why don't you watch where you are reeling?"

Fury erupted on Atwater's face. "We both know who was at fault," he said, dusting his shoulder. His fingers froze, and he frowned. "You tore my coat."

"Just as well. It doesn't suit you."

"I ought to call you out for that." Atwater smoothed Weston's exquisite creation. "Name—" His gaze sharpened, his eyes boring into Devall's face. In less than a second, his expression slid into a sneer, only the slightest catch in his voice revealing that he had read what was reflected there. "But one can expect manners only from a gentleman."

Turning away, he rapidly disappeared into Bond Street.

*Damnation!*

Devall watched until Atwater was out of sight. Still swearing over losing control of his face, he entered Hatchard's.

If only he had been prepared for this meeting! But it was too late for regrets. He had tipped his hand, losing the game even at the moment of victory. But the rubber was not over, though winning would now be more difficult.

He must choose his next encounter with greater care—and be sure they had an audience. Atwater would lose credit if he ducked an affair of honor in front of witnesses. Why had no one of consequence been nearby today?

A ball would provide scores of witnesses—which returned his mind to the problem of gaining entrée into society. He must seek out Lady Chartley after all.

Angela sighed as she added Byron's *The Giaour* to a stack that already held Jane Austen's latest novel *Pride and Prejudice*. The problem with bookshops was that she never left with only the volume she had intended to get.

"Well, if it isn't the soft-hearted hoyden," The unexpectedly deep voice startled her as she turned down the next aisle. "How much has he stolen?"

Lord Blackthorn leaned against a shelf. He was again dressed in black, but it was his eyes that riveted her attention—hard and black in the dim light, yet blazing with fury and hatred. Oddly, neither was aimed at her, despite his dripping sarcasm. Something had put him in a raging temper.

She shivered at this latest flash of mind-reading, trying to thrust it aside. But curiosity over his anger battled prudence and irritation. She ought to retreat lest others assume they were together. Yet the volume she most wanted was visible just beyond his left shoulder.

"Excuse me, sir." She looked past him in the hope that he would move. All kinds of people patronized the shops, but she was not obligated to talk with them.

*Even though you want to.*

She jumped at the inner voice. Blackthorn was clearly trouble. How could she wish to speak with an outcast? But she did. Even more urgent than discovering what had infuriated him, she needed to know why her reputation was safe in his hands.

"Playing the timid miss today?" he asked. "We both know it's not the real you."

This was the Black Marquess of rumor. His fury had faded, but his eyes still glittered like black ice. No hint of warmth entered his voice. His stance dared her to oppose him, promising instant retribution if she tried.

"Excuse me, sir," she repeated. "I must reach that shelf just behind you."

"Tell me your name first."

*Arrogant fool! How dare he?*

But she could never resist a challenge, especially when another's bad manners triggered her own temper. "Why? So you can ruin me like so many others? I already know too much about you, Lord Blackthorn. If you must know my name, find someone to introduce us. Not that any reputable person would do so, and I know no others."

"So, my first impression was right," he drawled, crossing his arms. "Do you enjoy brawling with street vendors?"

"When they are beating defenseless infants."

"Defenseless? The lad is a thief. You do him no favor when you let him get away with crime. You'd best run home and see how much he has stolen." Straightening, he loomed over her in a way that would intimidate a strong man, his piercing gaze more effective than Brummell's quizzing glass.

She ignored his glare. "Presumptuous, aren't you? And conceited, as well. Do you always judge without bothering to learn the facts? Or are you so sure of your own infallibility that you accept every impression as gospel? That boy is no thief."

"So naïve! Do you actually believe his claims? Boys like him are carefully coached in a variety of heartrending tales that can gain them access to homes worth robbing."

"As you know first hand? Maybe your friends lie and cheat, but not Jimmy." Her fists were clenched to keep from slapping him.

"So you made him your page. You would have been better off consigning him to the workhouse."

"Hardly. And why would I put so young a lad in service? No child should be exploited."

"Good Lord! He really got to you, didn't he? You'd best face the truth before he and his friends make off with all your possessions."

She was past caring what he could do to her reputation. Nor did she consider why she could argue with the most menacing scoundrel in London when she could barely exchange the time of day with reputable gentlemen. "You wrong me, sir. Jimmy has neither the incentive nor the opportunity to harm me. He is now in a well-run orphanage where his brother has lived for some weeks. Nor is he the hardened criminal you imply. Their parents were respectable before falling on hard times. Once the boys recover, they will remove to school."

"Soft-hearted wench, aren't you?"

"Odious wretch! Better soft-hearted than cruel. But why should I explain myself to you? You are hardly qualified to judge propriety. Now step aside so I can get my book. My carriage is waiting."

"Haven't you enough already?" He stared at the dozen books in her arms. "That should keep you busy for the rest of the Season."

"Determined to flaunt your ignorance, aren't you?" She ignored the voice that warned against goading so dangerous a man. "And making quite a cake of yourself. Move aside."

"Which one is it?" He settled back against the shelves, an immovable obstruction.

"*The Importance of Educating Members of the Working Classes.*"

"Not another reformer," he drawled.

"*Only the educated are free.* That is as true today as when Epictetus uttered the words seventeen hundred years ago, and he would know better than most. Without the ability to read, people can only believe what they are told, putting them at the mercy of unscrupulous masters, deceitful landowners, and other dishonorable folk. We've taken the first steps toward abolishing slavery in the colonies, yet we keep our own lower classes enslaved in ignorance."

His brows raised but he made no comment. Pulling out a volume not much larger than a pamphlet, he idly leafed through its pages.

"I had hoped it would be more detailed," she murmured, sighing in disappointment. But perhaps it contained different ideas than the others she had read.

Blackthorn said nothing, oblivious to both her disappointment and her growing anger.

"My book?" she demanded at last.

"Your name?" He narrowed his eyes, raising those sharply peaked brows.

"Lucifer himself," she muttered, shaking her head. "No wonder people claim you were spawned by the devil."

"And how pleased they are when I prove them right."

"That is the worst excuse for misbehavior I have ever heard!" She glared. "Give me my book."

"Your name, my little bluestocking reformer!" He lazily dangled the treatise just out of reach.

"Why? So you can pillory me by trumpeting my shortcomings to society?"

"Would I do that?" He pursed his lips as though deep in thought. "If I behaved in so ungentlemanly a fashion, you would retaliate by exposing mine. You could ruin me."

She gasped, eliciting a chuckle that sent excited shivers down her spine. Was he flirting with her? Or was this a veiled warning against mentioning those soldiers? But that would mean that he'd hired them to do something worse than any of his past deeds. The only worse crime she could think of was murder. The next shiver was icy.

His face lightened, bringing silver sparks to his eyes. "The fact that I've known damaging information about you for nearly a fortnight yet did not reveal it makes me look soft-hearted."

"Which might improve your image."

"Horrors! I work hard to maintain my reputation and don't care to have it damaged. Your name!"

She sighed. Teasing her was highly improper. But what did she expect? He had all but bragged that he enjoyed shocking people. Unless she told him her name, she must return for the book another day. "Miss Angela Warren."

"Lord Forley's sister?" Surprise blossomed across his face, proving that he really hadn't known who she was.

"I suppose you will now destroy what little credit I have. Haven't you ruined enough people?"

"Now you wrong *me*," he said, echoing her earlier charge. "I could have learned your identity long ago if that was my purpose."

"I can only pray you are telling the truth. My book, sir? If anyone sees me talking to you, that will be ruin enough."

He nodded, as if he had just realized the truth of that sentiment, but the book remained out of reach. "You really shouldn't jump out of moving carriages, Miss Warren. You could have been badly injured."

"True, but I wasn't thinking of myself." She pointedly held out her hand.

Smiling, he gently placed the book on her palm, brushing her fingers with his own. "It's been a pleasure." He winked.

"Has it?" Turning abruptly away, she stumbled out to her carriage.

Devall remained where he was, his eyes now narrowed in speculation. So that was Angela Warren. Very interesting. She was one of the girls Gabriel had danced attendance on in recent days, or so his informants had reported. Someone less like the first Lady Atwater he could not imagine. Was that the attraction? Or was Gabriel unaware of the passion that lurked beneath her surface? Perhaps cultivating Miss Warren could bring him closer to Atwater without following the lengthy—and onerous—path of charming Lady Chartley.

But he immediately rejected the idea. He could not destroy an innocent bystander no matter how urgent his feud with the earl.

He frowned. So what had he just been doing? His behavior astonished him. He was never rude to strangers, especially those for whom he had felt concern. Why had he done it? Surely he hadn't been trying to ruin her! It wasn't her fault that she had bothered him since their first encounter. And that would only get worse now that they had spoken.

Damn! He had misjudged her on several counts. Not only was she less naïve than he had expected, but she was much more intelligent. It was always possible that her brother had quoted

Epictetus, of course, but he suspected she had read it herself—perhaps even in the original Greek. She seemed familiar enough with the philosopher to know that he had started life as a Roman slave.

How much had she overheard that day on Piccadilly? He still didn't know, for asking her would have drawn her attention to the incident. Her demeanor gave him no clue. On the other hand, no one would believe the tale, so he was safe enough.

She was intriguing, though he was not quite sure what to make of her. Two very different images floated before his eyes. The first grew from his own impressions—a fiery reformer bursting with life and vitality; a girl who did not adhere to the strictures of society when they conflicted with her own beliefs; a woman whose red hair and green eyes lent emphasis to her passionate fury, making him want to hug her in delight.

He shook his head at the way she had confronted that vendor—in the middle of a public thoroughfare before the eyes of the world. That the gossips knew nothing of her escapade was blind luck. And talking to him was the height of folly. She had known his identity and reputation, yet had sparred with him in a bookshop patronized by all of society, meeting rudeness with rudeness, oblivious to who might have overheard.

A lingering hint of heliotrope teased his nose. An unusual scent for an unusual lady.

But a far different image emerged from his reports on Atwater's inamorata. *That* Miss Warren was shy and demure, rarely raising her voice above a whisper and seldom meeting any gentleman's eye. She was exceedingly proper and promised to make a biddable wife.

He shuddered. Her behavior matched that of the first Lady Atwater, though Lydia had been a blue-eyed blonde.

*Stupid!*

A wave of disappointment engulfed him—and fury at himself because he'd forgotten that she was one of society's daughters—and Lady Forley's daughter, at that. The opposing images meant nothing. She was putting on an act, mimicking Atwater's first wife to attract the earl's attention. And her reason was obvious. Title and fortune. It was what every chit wanted. She would be the Countess of Atwater, a big step up for Viscount Forley's impoverished sister. Her delayed come-out could only be blamed on failing finances. She was conventional, all right—greedy, selfish, determined, and willing to employ deceit and manipulation to improve her position in society.

How could he have been crazy enough to like her?

Picking up his own pile of books, he added a copy of the educational treatise and headed home, swearing profusely when that animated face stuck in his mind. She was far too enticing when enraged.

# Chapter Four

A week later, Devall leaned against a building in New Bond Street, watching the door of Grafton House, the linen draper's across the way. Miss Warren should exit at any moment, for she rarely wasted her time on idle browsing. It was further proof that her public image was a ruse. Conventional chits adored shopping.

*Why are you following her?*

The question surfaced daily despite his constant guard, but this time he couldn't suppress it. Ignoring the latest cuts direct—these from Ladies Horseley and Stafford—he considered his motives.

It was true that he hated pretense, but that was no reason for stalking Miss Warren—which he had been doing for a week now. She employed no more deceit than other young ladies.

He sighed. Atwater was a big reason, and not just because he despised the man. Miss Warren and the earl did not suit. Despite her greed, she deserved a husband who would appreciate her, but she was too naïve to recognize that Gabriel did not qualify. Somehow he must convince her that many gentlemen prized the traits she was hiding. By revealing herself as an Original, she could have much of society at her feet, including some who possessed the title and fortune she craved.

She emerged into the morning sunshine. Today's costume fit the role she was playing—an elegantly restrained but fashionable morning gown, a charming bonnet that completely concealed her fiery curls, and a mask of mindless *ennui* to hide her passions from the world. A very proper maid accompanied her.

Fury engulfed him. He hated charades. He hated dishonesty. So why did she insist on both?

Catching her eye, he bathed her with his most scathing stare. Within moments, she abandoned the meek facade. Good.

Or perhaps not. She countered with a glare that knifed into his head, sending shivers clear to his toes. Naturally she spotted that faint ripple. The corner of her mouth quirked in satisfaction.

This wasn't the first time they had silently fenced, but she was becoming too adept at probing deep into his mind. Thickening the armor that protected his darkest secrets, he deliberately fed his fury, hoping to divert her attention.

She was a deceitful wench. Greedy. And stupid, if she thought to manage Atwater after marriage. Inevitably her trickery would be exposed, but he doubted that she understood the consequences. His eyes bored into hers in warning, but she was too stubborn—or too ignorant—to heed him. He ought to wash his hands of her, but revulsion forced him to abandon the idea.

"Miss Warren," he mouthed silently, nodding in greeting. The clatter of hooves and wheels on cobblestones drowned out sound at this distance, so speaking could only draw unwanted attention. Approaching her openly would ruin her, but he must make her understand. "Be yourself. Stay away from Atwater."

She straightened, anger animating her face.

Ignoring the voice cautioning him to tread warily, he let his gaze travel over her body—and a very nice body it was. His eyes lingered on the best parts.

She returned the favor, flooding him with heat. Then her lips moved, and he flinched. Surely she hadn't just called him a lecherous rogue! But the satisfaction sparkling in her eyes confirmed it. She added something else that looked like *conceited ass*.

"Baggage!" he mouthed, stifling a laugh.

*Pompous popinjay!* she responded.

A carriage passed between them, blocking his view. By the time it was gone, she was ducking into a nearby shop.

"Damnation," he muttered as he strode away. His hands were trembling. What the devil had gotten into him? If anyone had noticed that exchange, she would be ruined. Fortunately, society always cut him, which required that they avert their eyes. But she lacked that protection. He must avoid further indiscretions.

*　　*　　*

Angela stared at the crowd packed into Almack's and sighed. Despite warnings from both Cassie and her mother, she had not expected the days to be so ruthlessly filled with activities. Balls, routs, theater, opera, drives in the park, picnics, morning calls, at-homes, shopping . . . The list went on and on. Some nights they took in four events. Lady Forley was ecstatic.

Angela was not. In this rush for quantity entertainment, quality got lost. As did enjoyment. Hundreds of events were scheduled during a Season that lasted only three months. And that didn't include the daily round of calls, the fashionable hour in the park, the theater, or the opera. No one wanted to miss anything, so they all scrambled to attend everything.

But the pace was so frenetic that she accomplished nothing, exchanging meaningless pleasantries at each stop before rushing on to the next. Despite spending most of her time with other people, she rarely talked to anyone—really talked; parroting gossip didn't count. The purpose of all this socializing was to find a husband, yet she knew little more about her suitors than their names and ranks.

Lady Jersey was watching, so she widened her smile and suppressed another sigh.

She had acquired a regular court, much to Lady Forley's delight. Most of the gentlemen who were seriously shopping for wives had already begun to narrow their choices, which reduced hers to those currently dancing attendance on her. One day soon she must bring one of them up to scratch. But which?

Not everyone was serious. Captain Harrington would be returning to the Peninsula as soon as his doctors declared him fit— probably next week. Several young sprigs just down from school occasionally hovered around her, indulging in small doses of polite society between visits to green rooms and gaming hells. Others flitted from one court to another, enjoying the variety.

Sir Alan was a different story. Lady Forley despised him, for he was only a baronet, her diatribes growing so obnoxious that Angela had seriously considered him for several days. But he was not a man she could live with in comfort. He cared for little beyond clothes and horses, his shallow mind incapable of original thought. If they wed, she would soon dominate him—not a situation she approved. She hoped her husband would consider her suggestions, but how could she respect a man who allowed her to ride roughshod over him? So it was time to hint Sir Alan away.

Garwood was another whom her mother disapproved despite encouraging him to remain in attendance—a large court enhanced one's credit. Angela had actually managed a reasonable conversation with him at the Clarkwell picnic, finding him intelligent and dedicated to his estate. And he made her feel comfortable enough that she had mentioned one of Andrew's agriculture experiments. Though surprised, he had accepted her knowledge, indulging in a lively debate.

Yet two questions remained. Could their relationship grow beyond idle friendship? And was he in the market for a wife? No one seemed to know.

She couldn't doubt Atwater's intentions. He made no secret of them. Surprisingly, he had narrowed his choices to herself and Miss Hanson, a baronet's daughter, abandoning both an earl's daughter and a duke's. The gossips favored her, both because of her higher rank and because Lady Forley enthusiastically approved a match.

Her mother's pressure annoyed her, as did people's assumption that she would automatically accept him because he was the most desirable *parti* in town. More than one girl had feigned friendship with her solely to fawn over Atwater. The gossips' sly innuendo was even more irritating than her mother's admonitions.

She could never relax with him. Perhaps it was his incessant flattery, which had grown even warmer since her ball. Perhaps it was the way he hovered, bringing her cool drinks when she was hardly aware of a dry throat and maneuvering her near the doors before she noted a heated ballroom. Or perhaps it was his notorious disdain. His credit was as high as Brummell's, and he used it in the same way—raising or lowering others' consequence by bestowing or denying his favor. She hated the way these arbiters of fashion played with people's lives. And knowing that he could destroy her on a whim increased her tension, for she was terrified of revealing her inadequacies. She couldn't converse with him beyond one-word responses to direct questions.

That must change. If she could not hold a rational discussion with him, then she must leave him to Miss Hanson—who clearly doted on him—and concentrate on bringing Garwood up to scratch.

But avoiding him would be difficult, she realized when Atwater arrived and headed directly to her side, passing Lady Jersey with only the barest nod. That easily insulted matron merely smiled.

"You dance divinely, my dear," he said as they took their places for a cotillion.

She said nothing.

The figure parted them, but he kept his face turned adoringly to hers instead of smiling at his new partner. It was clear to everyone in the room that he had made his decision and would court only her from now on. Miss Hanson seemed on the verge of tears. Lady Jersey's lips formed the words *young love* as she looked smilingly on.

Angela shivered.

Yet her reaction was silly. Now that he had singled her out, surely they would discuss serious subjects. Perhaps she could even figure out why Atwater terrified her while Blackthorn did not.

It was a question that had puzzled her for days. Blackthorn was the most dangerous man in Mayfair. Yet she had argued with him, insulted him, revealed interests that society would abhor, and not once considered herself in danger. And her instincts had been right. No hint had surfaced of their meeting. Yet his silence arose from neither prudence nor affection. He obviously loathed her.

She had spotted him several times since their encounter in Hatchard's—on Bond Street, in Hyde Park, and again near Hatchard's. Always he had caught her eye. Even from afar, he radiated anger. His appearances were too frequent to pass off as chance, so he must be watching her. Yet her reaction was inexplicable. His most ferocious glares failed to intimidate her, while Atwater's affections invariably did.

The movement of the dance brought her back to Atwater's side.

"So beautiful," he murmured, staring warmly into her eyes.

"Thank you, my lord," she managed.

"Call me Gabriel." He deftly avoided a couple who were so engrossed in each other that they had drifted out of their own set.

"I cannot, my lord." She could not consider such closeness. He was too much an enigma.

He nodded, looking even more pleased. "Of course not. So quiet and proper a lady must balk at unseemly familiarity. Society prefers that we wait."

*You don't understand!* But no words emerged.

Was that good or bad? Every exchange strengthened her impression that this man would not make a comfortable husband. His very presence prevented her from conducting a normal conversation on even innocuous subjects.

But she could not accept that as truth any more than she could believe society's facade of gaiety. He might not be at fault. Lady Forley's pressure was mounting. *You must snare Atwater . . . flirt with him . . . all it will take is a few lures . . . fortune and title are essential in a husband . . . he is the catch of the Season . . . you will be the envy of all society . . . don't waste any chances . . .*

Her discomfort might be no more than rebellion against her mother's manipulation. And it *was* manipulation. Lady Forley was being downright rude to Sir Alan and quite stilted toward Garwood. Yet she fawned over Atwater to the point of embarrassment.

But changing her mother's behavior was hopeless. The only way to halt her antics was to accept an offer—which meant sounding out Garwood's intentions so she knew whether she had a choice.

She stifled a sigh. Almack's was no place for serious discussions—or even for planning serious discussions. The patronesses watched everyone like hawks, frowning at any indiscretion.

When the dance concluded, Angela found Lady Forley engulfed in righteous indignation. "Are you implying that Lord Cloverdale did not die of natural causes? Lady Sefton swore he succumbed to a chill."

"What rubbish," said Lady Debenham with an audible snort. "Though it has never been general knowledge, I refuse to hide the truth now that *that man* is creeping back into society. He actually accepted what must have been an erroneous invitation to Lady Chartley's soiree last evening. The gall of the scoundrel!"

"Not Blackthorn!"

"Who else? He showed up, larger than life and even more devilish than usual. And Lady Chartley had the nerve to allow him inside. I was never so shocked in my life!" She furiously fluttered her fan. "But he is wrong if he thinks he can worm his way back into my good graces. I refused to speak in the past out of consideration for the families, but the truth must out. Blackthorn murdered Cloverdale."

Angela grimaced. Another body in the man's wake. And not one that could be passed off as fate or the suicide of a weakling. Surely this would banish that odd glow she experienced whenever he caught her eye.

"Murdered?" demanded Mrs. Bassington, another inveterate gossip, who had been shamelessly eavesdropping.

"He might consider it an affair of honor, but I cannot." Lady Debenham pulled herself straighter. "There were no seconds. No doctor. No witnesses. And Cloverdale was execrable with both sword and pistol. It was naught but cold-blooded murder, but without witnesses, none can lay charges."

"Without witnesses, how do you know what happened?" asked Lady Forley, surprising both Angela and Lady Debenham.

"What else could it be?" the gossip demanded. "Cloverdale told Lord Kingsley that he was meeting Blackthorn in the morning. Kingsley assumed it was to receive the crim-con settlement. Not until the body turned up did he deduce that the meeting had been a duel. But even that is not the sum of Blackthorn's crimes. Lord Coldstream's death must have occurred in the same way. The two had been at odds the day before. I tell you, Blackthorn is devoid of all honor."

"What is she going on about now?" murmured Sylvia, appearing at Angela's side. She had accompanied them to Almack's so Hart could keep a weary Cassie at home.

"Lady Debenham thinks Blackthorn killed both Cloverdale and Coldstream," she whispered.

"I remember the talk about Coldstream," said Sylvia. "He died while I was in town shopping with Cassie. He and Blackthorn had had an altercation at one of the clubs—Boodle's, I think—the night before, though it was never clear what caused it. One rumor claimed they argued over a girl; another swore it grew out of a card game. But they supposedly patched up the quarrel without a challenge."

"How do you know?" She moved closer to Sylvia so they wouldn't be heard. All ears were tuned to Lady Debenham's increasingly strident denunciations. "That is hardly drawing room talk."

"I overheard Hart and Cassie discussing it. He shares everything with her. But there was no hint of murder. I wonder if it's true."

Angela bit her tongue until Sylvia's next partner whisked her away. Why did she have such a strong urge to defend Blackthorn? It made no sense. In fact, nothing made sense. She was losing her mind.

She caught Lady Jersey's frown from across the room and smiled, forcing her face into a vapid mask to smooth her brow.

Just that morning she had seen him on New Bond Street when she emerged from the linen draper's shop. He had blessed her with another of his disapproving glowers, and had even gone so far as to mouth greetings. She could still feel his eyes boring through her.

Warmth suffused her body as his image obliterated the ballroom, returning her to Bond Street. Sunlight glinted off his curly-brimmed beaver. Menace rolled from him in palpable waves. It was the closest she had been to him since that day in Hatchard's, yet despite his antagonism, she still felt no threat.

The incongruity made her question her sanity even as a coach rolled past, blocking her view. Why did so notorious a scoundrel not intimidate her? Curiosity was an inadequate answer, though he had piqued hers since that day on Piccadilly. His silence over her misdeeds proved that he was less black than society claimed, yet his stalking supported even the worst tales. Was he playing some game with her?

Even as she grappled with his inconsistencies, their gazes locked, and she shivered.

He was a mass of seething emotion. Fury and disapproval were obvious. But his eyes contained so much more—warmth, irritation, pain, intelligence, wariness, arrogance . . .

An overwhelming urge to stroke that harsh face and smooth the furrowed brow graphically revealed her real enemy.

Herself.

No wonder she didn't fear him! Her own urges were far more dangerous. Blackthorn might be an enticing enigma, but she could not afford to explore his character. Satisfying her curiosity would destroy her. If rescuing Jimmy could make her a social pariah, what would compassion for the Black Marquess do? Someone would surely lock her in Bedlam—probably her mother.

Even as he mouthed another comment, a lady pushed past her into the shop, jostling her arm and reminding her that she was visible to the entire world.

Dear Lord! She was staring at him. Again. And again she had no idea how much time had passed. Even worse, she had replied—several times. The last thing she needed was for people to think she was besotted with the man. Caroline Lamb's obsession with Lord Byron had been the talk of the town for more than a year. Comparisons would ruin her.

Yet it was difficult to wrest her gaze from Blackthorn's. And she couldn't resist peeking over her shoulder as she ducked into a shop.

He hadn't moved an inch. And his eyes still bore into hers.

Shivering, Angela forced her attention back to Almack's. She must avoid Blackthorn, for she exerted no self-control in his presence. How could she have stared at him like a moonstruck pea-goose?

Garwood arrived to lead her into the next set. "What is that all about?" He nodded toward Lady Debenham.

"More rumors about Lord Blackthorn." She shrugged.

"Rumors abound in London. Many are exaggerated, though in Blackthorn's case, even the truth is severe."

"Meaning that stories about him are not exaggerated, or that they remain grim even when shorn of editing?"

"Definitely grim, though not entirely true. Take that gambling story, for example. He fleeced Graceford, right enough. Last Season, it was. But I saw no evidence of cheating. He is a better player than people suspect, for his mind is quite keen. Graceford, on the other hand, always had a little too much luck, though no one ever caught him at anything underhanded—at least not in this country. He died in a duel with an Italian *conte* who did not consider Graceford's fuzzed deck amusing. One of my friends recently returned from Naples and recounted the whole story. He witnessed the denouement."

"Heavens! But why does Blackthorn have a reputation for losing if he is such a good player?"

"I suspect he plays for idle pleasure and cares not whether he wins or loses. But let us forget the man, for despite exaggerations, he remains a blackguard. What he did to his betrothed can never be forgiven, and Lady Cloverdale was worse. There is a new exhibit at the British Institution you would enjoy—a retrospective of Reynolds. Shall we visit it tomorrow?"

"Mother has already accepted Lady Stafford's invitation to a Venetian breakfast. Perhaps Friday."

"Thank you. Would your brother and Lady Sylvia care to join us?"

"We can ask."

The arrangements were quickly made, and she moved off with Sir Alan. They had no opportunity to talk during the country dance, but afterward, when he offered to take her driving, she shook her head.

"I would enjoy it, but you should escort someone eligible to become your lady." He jerked as if she had slapped him. Damn! Her tact was severely lacking. In an effort to soothe his bruised feelings, she continued. "You are a good friend, and I want you to be happy. But you have often mentioned that you need a wife. Honesty compels me to point out that I will probably grow into a harridan much like my mother. You would be uncomfortable with such a person."

"Indeed I would," he said, much struck.

Angela grimaced once he departed. She had not handled that well. Yet what would have been better? Turning down an offer he had not yet made was frowned upon, but if she had waited, it would have been too late for him to look elsewhere this Season. The harridan comment had been an outright lie, but she could scarcely tell him that he was too weak-willed, even though it was the truth. After watching her mother dominate her father, she wished to avoid any chance of doing the same.

Lord Styles was chatting with Lady Forley, promising that the rest of the evening would be annoying. His giggling daughters would make their appearance all too soon.

Lord Styles laughed at one of Lady Forley's comments, and she thwacked him soundly with her fan. Atwater returned Grace to her father's side, bestowing a warm smile on Angela before moving off to find his next partner.

"I vow you are the luckiest thing," said Grace with a sigh, her eyes glued on Atwater's back. "I wish he would look at me that way. Isn't he the handsomest man? Golden hair. Blue eyes. And the most sensuous lips." She giggled.

"I suppose so," agreed Angela. Grace compared everyone to the heroes in her favorite gothic novels. "But looks are not everything."

"I know," said Grace. "Title and wealth count more. But it certainly adds to the package. Do I have any chance with Lord Atwater?" she asked Lady Hervey. "He dances with me every day and always has some compliment for my appearance."

"He only asks you because we are nearby when he claims his two sets with Miss Warren," replied her sister brutally, for once soberly honest. Her tone implied that the match was a foregone conclusion, making Angela shudder. "Turn your eyes to someone reasonable. Mr. Harley has been attentive the last few days. He may not have a title, but his uncle left him a fortune. And he's not bad looking. With only a bit more chin, he would be downright handsome."

"But he is such a sobersides," protested Grace.

"Not really." Lady Hervey understood the girl's penchant for pranksters. "Did you not know that he was responsible for that melee last week when three muddy dogs and a cat were released into Lord Houghington's hall just as he descended dressed for the opera?"

Grace laughed. "Lord Houghington is so fastidious that a speck of lint will send him home to change."

"One of the dogs shook himself right in front of his lordship." Lady Hervey giggled. "I heard his hysterics were a sight to behold."

*What a juvenile prank!* And the girls weren't much better. Lord Houghington might be more fastidious than Brummell, but the dogs had knocked over tables, breaking vases and starting a fire that scorched the drawing room carpet. The cat had sprayed the draperies. It would be long before the odor was gone.

When she returned from the next set, she found Lord Styles alone. Lady Forley had accompanied Grace to the withdrawing room to repair a flounce torn by Mr. Crawford, who was gaining a reputation for clumsiness, having damaged four gowns already this Season. Lady Hervey was across the room, laughing with friends.

"Silly chit to make such a fuss," grumbled Styles. Grace had been nearly hysterical over the accident, drawing disapproving glances from three of the patronesses.

"She is young yet," murmured Angela. The following set was a waltz, so she was neatly trapped here until her mother returned. The Countess Lieven had introduced the dance at Almack's the previous spring, but it was still considered scandalous for young girls. The Season would be considerably older before she received permission to try it.

"I don't know where she comes by these jumped-up ideas." He seemed determined to air his complaints. "Her sisters found perfectly good husbands at the York races. There was no call to waste good money on London."

"It is rather expensive."

"Stupid widgeon. Just because I inherited a title, she thinks to land some rich lord. I must have had rocks in my head to agree. I hate London."

She could understand that. Ignoring Lady Forley's dictums for once, she answered truthfully. "Hate is a bit strong, but I, too, prefer the country, as does my brother. Life is too hectic here, too shallow, too phony. Though it can be fun in small doses."

He seemed surprised, but also gratified. "Not even in small doses. Even York is too hectic for my tastes."

"You prefer your estate then?"

"Definitely. It offers marvelous hunting. The open moors are more real than this stuffy ballroom."

"How fortunate that you love them," she said lightly. "Your home is quite isolated, I understand."

"As is your brother's."

"We have a few neighbors, but we are in a pocket of hills separated from most other estates by Romney Marsh, and now by the military canal."

"Will you pine for it once you leave?"

"Some, but with my brother's impending marriage, I have no place there any more. Lady Sylvia will assume running the house."

An odd expression flitted across his face. "That's what the old harridan meant."

"What?"

"My housekeeper. With Grace gone, who will run my house? Who will see after my tenants? She's my youngest."

Heavens! Was he hinting that she would make an adequate wife? But his next words dispelled that fear.

"I suppose I must look over the widows when I get home. There is one in the village and several in the nearest market town. Someone accustomed to living modestly would be best. I cannot abide waste."

She was saved from responding by a commotion outside the ballroom.

"No one gets in after eleven," swore a distant voice, recognizable as the porter's. "No exceptions."

A man answered, but his voice was muffled.

"Good God! It's a bloomin' footpad!" exclaimed a sprig near the window that overlooked the entrance.

"We'll be murdered!" gasped a matron.

Half a dozen ladies screamed, prompting several gentlemen to turn censorious quizzing glasses on the lad.

"Nonsense!" declared Captain Harrington from his post at another window. He caught Angela's gaze with a reassuring wink. "It's only a jarvey trying to deliver a message."

This assessment proved accurate, for the porter appeared in the doorway, where he exchanged a few words with Lady Jersey. She then sought out Lady Hanson, who gasped. Only the timely appearance of a vinaigrette prevented a swoon. She left immediately, supported by her teary-eyed daughter.

Within seconds everyone in the ballroom had heard the news. Sir Gerald Hanson had been stricken at his club, collapsing onto the hazard table—dead.

Angela was shocked, though not by the death. Society's reception of the news appalled her. The orchestra never missed a beat. People parroted brief regrets, then returned to the serious business of revelry, social smiles firmly in place. Not that she grieved for a man she had never met, but many of those in attendance knew the family well. And she *did* feel sorry for Miss Hanson, who had lost her father and the man she cared for in the space of an evening.

Lady Forley returned as Atwater escorted Angela into a set.

Grace simpered at Mr. Harley, clinging to his arm. "I'm so glad we finished in time. I would hate missing a set with *you*."

"Silly chit," Styles murmured.

"She must be a trial," Lady Forley agreed. "Thank heaven Angela is not prone to such starts."

"She seems calm and sensible."

"Yes. It is gratifying when I see myself in the girl."


Devall lounged in a doorway across King Street from Almack's, waiting for society's elite to emerge. Gabriel must be inside, for he never missed an assembly—or any other activity that might flaunt his exalted position in the *ton*. What better place to provoke the earl than before the *crème de la crème*?

Snapping his pocket watch closed, Devall scanned the revelers now streaming from the building. Carriages crowded the street. Ladies and gentlemen crammed the sidewalks.

*Devil take it.* He had forgotten the confusion that always followed an assembly. How was he to stage an accident in this melee?

But he had no time for planning. Atwater emerged, heading toward a carriage a short distance away.

Devall kept his eyes fixed on the earl's hat as he hurried to cut him off. And that was a mistake. He was so intent on his target that he slammed into a lady.

"Beg pardon," he mumbled, absently catching her to prevent a fall.

"Why should I?" she demanded.

*Miss Warren!* Searing heat burned through his gloves. He dropped his hands, but the crush prevented him from backing away, so she still pressed against his chest. Warmth exploded through his body.

"Are you trying to ruin me?" she hissed, glaring into his face.

"N-never," he stammered. Her ball gown was stunning—embroidered ivory silk embellished with green ribbons that made her eyes glow. Her hair blazed with vitality, threaded with more ribbon that begged his fingers to follow. He restrained himself—barely. He had already done enough damage for one night.

"Your actions belie your words." Her voice steadied his swirling thoughts.

"Shh," he warned, guiltily tearing his eyes away while keeping his face impassive. A quick glance confirmed that his actions so far remained unnoticed. "I had no idea you were here," he added, keeping his lips immobile. "Forgive me." He wanted to say more, but danger prickled the back of his neck. Unless he left immediately, her reputation would suffer. Giving her no time to respond, he turned toward Atwater.

The earl was gone.

Cursing himself, he fled. What the devil was wrong with him? He never lost sight of his goals. Yet he had allowed a word and a touch to divert him, and had thus endangered an innocent. Seriously endangered her. He must have stared at her for well over a minute if Atwater had had time to board his carriage and pull away.

Pain knifed his chest. Closing his eyes, he shuddered. Never again. He must ignore Miss Warren from now on. No more stalking. With luck, she would escape censure this time, but he risked her reputation every time he approached her. She did not deserve ruin.

Angela watched Blackthorn stride away, oblivious to the people around her. What had just happened? She had accused him of trying to ruin her, but it wasn't true. He had not even noticed her until he nearly knocked her down.

She frowned. Only after she spoke had he actually looked at her. And then he had recoiled—and immediately taken steps to protect her. So what had been his purpose? His presence outside of Almack's had to be deliberate.

"I told you that man would ruin you," hissed Lady Forley, already waving her vinaigrette.

Angela had no recollection of entering the coach. Andrew

must have maneuvered her inside. Because of Blackthorn? Or had he even noticed? He and Sylvia were already murmuring to each other on the facing seat, oblivious to anything else.

Lady Forley dabbed at her eyes. "How could you allow him to touch you? Atwater may not have seen it, but there is little doubt that he will hear of your disgrace."

"You are being ridiculous." Angela faced her mother. "The man saved me from falling—I had slipped," she added untruthfully. "There was nothing untoward in the incident. The moment I regained my balance, he released me. Would you prefer that I had disgraced myself by sprawling on the street?"

"Fustian!" Her voice was rising. "I am not stupid. Why was he there if not to ruin you? And he has. He actually touched you! And instead of protesting, you spoke to him. Atwater will surely take you in disgust."

She continued, but Angela was no longer listening. How could she explain her reaction when she didn't understand it herself? The Black Marquess was an enigma. She could not account for his anger, for she had done nothing to him—well, she had called him some rather unladylike names, but he had already embarked on his campaign by then. What was its purpose? Despite that folderol he had fed her at Hatchard's, she was incapable of harming him.

Lady Forley's diatribe grew more strident once Andrew climbed down to escort Sylvia to the door. But it abruptly ceased when Andrew motioned the footman to bring them inside. The butler led them to the drawing room where Hart paced nervously about, a frown on his face.

"What is wrong?" demanded Sylvia, laying a quivering hand on his arm. "Is it Cassie?"

Angela choked.

"Nothing serious," said Hart with a nod. "But a month in town has been too much for her. We will leave for the Grange in the morning."

"Oh, no!" Sylvia blanched.

Angela caught Hart's glance and understood the question in his eyes. "Sylvia needn't accompany you, surely. We would be delighted if she could stay with us until your sister arrives. With both Mama and myself in residence, there will be no impropriety in residing with her betrothed."

He relaxed. "You should discuss this with your mother first, Angie." But both understood that the offer was what he had hoped for when he invited them in.

"Mother?"

Lady Forley's mouth had gaped at the suggestion, but the look in Andrew's eyes stopped her protests. "Of course it is proper," she agreed.

"Thank you, Lady Forley."

Sylvia and Andrew were smiling in obvious rapture.

"How is Cassie?" murmured Angela some minutes later, slipping close to Hart when the others converged on Lady Forley for belated thanks.

"Exhausted, but otherwise sound. She has not yet done herself any harm, but I mentioned before that I would eventually have to put my foot down. That time is here."

"She is fortunate to have someone who cares. I trust Sylvia will join us in the morning."

He nodded. "I will loan her a carriage and grooms so you will have an easier time getting around. Thank you for taking her in."

"It is nothing. Andrew will enjoy having her so close. Perhaps this will compensate him for having to wait so long for his nuptials."

He laughed.

# Chapter Five

"Thank you for inviting me to stay with you," said Sylvia as she and Angela dressed for the theater the following evening. The smallness of the Clifford Street house meant they shared a room. "I was afraid Hart would make me leave town."

Angela grinned. "We are delighted to have you here, though Andrew is drooling so badly that we may have to lock him in the cellar."

Sylvia giggled, then sobered. "I hope Cassie is all right. If anything happens to her, I will never forgive myself for dragging her to town."

"Relax. Hart and I discussed the situation weeks ago. I knew he would eventually take her home. She has not overextended. He merely fears she might."

"He does take awfully good care of her." She sighed.

"And Andrew will do the same for you."

"Will Atwater treat you that well?"

Angela frowned. Too many people assumed that she would accept the earl. "I don't know if he will have the chance. I cannot feel comfortable with him."

"I thought it was settled." Sylvia sounded surprised. "That is the impression your mother gave."

"Drat the woman!" Dismissing her maid, she collected her reticule and fan. "I will have to speak to her. Again. She is pushing hard for a match, but frankly I prefer Garwood."

"Well, you must admit that Atwater is gorgeous."

"He is indeed. Perhaps Mother is right and my sense is wanting. Or maybe my background prevents me from fitting into society." She shrugged. "For now, I wish to think only of the theater. What are we to see?"

*"Hamlet."*

"Not *poor Yorick* again. I saw that last week." She hid her grimace as she followed Sylvia downstairs. This Season's version of *Hamlet* bore only a passing resemblance to Shakespeare's original. And since Atwater was escorting them, it promised to be a very long evening.

Andrew was waiting for Sylvia in the hall. Their eyes locked as she descended the stairs, the sparks that sizzled between them nearly igniting the air. Suppressing her envy, Angela passed them and entered the drawing room where Atwater waited.

"You look ravishing, my dear," he said, his eyes revealing a feral gleam as they caressed her face and figure. She shivered, refusing to respond.

Lady Forley cloaked her silence with a burst of enthusiasm that carried them all the way to the theater.

Drury Lane was ablaze with light, welcoming the line of carriages that inched forward to disgorge their loads of dazzling lords and ladies. Clustered before the entrance were the usual assortment of fruit and flower vendors, link boys, pickpockets, and beggars. Later their ranks would swell with prostitutes.

Angela allowed Atwater to help her from the carriage, though her arm shuddered at his touch—and not from pleasure. What was it about this man that troubled her? He was handsome and attentive, lavishing her with care. She no longer believed that her antipathy arose solely from his effusiveness—or even from Lady Forley's pressure.

Perhaps avoiding him for a few days would give her a chance to examine her heart—not that she had any hope of doing so. Despite numerous protests, her mother insisted on accepting invitations to any event that Atwater was attending, which often meant skipping activities Angela would have liked, such as musical evenings. Her own playing was average at best, but she enjoyed listening to that of others.

The only alternative was to elicit his cooperation for remaining apart for a few days. She was struggling for the words that could make such a request without insulting him when his brows snapped into a furious frown.

"Devil take it! How did you get here? Out of the way!" He

backhanded a beggar who had stepped forward to block their progress. His other fist slammed into the man's ribs.

She gasped. The man was hardly more than a skeleton. One shirtsleeve hung empty, the tattered remains of an infantry uniform providing little protection against the night chill, battle scars visible through its holes. His left leg was twisted from a badly set break. No sound escaped his lips, even when Atwater's blow shifted all his weight onto the crooked leg, which collapsed. Pain exploded through his eyes when he slammed into the ground. And hatred.

"Oh, no!" Her involuntary cry attracted Atwater's attention.

"Save your sympathy," he ordered, grabbing her arm to drag her into the theater. "He deserves none of it. Army doctors do no favors when they amputate limbs. Better to die quickly of gangrene than slowly of starvation."

Shock stilled further protest. Shock at his callous words. Shock at his violence. Shock at Blackthorn, who appeared at the top of the steps, the hatred blazing in his eyes ferocious enough to repel the strongest warrior. In that instant she could believe every black tale of the man. And more. He seemed unbalanced. Had all her impressions been wrong?

Devall watched them go. Nothing was making sense—except Miss Warren, of course. Despite his warnings, she was still playing the part of Atwater's first wife, still pursuing titled wealth. Her acting was superb. That demure smile as she descended from the carriage was Lydia to a tee. A knife twisted in his heart. Yes, her natural passion for justice still blazed. She had grimaced in pain when the beggar hit the ground, but she had not castigated Atwater for his appalling attack. If her hand had rested on anyone else's sleeve, she would have created a scene worthy of Siddons in her prime, but her greed ran too strong. He despised her for it and had let her see his contempt. Not that it would sway her from her course. She would continue until she brought Atwater up to scratch, then revert to her normal self.

*You're overreacting,* his conscience chided him. *No one could have expected that assault. Shock froze her. You saw how he practically dragged her away.*

He brutally stifled the voice. Overreaction was alien to his constitution. Every move he had made in the last six years had been carefully planned. Emotion never swayed his judgment. Not even his admiration for Miss Warren would forgive her scheming. Forcing her eyes from his mind, he returned to business.

Atwater was a serious problem. The man refused to act like a gentleman, which was another disgrace that deserved censure. Oh, he could understand why Gabriel was ducking a challenge, but the affair with the beggar made no sense.

Why would a high-ranking lord, renowned for his benevolent charm, assault a lowly beggar with half the *ton* as witness? And with such violence! Atwater was too beloved for the incident to tarnish his reputation, but displaying his true colors to Miss Warren was odd. Even though she hid her own character behind a mask, any man who was seriously courting her would take pains to present only his best face.

And the beggar's behavior was little better. Crippled veterans littered London, congregating around public places to beg for pennies. But he had never seen one deliberately block an entrance. Nor had he witnessed one who singled out an individual for contempt. In fact, the man's eyes had gone beyond contempt.

He'd recognized the expression, of course. It was the twin of the one he had bestowed on Miss Warren—blazing, unadulterated hatred. What was the man's grudge against Atwater? Obviously, he was no ordinary beggar. Despite a steady stream of new arrivals, he was already limping away.

Turning on his heel, Blackthorn abruptly abandoned the theater and followed, waiting until they were out of sight to accost him.

"I'd like an explanation for that confrontation in Drury Lane," he said quietly.

The beggar heard the menace in his voice, but ignored it. "'Twas a private affair, sir, of no interest to others."

"I doubt it." He raked the beggar with a comprehensive gaze, taking in every detail, including a growing bruise on his ribs and the blood seeping from a cut Atwater's signet ring had made on his cheek. "I've a bone to pick with the earl and could use more evidence against him."

The beggar's mouth thinned to a grim line, but no words emerged.

Devall frowned. "Do you think Atwater sent me to harm you?" It was a shot in the dark, so he was surprised when the fellow nodded.

*Well, well!* Atwater was even worse than he had thought. "I am Devall Sherbrooke, Marquess of Blackthorn. If you know him at all, that should convince you that I have a legitimate complaint."

Relief filled the beggar's eyes. "That you do, my lord. That you do." Relaxing, he nodded toward a nearby tavern. "I'm Ned Parker, and I have a tale you'll not soon forget . . ."

Angela lay awake long into the night. Atwater's behavior had gone far beyond civility. Why had he assaulted that beggar?

It was possible that he merely despised deformity. Some people could not tolerate imperfection, as she well knew. A neighbor had been caught in a burning house some years earlier, which left his face badly scarred. Many now shunned him, unable to cope with his appearance.

But Atwater's reaction was too violent to explain away in general terms. Other disabled veterans roamed the streets, but he had never heeded them. So this was personal. What had the man done? Or was Atwater himself the transgressor? She shook her head as lurid possibilities filled her brain.

In the end, it didn't matter. Nothing could excuse so public an assault. Some character defect lurked beneath Atwater's smooth exterior—which explained why his touch made her skin crawl. She must have sensed it. Discovering the truth would make it easier to turn Lady Forley's attention to Garwood.

But learning the details would be difficult. The gossips apparently knew nothing. The beggar was anonymous. Talking to Atwater was hard under any circumstances, but he would never discuss this.

She'd already tried, making several attempts at the theater, but he had refused to respond to even innocuous questions. His intransigence had settled her feelings once and for all. He must want only an ornament for a wife. The fact that he had asked her nothing beyond basic questions of parentage and dowry proved it. He had no respect for intelligence, no interest in her thoughts, and no intention of sharing more than a bed with his wife. That wasn't the life she wanted.

So how was she to convince her mother to cease encouraging the man? She could hardly turn him away by herself. This evening's show of temper precluded even a refined version of how she'd handled Sir Alan. At the very least, he would snub her, and his standing in society would prompt others to follow suit.

She couldn't afford ostracism. But if she could dampen her mother's enthusiasm, perhaps she could gradually back off, cutting his dances to one a night and skipping some of the balls he patronized. So she must discover the details. Only something truly reprehensible might sway Lady Forley.

Mulling the problem made sleep almost impossible. Her mind raced in circles. The more she thought, the more she cursed herself for her inability to take control of her life. Atwater was touchy; Lady Forley was determined; and she was caught in the middle.

By dawn, she was groggy and out of sorts. Leaving Sylvia snuggled warmly in bed, she called for her horse and headed for Hyde Park. It was generally empty at this hour, allowing her the freedom to gallop.

Removing her hat the moment she was alone, she let the air wash through her hair. Weariness, irritation, and her longing for home flowed away with it. Not until she reined in near the Serpentine did she spot another early riser. The Marquess of Blackthorn sat atop a powerful black stallion, half hidden by a thicket of shrubs.

"Good morning, Miss Warren," he said icily. "Did you enjoy the theater last night?"

She grimaced, slamming the hat back in place. Removing it was yet another aberration that could damage her.

She had wondered whether her imagination had conjured that black stare on the theater steps, for he had appeared in none of the boxes and had been conspicuously absent when Atwater promenaded her through the corridors during the intervals. All Mayfair had buzzed for days with reports that Blackthorn was stalking Atwater, and his appearance outside Almack's supported that notion. But the theater was open to anyone, so why had he not followed them inside? One malevolent gaze was hardly worthy of his reputation.

"Cat got your tongue?" he asked when she ignored him.

"You are not a man to accept cuts, I see." She sighed. "The building was opulent, the acting acceptable, the morning sunlight delightful, the ride invigorating. Good day to you, sir." She turned to leave, only to find him trotting at her side.

He was a superb rider, sitting his stallion like a centaur. Anyone familiar with horses would recognize the skill that exerted seemingly effortless control over his high-strung beast.

"Why must you persecute me, Lord Blackthorn?" she demanded. "You know my reputation will be in shreds should anyone see us together. And you swore just two nights ago that you meant me no harm. Did you lie? Or are you using me to punish Lord Atwater?"

"I admit he is not my favorite person," he said almost pleasantly. "But that is not my reason for speaking with you. I pursue my quarrels privately."

"The last person with whom you had a private quarrel is dead." She glared at him, shocked at her own temerity.

"But not by my hand." He glared back, his expression marred by a wayward lock of hair that curled across his forehead.

"I know you didn't kill Graceford—unless you disguised yourself as an Italian *conte*. I was referring to Lord Cloverdale. Or was Coldstream the latest? I don't recall the chronology of your misdeeds."

"My, what a gossip the lady is." But his eyes seemed suddenly apprehensive. "Though that is more in keeping with female character than haranguing a street vendor."

"Cynical, aren't you? We've held this conversation before. There is no need to repeat it."

"Truth is not cynicism. Like all girls, you spend your time fawning over the harridans who have established themselves as arbiters of taste. Woe be unto anyone who dares to think for herself. Have you no better use for your time than making and breaking reputations? Or do you enjoy playing with people's lives?" Bitterness tinged his voice; and pain. But she ignored them, furious over his unfair portrayal of both herself and society.

"Beast!"

"You forget your training, Miss Warren. Run along home before you jeopardize so glorious a future. You can hardly move into society's inner circles by flouting its rules."

"I already tried to leave, but you chose to accompany me," she snapped. "Your faulty judgment is again trumpeting itself to the world, my lord. You may enjoy sounding like a fool, but I do not. I won't be treated as a brainless widgeon. Certainly not by so notorious a scoundrel."

"I didn't—"

"You did. Condescending toad! Don't you dare pat me on the head and utter soothing platitudes. And quit judging people you don't know."

"You pass your time prattling in drawing rooms, then claim you are not a gossip? You must think me a fool."

"Girls have no control over their schedules," she reminded him bitterly. "Not even those of us who are nearly on the shelf. Nor are we allowed to prattle, not that it makes any difference. Society's denizens are so intimidating that they freeze my tongue with a glance. I've not met a soul I could talk to since our arrival."

"You aren't tongue-tied today."

"You don't count," she retorted tartly, then blushed. "I mean, you are not part of society and can already ruin me. Nothing I say now can make things worse."

"Yet most people find me intimidating." He raked her with his most devilish stare.

"No." She frowned. "I would sooner describe you as infuriating, especially the way you consistently jump to false conclusions based on no evidence whatsoever."

"What am I supposed to think? If you are not a gossip, how do you know so much about me?"

"My mother warned me against you, of course. And one can go nowhere without hearing stories about you. Every tabby in town is incensed at your presence. Surely you know enough about society to expect that."

"Your mother warned you against me yet allowed you to make a spectacle of yourself over a street urchin? I'm out of short pants, Miss Warren."

"You are also the most odious man I ever met!" She reined in her temper, but not before her horse sensed her fury and began to nervously prance. "I gave her no choice, if you must know. Her hysterics lasted all of two days."

"My, my! I believe I have hit a nerve."

"What you believe is irrelevant." Turning aside, she cantered away.

She had gone barely twenty feet before he grabbed her bridle and halted her progress. Her horse snorted, twisting his head to glare at her as if demanding she make up her mind.

"Not so fast, Miss Warren." He released his hold. "First let me explain why I risked both our reputations by approaching you. You are equally quick to judge, by the way. I have no wish to ruin you."

"I hadn't thought so until you started hounding me. Now I don't know what to think. First you expose me to censure, then you help me sidestep it. What will you do next?"

He frowned and opened his mouth, but bit back whatever he had started to say. "We will not brangle further this morning. There's another street urchin you might be interested in—an orphan who has been sharing a shed in Haymarket with three crippled soldiers. None is in very good shape, but Mickey is in urgent need of care. He was injured last week and can no longer look after himself. If you really do know of a good orphanage, he's yours."

"Where is he?" Her anger dissipated, leaving behind only concern.

He gave her the direction. "Don't go alone. That neighborhood is no place for a lady."

"I will not go at all. My friend will handle everything." She frowned. "It may take two or three days, though. My friend is out of town. Could you see after Mickey until then?"

"Too good to take care of him yourself? Or are you afraid Atwater will disapprove your real character?"

"Of course not! But you do not know my mother. Even living on the streets is preferable to what she would visit on him."

He sighed, for he did indeed know her mother. Or had, before he had severed all connection to society. "I suppose I can see that he has enough to eat for a couple of days."

"Thank you. And despite what you think, the effort won't kill you."

He watched her ride away. To which question had she objected? Not that it mattered. She could not afford to reveal her heart, for Atwater could still escape her clutches. Cold-blooded wench. Had she fallen in love with the man as well as the fortune? Women had fawned over the earl for years. And Atwater was skilled at feigning adoration. Not that it mattered. After living in near-poverty for so long, she would convince herself that she was in love. So why was he trusting Mickey to her care?

And why did picturing her on Atwater's arm curdle his stomach?

# Chapter Six

Angela smiled at her partner as he escorted her back to her mother. But the smile did not reach her eyes. Atwater lounged at Lady Forley's side, though his second dance was three sets away. He had hovered more and more in recent days, his lurking presence shouting to the world that he had marked her as his own. And the message was understood. Most of society had already married them. Few gentlemen danced with her, the rest intimidated by Atwater's cold stares. Only Garwood remained in her court.

And she blessed him every day. He had hinted that he was ready for marriage. She had made her preference clear by criticizing both her mother's devotion to society and her encouragement of Atwater.

They had enjoyed a pleasant afternoon at the British Institution, admiring Reynolds's work as well as a second exhibit of current artists. She could relax with him, conversing easily on many topics. And she no longer censored her tongue, allowing him to see her education and her interests. He accepted both, which boded well for the future. Their time together might lack any spark of excitement, but he was comfortable.

And he was all that kept her going. Between Atwater's hovering and the insipid silliness of the Styles clan—they were never far away, either—she was not enjoying the Season.

Atwater's glare made her partner grimace. He was young and had not yet acquired sufficient town bronze to hide his feelings. Poor lad. He would never dance with her again. It was the fourth sprig in two days that Atwater had scared off. Some girls might enjoy such a public display of infatuation, but not she.

She had frequently bitten her tongue, loathe to create a scene, but this time she gave full rein to her anger. What right had he to control her life? By whose authority was he changing the rules that all of society followed? No gentleman could dance more than twice with any lady. Her reputation would diminish if she did not dance with others. Sitting out excessive sets would ruin her.

"That was not well done," she hissed the moment her mother turned toward Sylvia. If Lady Forley joined this dispute, the brangle would become very public.

Shock filled his eyes. It was the first time in days that she had initiated a discussion with him. He looked as though one of the decorations had spoken.

"The pup is unworthy of you."

"He is perfectly harmless, but that is not the point. It is not your place to approve my dance card. Nor is it your place to choose my friends. This hovering makes fools of us both. You should be attending others. I don't want to see you again before your next set."

His face twisted in fury, but he bowed stiffly and left.

"Whatever sent Atwater off in such a huff?" demanded Lady Forley.

"He has been frightfully rude to several of my partners, Mother. Such behavior is unacceptable."

"How dare you criticize the man you will marry?"

"This is neither the time nor the place to discuss the future, but I must remind you that I have made no such decision. Nor am I likely to. Enough."

She smiled at Garwood as he approached for the next set.

"What was that all about?" he asked when they took their places for a quadrille.

"Nothing. Mother was just being her usual overbearing self. She will never understand me, for our interests are as chalk and cheese."

He nodded. "Parents so often try to relive their own lives through their children. My father was the same, but I never could share his love of the sporting life."

"We have a neighbor like that. He lives for the hunt, neglecting all else, including his family."

"Forget your mother," he urged as the music began. "She will not control your life much longer."

She smiled. If the warmth in his eyes was any indication, he would make his offer any day now. Thank God! Her mother's pressure had become nearly unbearable. Philip. She tried his name in her mind. Would she grow to love him? She would certainly try.

He brushed against her as they moved into the next pattern, squeezing her hand in reassurance.

Devall sat in an isolated corner of White's reading room, his face ostensibly buried in a newspaper. Few men approached him, but clubs were more tolerant than drawing rooms. None had seriously considered terminating his membership. The room was sparsely populated now that Brummell's set had deserted the bow window in favor of the card room, where they were looking to break a run of bad luck.

The door opened in a swirl of raindrops, the night having turned blustery and wet. The new arrival removed a sodden cloak and handed it to a footman, revealing a braid-encrusted red uniform jacket on a tall, lanky frame.

An unaccustomed smile creased Devall's face. "Jack!" he called. "When did you get back?"

Major John Caldwell grinned as he limped across the room. "This is the last place I expected to find you, Devall." He pulled a chair closer and sank gratefully into its depths. "In fact, I was planning to run down to Wyndhaven next week."

"What happened to your leg?" A footman delivered a second glass and poured wine for the major.

"Sword cut to the thigh. It festered so Hooky sent me home for a spell, but it should heal without a problem."

"You just arrived then?"

"Yesterday. What in the name of all that's wonderful are you doing in London? And looking as devilish as ever," he added, taking in the stark black clothes and a countenance only marginally lightened by his own unexpected appearance. "Did you finally decide to redeem your reputation?"

"No. It serves its purpose. But this is hardly the place for private discussion." The words halted further inquiry even though the room was practically empty. "How goes the Peninsula Campaign?"

"I think the tide has turned at last. Napoleon cannot possibly recover after that disastrous retreat from Moscow."

Devall's glass paused midway to his lips. "Did he really lose half a million men, or has the number been exaggerated?" Speculation had been rampant for months, ever since the remnants of the Grande Armée had stumbled back across the Niemen, but estimates of the French losses varied widely.

"More. He started with six hundred thousand. The Tsar's troops captured a few thousand—a very few. Only eighteen thousand survived the retreat, and many of them were in pitiful shape."

They settled down for a long discussion of the war.

"So we are finally winning?" Devall asked at last.

"One cannot be overconfident, and many call me an incurable optimist, but I believe it will be over within the year."

A new gust of wind blew into the room as the porter hurried to assist another arrival.

Atwater.

Devall's good cheer vanished. Refilling his glass, he motioned Jack to stay put and casually sauntered toward the porter's desk as Atwater headed for the gaming room.

The collision almost appeared accidental—two preoccupied men bumping into each other—but the wine that spilled down Atwater's cravat, waistcoat, and evening jacket was no mistake. Nor was the hatred that blazed from Blackthorn's eyes.

"You just cannot avoid running people down, can you?" he demanded icily.

Atwater's face contorted in rage, but he turned without a word to accept the porter's help.

Devall cursed himself for again forcing a confrontation without the audience necessary to assure success. For some reason, he couldn't keep his mind on the job this time. First Miss Warren had intruded, and now Jack. Never had he been so careless with a mission.

But never had it mattered so much. Recognizing his emotional involvement gave him pause. He must keep a clear head. Lydia deserved better.

Sighing, he resumed his seat.

"What is your quarrel with Atwater?" asked Jack quietly. "If it is justified, I'll second you."

"We will discuss it later." He returned to their interrupted conversation, but it was long before he could relax and enjoy Jack's company. No matter how hard he tried, suppressing his fury at Atwater was impossible.

Dawn was approaching when they adjourned to the gaming room.

Atwater had repaired his wardrobe and was now enjoying an evening of piquet. Harley announced that he had lost enough, starting a jovial discussion over who would next partner the earl.

Devall's hatred again burned white hot. At last he had a perfect opportunity. "I would never be so foolish," he commented to Jack, pitching his voice just loud enough to carry to the table.

"Is he that good a player?" asked Jack carefully.

He suppressed a grimace. Jack might be his closest friend, but until he knew the details, he would steer clear of this feud. So he must go it alone for now. But at least he could bounce barbs from Jack to Atwater.

"He wins uncommonly often," he replied, his tone implying that it was not due to skill.

Gasps rose from every corner. The sanctity of White's made the allusion even more serious.

"Are you going to take that?" demanded Shelford, staring at the earl.

"I'd call out anyone who implied such a thing," slurred Harley, who had imbibed more than was good for him. But his eyes drifted to the pile of vowels in front of the earl.

Atwater's face remained impassive. Several voices rose in support of his integrity, though the consensus was that such a charge could not go unpunished.

Devall locked gazes with Atwater, the ice passing between them nearly visible. He could feel the earl's fury—and his rigid control.

Atwater lowered his gaze first. "Shelford, would you care for a game? Ignore his feeble attempt to divert our memories from Graceford's very odd losses."

*Nice recovery,* Devall had to admit, though disappointment

coursed through his breast. Atwater had turned the tables completely. Several gentlemen were already looking at him askance.

"Trying to deflect attention from yourself, Atwater?" demanded a voice from the far corner. "We all know Graceford was caught cheating in Naples. I'd say losing to Blackthorn was no more than he deserved."

Garwood. Devall identified the speaker even as men perked up on all sides, but this wasn't the time to consider his unexpected support.

"I say! He's right!" exclaimed someone.

"We were all nicked by Graceford," slurred another. "Owe thanks for recognizing a sharp."

"Maybe his eye is still in," suggested a third, trailing off into hiccups.

"But Atwater's luck is no better than mine," said Shelford quietly.

"Or mine," agreed another. "Should call out anyone who thinks otherwise."

Atwater gritted his teeth, indulging in one hate-filled glance at Devall before turning back to Shelford. "Ignore the rogue. He is no gentleman so cannot be treated as one."

Devall twisted his mouth into a sneer. He'd almost had the bastard. What now? Gabriel apparently planned to ignore the rules of gentlemanly conduct—hardly surprising when set against his other crimes. The hell of it was that he could get away with it. His reputation was so solid that society would forgive him nearly anything.

So he needed a new approach. Somehow, he must weaken the man's credit. Turning on his heel, he left, Jack at his elbow.

"If you have a legitimate quarrel, why not just challenge him and be done with it?" Jack asked as they hurried through the rain.

"I prefer swords."

Enlightenment struck. "He is no fencer. I take it first blood won't end the fight."

He nodded.

Jack's eyes closed briefly. "Dammit, Devall! Won't you ever learn? What has he done to draw such ire?"

"Murder."

\*     \*     \*

Hyde Park was sparkling clean as Garwood and Angela joined the crowds for the fashionable hour. Last night's storm had washed all trace of soot from the trees and shrubs, leaving every leaf sparkling. The sight raised her spirits.

Lady Forley had kept her up half the night, haranguing her for her set-down of Atwater and vowing that she would never approve a betrothal with anyone else. When Angela had reminded her that Andrew was her guardian and thus responsible for approving any suitors, the woman's fury had erupted into a full-fledged fit. Filial duty required that she accept her mother's guidance; only a title and fortune would enhance her social position; and on and on and on . . .

She shuddered. She cared nothing for social position, but her mother's mind was closed. The woman flatly refused to believe that Angela's interests did not mirror her own. Thus it was vital to bring Garwood up to scratch as soon as possible.

But she had no idea how to go about it. Too much pressure could send him running—as she herself longed to do whenever her mother launched one of her lectures. Eliciting proposals was probably another of those skills most girls had learned along with flirting and making pretty conversation, but she lacked that sort of training.

"I see Lady Stafford has recovered from her brief indisposition," said Garwood, breaking into her reverie.

"Then it must not have been a chill after all, for she was abed only one day." Angela returned her gaze to Garwood. "And just as well. She is increasing again."

"I had not heard." He sounded aggrieved.

She laughed. "Does a list of those in a delicate condition make the rounds of the clubs? I thought the topic more suitable for drawing rooms. Lady Debenham mentioned it last night, and she usually knows such things."

"You would be surprised what gets discussed at White's, to say nothing of wagered upon. But did Lady Debenham actually steal a march on Lady Beatrice?"

"Pigs will fly first. I swear Lady Beatrice has an informant in every house in town. How else can she learn what happens almost before the participants? But what was that about wagers?"

"Gentleman frequently bet on odd things," he admitted sheepishly. "Which of two water drops will descend a window first; whether the next horse to turn down St. James's will be brown or black—silly wagers."

"How did that come to mind in relation to Lady Stafford?"

He grimaced. "I should have kept my mouth shut. There are those who wager on human events—whether a couple with four boys will next produce a girl, or the exact date of a birth."

"And I suppose they also speculate on how soon after a wedding that birth occurs? Or the nature of the Season's attachments? Will Lord A succeed in winning Miss B? Or Lord C manage to seduce Lady D? What a despicable practice, reducing people to pawns." Undoubtedly they were also betting on when she would accept Atwater. It was yet another strike against his suit. She had a perverse desire to confound every betting man in London.

"There are those who will bet on anything, but I am not of their number."

She relaxed. "I know, and I apologize for my outburst. It just seems so degrading to find ladies' names being bandied about the clubs."

"Your outrage does you credit and is one reason I care so deeply for you." He must have realized how close he had just come to a declaration, for he bit off further comment, determinedly switching to neutral topics.

She sighed but could only follow suit, reverting to park chatter as they greeted friends. It was frustrating. He was so close, but hadn't yet taken the plunge. And so she faced yet another evening of Atwater's hovering and Lady Forley's pressure.

She caught sight of Blackthorn in the distance, locking onto his eyes as usual. She had sent word to Hart about Mickey, but she had no idea when he would collect the boy. Nor could she figure out why Blackthorn had brought Mickey's plight to her attention. Aiding an orphan hardly fit his reputation, but even discounting that, he surely could have handled the problem by himself. Hart did not run the only orphanage in England. Was he testing her for some reason?

"He tried to force another argument on Atwater at White's last night," said Garwood, following her gaze. His voice contained an odd mixture of disgust and approval.

"Does anyone know why?"

He shook his head. "His innuendo was patently false, so he must have been manufacturing a quarrel to cover his real complaint."

"If he has a legitimate charge, why does he not make it public?"

"Honor does not always allow such exposure."

Men! They could cloak the oddest behavior in honor. More than one tradesman was in dire straits because honor demanded that a gentleman pay gaming debts before bills for goods and services. And settling disputes on a dueling field was barbaric, recalling the *I'm-stronger-so-I'm-right* bullying so prevalent in medieval days.

"Honor is laudable," she said carefully, "but I will never agree that violence solves anything."

Blackthorn's actions with Mickey had made her wonder if his core was less black than rumor suggested. Had she jumped on that idea because she wanted him to be good? It would make her feel less guilty for liking the scoundrel. She shivered. After such an admission, could she ever trust her judgment again?

But the situation was even worse than that. She had felt an unaccountable link to the marquess since the first time she had met his eyes. Was a misplaced infatuation responsible for her inability to love Philip? Such a disaster could destroy her life.

Garwood put on a determinedly cheerful face. "Enough of unpleasant topics. Did you see the way Miss Sanderson stared at Mr. Crawford last night?"

"Yes. How shameful that her chaperon retired to the card room. What Lady Sanderson was about, to leave her daughter in the hands of so avid a whist player I cannot imagine. Of course, I also have trouble believing the girl has developed a *tendre* for such a cawker. They disappeared into the garden for one whole set. Heaven knows what they were doing."

"I think heaven knows quite well." He chuckled. "It is the gossips who lust after the details."

"Or envy them. Their speculation contains more excitement than condemnation."

He laughed, then abruptly sobered. Glaring at an approaching curricle, he deliberately turned his eyes away and set his horses to a trot. Pain exploded in the other driver's eyes.

"What was that all about?" she asked.

"I cannot abide dishonesty."

"Nor can I. What has he done? That was Lord Renford, was it not?"

"Yes. He used to be a close friend." Agony underlay his voice. "I just discovered that he stole some papers from my study."

Her eyes widened. "Why would he do such a thing?"

"They concerned investments I am considering, including detailed information about some property. Whoever buys it should reap large profits as soon as certain plans become general knowledge. They were on my desk when he called yesterday morning, but gone after I had seen him out. He wasted no time. When my agent offered for the property at noon, it had just sold. I can still make a profit, but not what I'd expected."

"Is he so desperate?"

"No. He is wealthier than I, which makes his behavior incomprehensible."

"He did not explain when you asked about it?"

"There was no point in starting an argument. No one else had access to them. I will not countenance deceit among my friends."

She nodded. "Nor I. Trust is vital to any relationship. As is honesty."

"I'm glad you understand, for not all ladies are so insightful. Perhaps you have been equally cursed by liars and cheats."

She silently nodded. A neighbor had been caught working for Napoleon. Another had tried to cut his older brother out of an inheritance. The world unfortunately held too many liars and cheats.

"Renford is not the only gentleman I have been forced to cut," he said with a sigh. "A schoolmate seduced one of my tenants, then lied about his responsibility for her resulting condition. And one of my cousins fleeced a friend, though he also lied about it. I cannot understand how anyone can deny his own actions. It only makes matters worse."

"True. Much better to admit a fault and take steps to correct it. Repentance can lead to forgiveness, but obstinacy merely adds new grievances."

They left the park in companionable silence. His high standards matched her own—honorably moral yet broadminded about her education. Even his willingness to uphold the rights of tenants by condemning a friend boded well. They could forge a good partnership out of a marriage.

# Chapter Seven

Devall halted in amazement. Miss Warren was leaning over a ragged soldier on Piccadilly, pushing something into his filthy hand. Every time he thought he understood the chit, she did something to blast the image to pieces. He had considered her sympathetic to helpless orphans, yet Mickey had still been huddled in that derelict shed two days before. So he'd decided she had been playing him for a fool, yet here she was, succoring a beggar.

The man grasped her hand as she turned away, mouthing a seemingly emotional entreaty.

Devall stiffened. Had he been wrong? The fellow was undernourished but able-bodied and might be trying to force his attentions on her. But she smiled and patted the man's arm before turning to leave.

His unexpected concern for her safety made him furious. She had occupied his thoughts far too often in recent days.

"Such sympathy!" He fell in beside her. "Do you feel worthier if you toss a penny to a beggar now and then?"

She pulled her pelisse closer and tried to brush past, but he grabbed her arm, forcing her to face him.

"Let go!" she demanded. "Even your reputation does not include assaulting ladies on public streets—or are you embarking on a new vice to keep boredom at bay?"

"What a waspish tongue, but more believable than alms for the poor. Why the pretense? Are you trying to impress me?"

"Conceited, aren't you," she observed caustically. "Do you actually believe that you are so important that your very presence can influence everyone's behavior? Frankly, I didn't see you. Besides, no one of sense would seek to impress you. What I want is for you to leave before you ruin my reputation."

"Always so concerned for your reputation."

"As I must be. Why do you insist on accompanying me when you disapprove of everything I do?"

"Accosting beggars is unsafe for women."

"Talking to you is even more dangerous."

"So you really do distribute alms to street beggars?" He carefully kept his voice neutral, not revealing his own very private support for the flotsam of war.

"I wish I could, but I haven't the means. If you must know, I was attracted to Mr. Jacobs by his uniform, which is identical to that worn by one of our tenants who died last year at Badajoz. I wondered if they had been acquainted and if he could give me an accurate description of Robin's death, for the letter from his commanding officer was clearly a formula he used for any death in action. A heroic demise fits neither the realities of war nor poor Robin's character."

He stared before signaling his groom to help her maid onto the perch. "Get in."

"Why?"

"So we can finish this discussion away from prying eyes." She was right. And harming her reputation would add yet another blot to his, making his efforts to gain access to society balls more difficult.

She stared a moment, then shrugged and allowed him to hand her into his curricle.

"So did he know your tenant?" he asked, turning away from Piccadilly.

"Yes." Her eyes filled with sadness. "It was as I thought. Robin died in great pain from wounds incurred when a riderless horse trampled him as he tended spare mounts behind the lines. His mother must never learn that, of course, but his father will appreciate the truth."

"So you gave him your tenant's direction?"

"No, I will tell him myself. I asked him to contact my brother. If Andrew cannot find work for him, I know our neighbor can."

He remained silent, mulling her words. Was she really this caring, or was this an easy way to thank the man for answering her questions? "Why did you not help Mickey?" he asked.

"I did."

He stared.

"I told you it would take time to arrange. He was picked up yesterday and should have reached the orphanage by now."

"What orphanage is that?"

"My friend prefers anonymity."

He dropped the subject, choosing a roundabout route to Clifford Street. Her direction was one of the bits of information he had collected on Atwater. Should he try again to warn her about Gabriel? Whatever her motives for hanging on the earl's arm, she did not deserve to be bound to him. No lady did.

"If you are truly a caring person, you should avoid Lord Atwater," he said at last. "He does not condone charity. Nor does he approve of females showing any sign of independence."

"Would you be more specific? I must make a match this Season."

"Is your home so terrible that you need to escape?"

"As usual, you leap to unwarranted conclusions. My brother will marry in a few weeks. My remaining at home would be unfair both to him and to Sylvia, and I can't waste the sacrifices he made to provide me a Season. By the time he can afford another, I will be too long on the shelf to be marriageable."

"Such concern. Again she seeks to impress me."

"Fustian! Your opinion means nothing. In fact, your regard would harm my credibility beyond redemption."

"You are incapable of wounding me, so don't try," he lied. But her taunt hurt. He thrust the pain aside. "Why not admit that you are after Atwater's title and fortune and be done with it?"

"You wrong me, as usual."

"How? Girls fawn over the most debased monsters to improve their consequence."

"So cynical." She sighed. "You can't force everyone into the same box. Are you like every other man in London? Even the stupidest people know that there is no label that applies to all. Can you compare Lord Castlereagh, who heads the Foreign Office, with Lord Petersham, who cares for naught but snuff and tea? Why should women be any different? Does Maria Edgeworth indulge in London gossip? Is Jane Austen interested only in finding a titled husband? And there are as many differences within a class as between classes. Why don't you try to make something of your own life instead of needlessly lashing out at others?"

"I already knew you were a bluestocking," he reminded her.

"Yet another fact that can ruin me," she admitted. "I might as well resign myself to life as a spinster."

"You should know by now that I have no desire to harm you. I am not as black as my reputation claims."

"Then why am I in this curricle?" she demanded. "One whisper and I am doomed."

"You will notice that we are not traveling fashionable streets," he pointed out. "I do wish to protect your honor. But I had to warn you about Atwater."

"Why do you hate him?"

He stared her down. Only after one more attempt to draw Atwater into a duel would he make the truth public. This time he would confront him before the matrons responsible for his matchless credit. But not in the chaos outside a ball. "I have my reasons, which I would prefer to keep private. But he is not what he seems, Miss Warren. His heart is blacker than my reputation. At least look beneath his surface."

"I wish you would explain. He has always made me nervous, but I don't know why. Distancing myself from him is proving to be impossible without facts. Even people I don't know try to push us together."

"Perhaps you are smarter than I thought. Just stay away from him. You will regret it if you don't. And that is not a threat," he added, drawing up before her house.

Her fingers burned through his glove as he handed her down, startling them both. But he ignored the heat.

His face twisted into an even blacker scowl than usual as he drove home. His motives had not been as straightforward as he had claimed. Turning her against Atwater would crack the man's armor. Atwater had been hovering so closely that no one was willing to offer odds against a marriage. The betting books held wagers only on the date the announcement would appear. Maneuvering Miss Warren into repudiating him would cause a sensation, infuriating Atwater—which should make it easier to goad him into a challenge—and raising questions about his character among society's gossips, thus eroding his consequence.

So his warning had been selfish and deliberate. But he had not expected her reaction. It wasn't the first time she'd thrown his thoughts into turmoil, of course. Every time they met, she confounded his perceptions. And not always benignly.

Her claim that people were forcing her into Atwater's orbit had pierced one of his more vital ramparts. Memories were oozing to the surface that he had no desire to confront. She wasn't the only girl who had little say in her destiny.

Frantically scraping the hair off his forehead, he strode into the library and poured an oversized glass of brandy, rapidly draining it and pouring another.

Penelope.

*Go away,* he ordered, trying to turn his thoughts to Atwater. To Miss Warren. To anything else. But it was hopeless. Pain ripped his chest.

His betrothal to the Honorable Penelope Quincy had been arranged by their respective fathers. He had first heard of it by reading the announcement in the morning paper. The shock had died a quick death, of course. A lifetime of lessons had taught him that opposing his father's wishes led to very unpleasant consequences.

He slammed the door on those memories, for they were even more painful than thinking about Penelope.

Draining the glass, he paced the library. Damn his father to hell! And hers. His life would never be the same. That announcement had established his course, defining an inescapable destiny. Not that he had bowed to orders in the end.

His feet moved faster. Even if he could magically return to that night six years ago knowing what the future held, he would change nothing. The die had been cast. Their fathers' scheming had left him no choice. Jilting Penelope in a less public arena would not have worked. Wedding her would have been worse. But he had been a social outcast ever since.

Not that he minded—most of the time. He had even turned the situation to his advantage. But occasionally the loneliness overwhelmed him. Like now.

He dropped into a chair, pressing his hands to his eyes. He had once naïvely dreamed of finding a wife who could share his concerns. He had even dreamed of children, though he had never admitted to a soul that he liked the little beasts. Now he avoided even the thought of them. Marriage was forever out of reach, and not just to daughters of the aristocracy. He could condemn no woman to permanent ostracism. Nor could he produce an heir. School was brutal enough without the added stigma his son would carry. And the thought of siring an unmarriageable daughter made him cringe. It was a reality he had accepted long ago, and one that rarely bothered him. The fact that it did today was Miss Warren's fault.

Why had she reminded him that even casual friendships were impossible? He knew that better than anyone. His very presence could destroy anyone he favored. The pain accompanied him every time he left home, which was why he could relax only at Wyndhaven. He had so few friends, and only Jack willingly approached him in public. The servants who carried out his business were too aware of his title—and too afraid of him, he had to admit—to drop their formality.

Damn her! Angela would make a wonderful friend. He enjoyed debating with her, watching for that exhilarating moment when her face would flush with passion as she countered an argument or delivered a well-deserved set-down. He enjoyed probing a mind that matched his own in so many ways. But beyond that, she treated him like a normal human being—and continued to do so even when he was at his most obnoxious.

*Conceited . . . odious . . . cynical . . .* He grimaced, admitting that he merited such censure. *Conceit* was wrong, of course. No one with his history could ever sustain an exalted opinion of himself. But the cynicism was real enough. He knew the hidden face of society too well to believe its facade.

Closing his eyes, he leaned his head against the back of the chair. With him, Angela donned no facade. His accusations had been unfair, for she was not a conscienceless fortune hunter. Labeling her as such had been an excuse to avoid probing her character. Something lurked beneath her surface that he didn't want to discover.

But he could no longer avoid an investigation. If she was as innocent as he feared, he must help her. She was at the mercy of events—perhaps not as helpless as Penelope had been, or himself, but she was clearly under pressure and being shoved into a union that would destroy her.

So here was yet another reason to garner some invitations. He could hardly lend her an invisible hand if he was barred from society.

Lady Chartley had done as much as she would. Recalling her glee when a particularly stuffy matron abandoned the room in a huff the moment he'd arrived brought a fleeting grin to his lips. But truth quickly stifled any real pleasure. She had opened the door that vital first crack, but that was all he could expect. She wouldn't risk her own credit by championing his cause.

Perhaps Jack could help.

Angela thought long about Blackthorn's warning. Why hadn't he just told her the truth? His tone had made Atwater's crime sound dire—which explained why he was bent on forcing the earl into a duel, not that she condoned violence—yet none of society's gossips had a clue. Not even Lady Beatrice, who generally knew everything that happened, even in the farthest corners of the country. Lady Debenham had an equally impressive network of correspondents. And both heard everything the servants knew. Could she really believe that they had overlooked even an innocuous indiscretion?

She sighed. He should have spelled out the details. Vague warnings wouldn't help her, for Lady Forley would believe nothing without evidence. And that evidence would have to be powerful and irrefutable. The woman considered herself infallible. Having judged Atwater to be perfect, she wouldn't back down.

So Angela was again stuck between a rock and a hard place. Since Lady Forley refused to distance them from Atwater, all she could do was act warmer toward Philip and cooler to the earl. Any man with intelligence should get the message. Of course, if he paid attention to her, he would have gotten it already.

*On-dits* revealed Blackthorn's grievance the very next day. Lady Beatrice was the first to report the news.

"Lord Atwater is not the sweet innocent he likes to pretend," she teased her visitors as she poured tea for the latest arrivals.

"What did he do?" asked Lady Marchgate, accepting a lemon biscuit from a circulating footman.

"He killed his first wife." Everyone in the room gasped. "Not murder, mind you, though it comes close. He struck the girl, triggering the miscarriage that killed her."

"Really?" asked Lady Debenham, her obvious disbelief goading Lady Beatrice. Their long rivalry was well known.

"Absolutely. And it was not the first time."

"Poor Lydia," mourned a dowager. "She was such a sweet girl."

"But shy," offered another, her own disbelief evident. "Not the sort to defy a husband. She would have done anything for him. And Atwater is too considerate to raise his hand to anyone."

"He doted on her," agreed Lady Marchgate. "Never have I seen so loving a husband. It was almost scandalous the way he wore his heart on his sleeve."

"So did she," Lady Debenham reminded them. "The love of the century, as I remarked at the time."

Lady Beatrice's face matched her purple gown at this tacit condemnation of her news, and she took careful note of each speaker.

Angela did not participate in the talk, but she had to bite her tongue to stay out of it. For once, she could think of too much to say. Atwater's courtship of Lydia closely resembled his treatment of her—which she found suffocating. Had Lydia felt the same? Perhaps not, if she had loved him. But whether the tale was true or not, why had it surfaced now?

Instinct blamed Blackthorn, for the charges fit well with his campaign to force a duel on the earl. Yet only yesterday he had refused to describe his quarrel. Was this tale a lie? Philip claimed that Blackthorn wished to keep his real feud private. Would the marquess have changed tactics so quickly? Or was some other man responsible for this rumor, making it unrelated to Blackthorn's campaign? This last possibility was frightening, for it hinted that Atwater had injured at least two people. But it didn't seem possible that he had successfully fooled every member of society, not even if both misdeeds had occurred very recently. She found it hard enough to believe that Blackthorn had a legit-

imate complaint. Her own discomfort around Atwater notwith-
standing, the gossips were simply too knowing.

Events supported the theory that Blackthorn had spread the
tale. He somehow wangled an invitation to the Cunningham ball
the next night. Lady Forley was not the only guest to gasp in
shock. Several people left in righteous indignation. Others can-
celed plans so they could move on to later gatherings so they
could witness his confrontation with Atwater.

Rumors of the earl's brutality had swept Mayfair, though few
believed them. Every word was attributed to Blackthorn's imagination. Most swore that his motives were envy for a man who
was everything he was not, and jealousy over Atwater's standing
in society.

True to his name, the Black Marquess was dressed in black relieved only by snowy linen and an enormous ruby nestled in the
intricate folds of his cravat, which flashed like the fires of hell in
the gleam of a thousand candles. Black hair. Demonic visage.
Sneering expression. Never had he looked more satanic. His
peaked brows lifted in mocking challenge as his dark eyes raked
the room.

What a nightmare! Angela was terrified lest he approach her
or indicate that he knew her. Lady Forley squeaked and
squawked, using both Atwater and the Styles family as shields,
all the while lamenting the fact that Andrew and Sylvia had accompanied Lady Ashton to a musicale that evening. Atwater
hovered more determinedly than ever, even glaring as Garwood
led her into his two sets. They were the only dances she enjoyed.

Blackthorn remained nearby, staring at Atwater, never moving
more than twenty feet away, dancing with no one. Most of the
guests relaxed when it became apparent that he would not inflict
his conversation on them or approach their daughters. And the
rumors piqued curiosity. Atwater had been under more pressure
than any gentleman should have to bear. Most people believed he
should strike back. A few even speculated that his refusal to issue
a well-deserved challenge indicated guilt over the private feud
that had prompted Blackthorn's campaign. Thus every eye in the
room watched them. No one wished to miss the moment if the
earl's composure cracked.

By supper Angela had a raging headache. Rather than endure

a meal with Blackthorn's gaze burning into her back, she excused herself to the retiring room. But even that provided no refuge. Speculation raged nonstop. Though the participants constantly changed, only one topic surfaced this night. She was returning to the ballroom in defeat when Blackthorn himself appeared in the hallway.

"You look unwell," he commented.

"Why should that surprise you? Are you enjoying yourself? You've certainly made the rest of us miserable."

He pulled her into a nearby anteroom and shut the door.

"Pull yourself together, Miss Warren. I have no quarrel with you."

"No, you don't. I'm just the innocent bystander who gets hurt by your feud. But what do you care? All's fair, is that it?" She burst into tears, infuriating herself even more.

"My God!" Pulling her into his arms, he muffled her sobs against his coat. The spicy scent he used permeated the fabric. "I did not intend to hurt you and had no idea I was doing so."

"Just because Atwater ignores you does not mean he is immune to your hatred. He may make a pretense of serenity, refusing to create a scene in public, but he takes out his frustration on his companions. I already have bruises where his fingers dug into my arm while we were dancing. How long do you expect him to put up with this before he explodes?"

He blanched. "You need not remain in his vicinity."

"So quick to judge," she countered wryly. "It is true that he did not officially escort us tonight. But he has chosen to remain at my mother's side—with her enthusiastic encouragement. I raked him over the coals for it several days ago. Mother read me lectures, threw hysterics, then encouraged him even more. Your animosity makes her cling even harder. What would you suggest I do to discourage them? Read the riot act? Even that might have no effect. And unlike you, I have a reputation to protect if I ever hope to wed. Such a show of temper would ruin me."

"I was impertinent. Forgive me?" He handed her a handkerchief.

Shocked that she was still in his arms, she pulled away. It had been amazingly comforting to be held against that hard body. "Very well, but can you please refrain from ruining the remainder of my evening? It's hard enough to relax given the people Mother keeps around."

"This is not working as I envisioned anyway." He restlessly paced the floor. "I will find another way."

"And who will you hurt this time? Give it up, my lord. Vengeance rarely works. Haven't your rumors exacted payment enough?"

"I started no rumors."

"Then who?"

"The truth will out on its own."

"What is the truth?" She stared at him, willing him to trust her.

He tore his gaze away, shaking his head. "I will leave you to discover that for yourself. No one ever believes anything I say." Striding from the room, he left the ball without another word. She didn't know if that flash of fury in his eyes had been for her, for Atwater, or for someone else.

She stayed in the anteroom until all trace of tears had vanished. When Blackthorn was rudely abrupt, she could believe every indictment against him. But usually she liked him—or was that her well-known perversity speaking? Perversity might explain why society's rogue attracted her while its hero only repelled. Sense certainly had nothing to do with it. Did she actually believe that her judgment surpassed that of every other member of the *ton*? Yet accepting their view was an admission that she was either stupid or incompetent.

She sighed.

So what was the truth? *I started no rumors.* While he often refused to answer questions, she had never known him to lie. Nor was lying included in society's litany of his faults—which raised questions about his parting comment. She shook her head. She would consider that later.

If Blackthorn was truthful, then Atwater must have more than one enemy. If he had even temporarily pulled the wool over the eyes of society's most knowing gossips, could she trust anything they said—including tales of Blackthorn's own crimes? A shiver almost of excitement tickled her spine. Was he less black than people claimed? It was a difficult question because no one in society seemed capable of thought. They blindly followed a handful of fashionables like a flock of unusually stupid sheep.

Blackthorn was rude and possibly crude, but he had never treated her dishonorably—not even when she argued with him. Meeting away from the eyes of the polite world had allowed them to speak freely. Neither had any reason to put his best foot forward, so she could trust her impressions more readily than with other people.

In a way, Atwater also gave her glimpses of truth. He *was* on his best behavior. But that revealed what he thought she wanted from him. His extravagant compliments implied that she was empty-headed and vain. He made even the most innocuous decisions for her, implying that she was incompetent and biddable. None of it was true.

Tucking the handkerchief away, she sighed. She must discern the truth about Blackthorn and Atwater for herself. Other people's claims were suspect. But answering all her questions would take more time than she had.

She glanced in a mirror to check her face, then pleaded a headache, forcing her mother to take her home.

Had Atwater killed his wife? Perhaps a tendency toward violence was what disturbed her about the man. Yet Blackthorn never incited even a flicker of unease despite being the most violent man she had ever met. Fortunately, studying their characters was no more than an intellectual game. Thank God for Garwood.

"How is your head?" asked Sylvia when they had settled into their respective beds. She had heard about the ball from Lady Forley.

"Better. Any other night it wouldn't have mattered, but I could not remain another minute."

"Who can blame you? Blackthorn sounds unhinged. What did Lord Atwater say?"

"Very little, and nothing to the point. But he was coiled so tightly, I feared he would explode."

"Do you think they came to blows after you left?" she sounded excited by the prospect.

"I doubt it." She would never admit knowing that Blackthorn had left during supper. "Atwater resists every provocation."

"The marquess is mad. Why else would he press so adamantly?"

"Perhaps he believes the tales about Lady Atwater's death."

"Do you?"

"I don't know what to believe, but I will accept Garwood, so it is irrelevant. Atwater would never make a comfortable husband. He treats me like a four-year-old who is incapable even of eating without his advice and assistance. In his mind, female intelligence is a contradiction in terms."

"Gracious! Thank heaven Andrew does not embrace that notion."

Angela laughed. "He will be a supportive and loving husband, though he is so frustrated right now that male intelligence seems the contradiction."

Giggles rippled through the dark. "If you plan to accept Garwood, why haven't you told your mother?"

"I have, but she ignores anything she does not wish to hear and is determined to change my mind. Since all she cares about is title and social position, she considers Garwood utterly ineligible. She'll never understand me."

"I'll try to help you convince her. Do you love Garwood?"

"No, but we are comfortable."

Sylvia subsided into sleep, but Angela had felt that flash of sorrow at her admission. The girl was too young to accept that few marriages were based on love. But love wasn't necessary. Philip would make a good husband. And she would work hard to keep him content, though his touch was no different than Andrew's. Could she enjoy intimacy with a man who felt like a brother? Why couldn't he be as stimulating as Blackthorn?

What an unfortunate thought to fall asleep on, she reflected in the morning. Her dreams had been haunted by furious eyes in a harsh face. And oddly enough, by compassionate arms that comforted her while she wept.

# Chapter Eight

The rumors about Atwater's first marriage echoed in drawing rooms and men's clubs, ballrooms and theaters—anywhere, in fact, where two members of society met. New details emerged hourly, accusing him of brutalizing his wife from the first day of their marriage, of mistreating his tenants, of visiting excessive punishments on miscreants. Everyone embraced the scandal, though few believed it. And because they assumed Blackthorn had fabricated the tales, many added new charges, willingly changing details to make the stories more dramatic. What difference could embellishing fiction make? Sprigs whose behavior had drawn Atwater's censure leaped on the chance to retaliate.

Blackthorn dogged Atwater's footsteps, the hatred that pulsed between the men nearly visible. But Angela at last understood his antagonism. Atwater's first wife had been Blackthorn's cousin. He must believe that the earl had killed her. And since he had not started the rumors, someone else also believed it. Thus an element of truth must underlie the tale. Atwater's refusal to assume mourning supported his guilt.

Society waited expectantly for Atwater to challenge Blackthorn. All eyes followed him. All ears pricked to attention whenever he opened his mouth. Every muscle in his body noticeably tightened whenever Blackthorn appeared. The betting books bulged with wagers about when and how the duel would proceed.

But he confounded London's gamesters, for when he broke, he eschewed a physical confrontation, instead choosing to counterattack in the arena where he was the undisputed champion.

"Lord Atwater has confessed the truth of his wife's death," Lady Debenham announced one afternoon to the ladies assembled in her drawing room. "And it is obvious why he hoped to hide the circumstances." She smiled sympathetically at Angela, confirming that despite the stories, society still expected her to become the next Lady Atwater.

Angela hid her grimace. She had been trying to distance herself from the earl for days, hoping that the scandal would make the break easier, but her mother and Atwater between them had blocked every effort.

"What is the truth?" demanded an elderly dowager, sounding gleeful that Lady Debenham had apparently stolen a march on Lady Beatrice, whose purple face and dagger eyes glared at her hostess.

Lady Debenham deliberately poured tea for a new arrival before responding. "He admits to striking his wife, knocking her down, and bringing on her miscarriage." Satisfaction blazed in her eyes as gasps rolled around the room. "But we must sympathize with the poor man. He loved her with all his heart and was thrilled that she had conceived so quickly. He showered her with attention, catering to her every whim. Then his entire world collapsed." She paused until the silence was nearly unbearable. "Another man had fathered the child."

Someone shrieked.

"How awful!"

"Poor Atwater."

"How could so shy a girl be so unscrupulous?"

"Who?"

All eyes returned to Lady Debenham.

"When he confronted her, she laughed, bragging at the ease with which she had deceived him. She had carried her lover's child on her wedding day."

More gasps echoed.

"Who?" demanded Lady Beatrice.

"Her cousin, Lord Blackthorn." Lady Debenham smiled, raising her teacup to her lips as her visitors' shock gave way to avid chatter.

"Scandalous!"

"That man should have been hung long ago."

"The entire Sherbrooke family should be ostracized."

"How like him to turn the tale against Atwater."

"It is no wonder Atwater cannot mourn her."

"How did the poor man survive such betrayal?"

Angela hardly heard the talk as it swirled around her. *The truth will out* . . . Well, the truth was out with a vengeance.

Or was it?

She followed Lady Forley to their carriage as she tried to pin down that elusive feeling that something was wrong.

"I told you there could be no basis for those malicious rumors," said Lady Forley as their carriage circled Berkeley Square. They passed the crowd outside Gunter's, where footmen raced in and out filling orders for ices. "Perhaps now you will believe that I know what is best for you. You must support your intended husband in his time of trial. Let everyone know that you accept his innocence."

"He is not my intended husband!" Her mind finally brought that elusive thought into focus. Lady Atwater had died nine months to the day after her marriage. If she had been increasing before her wedding, why did everyone attribute her death to a miscarriage? The timing did not fit. "He struck his wife, Mother," she continued. "Such behavior is unacceptable."

"Nonsense. He had cause. The worst thing a woman can do is foist an ill-gotten heir onto her husband. You must support him, and the best way to do so is to dismiss Garwood. You demean yourself by allowing him to dangle after you when you have no intention of wedding him."

"Stop forcing your own views onto me," she demanded coldly. "I refuse to consider Atwater as a husband. He makes me uncomfortable. And his explanation clearly prevaricates. If she was already increasing when she wed, why had she not delivered before this so-called miscarriage?"

"Fustian. Rid yourself of these ridiculous phantoms. Only Atwater can assure you a place in society. Garwood will never bring you to town every Season as is your due. You will die if you are immured in the country for years on end. And you have no idea how demeaning it is to have one's wardrobe stripped to the bone, to have to entertain while living in a neighborhood of cits, to use a traveling coach for making town calls. If you wed Garwood, you would soon find yourself barred from the highest circles. As the Countess of Atwater, you will be a pillar of society. His credit is high, his position inviolable, his town house properly situated in Upper Brook Street . . ."

Angela tuned out the familiar refrain. It was true that she did not consider their present circumstances demeaning. She cared nothing for such trivial matters. Nor did she covet the annual treks to town. She had spent her entire life on the estate, working with its tenants, helping Andrew rebuild his inheritance, supervising the household Lady Forley disparaged as beneath her touch—this despite the fact that her own father had been a baronet, so her marriage had been a huge step up.

Forley Court was the life she knew and loved. That was the sort of life she wanted after marriage—a husband with whom she could feel comfortable and who would install her as lady of the manor on his own estate.

Atwater would never be such a man, regardless of the truth about his first wife. Yesterday's confrontation had been the last straw. He had unexpectedly appeared at her modiste's to collect her from an appointment.

"My own carriage is waiting," she had protested.

"Lady Forley needed to go out. I have already dispatched it and will look after you myself." He'd smiled.

She had been furious but helpless. Her mother had obviously seized yet another opportunity to force her into Atwater's company and inextricably link their names. Even if some emergency had arisen that demanded use of a carriage, Hart's town coach was available. Sylvia had remained at home.

"Come," he ordered, motioning her toward the door.

"I am not finished." She turned back to Jeanette. They had been discussing the details of a new evening gown and had the fabric spread over a table while they compared it to a fashion plate.

"Let the dressmaker do her job," he snapped, an iron grip forcing her hand onto his arm, "if she is capable of doing so. I cannot believe you would patronize a country upstart. There are any number of top modistes in town. Your beauty deserves only the best."

Angela cast an apologetic glance at Jeanette, but she could not resist his force without creating a scandalous scene that might harm Jeanette's business. Without her own coach, she had no choice but to go with him.

"You have more important duties today." He glared as he all but threw her into his phaeton. "Why are you not at Atwater House overseeing the preparations for tomorrow's rout?"

"Mrs. Lincoln knows what to do. How many times must I remind you that I am not your hostess?"

"You should be. Your place will always be at my side. You are the light of my life, the love of my heart, the ornament I need to brighten my home after so much agony."

She shook her head. Did he really believe that pouring the butter boat over her head would influence her? She was possibly above average in looks, but was certainly no diamond. And she had protested often against involving herself with his rout. Lady Forley had volunteered her services, of course, but this was one instance in which she had dug in her heels and refused. His housekeeper was capable of handling the arrangements. The subject had come up often during the last fortnight, but she had continued to refuse. His deliberate disregard of her wishes triggered her temper.

"You will take me home, my lord," she said firmly. He had turned toward Brook Street. "Immediately."

"There is too much to be done for you to turn missish," he countered, eyes glittering dangerously.

"Quite right. I have much planned for today—at my own home. You have already interfered too much, without my invitation and over my repeated objections. It is time to prove that you deserve the title *gentleman*. Take me home."

Fire flashed in his eyes, and for a moment she feared his reaction, but he relaxed his grip on the ribbons and turned his charming smile on her.

"My apologies, Miss Warren. Lady Forley disclaimed any plans for the day."

"Mother is often muddled. You cannot accept her word for anything, my lord. She is stupid and selfish, and deliberately forgets that my brother is head of the family."

Another sharp glance pierced her, but he had turned his horses toward Clifford Street.

Thrusting the memory aside, she sighed in despair. She could not face Atwater's hovering another minute.

Philip would be at tonight's rout. It was time to end this farce of a Season and settle her future. She would bring him up to scratch if she had to turn the tables and ask for *his* hand. She was sick of games, sick of insincere smiles and flattering falsehoods, sick of the endless posturing. That furious gleam in Atwater's eyes still made her skin crawl. She could easily see him striking down so insignificant a creature as a wife.

Atwater's rout was little different than a hundred others, though Lady Forley sulked during the entire ride to Brook Street. She had wanted to be the first arrival, thus fostering the image that Angela was the hostess. But Angela had anticipated the strategem, deliberately procrastinating over her *toilette* so that his house was crowded when they entered. If she had been given a choice, they would be at the opera tonight—she'd not yet seen von Weber's *Abu Hassan*—but when had her desires ever mattered?

It took only half an hour to discover that this was the most enjoyable evening since her come-out ball. Atwater was stuck in the receiving line, leaving her free to laugh, to talk, to lightly flirt. He wasn't at hand to restrict her companions or to dampen their spirits with that proprietary stare she was coming to loathe.

If she'd had any doubts over accepting Philip, they were now gone. She only hoped he would arrive soon. Tonight's freedom provided a perfect opportunity to settle their betrothal.

Atwater would be tied up for most of the evening. His public admission that he had struck his wife guaranteed that every member of the *ton* would be here tonight. And he would have to greet them. Lady Forley lurked determinedly at his side, leaving Angela to her own devices.

But Philip was late. The excessive crush made it difficult for carriages to negotiate the street, and the rooms were so crowded that she could barely move. Eventually, the heat and oppressive air that signaled an approaching storm drove her away. But the retiring room was full of ladies gossiping about Blackthorn. Unwilling to listen to the self-righteous prattle, and equally unwilling to draw attention to herself by pointing out the discrepancies in Atwater's claims, she sought a small anteroom outside Atwater's office where she could recover in peace. It was usually used as a waiting room for tradesmen.

She had risen to return to the drawing room when the office door slammed shut. Angry voices stopped her in her tracks.

"Imbecile!" snapped Atwater. "How dare you allow Garwood into the house! I expressly forbade his appearance."

"Forgive me, my lord," whispered a shaken voice—the footman who had been stationed at the front door. "I do not know how he got in, for he did not pass me."

"Liar. I saw him come up the stairs. You were fawning over his grace of Woburton and paid him no heed."

The footman gasped.

"I do not countenance incompetence, James, as you well know. You will leave my employ immediately. There will be no reference."

Angela stifled a protest. The last thing she needed was for Atwater to corner her alone in this room. Being compromised had no place in her plans.

Again the door slammed.

She could not believe such high-handed cruelty. And why had he tried to bar Garwood? She knew Philip had received an invitation, for he had mentioned it only yesterday. Had Atwater planned to embarrass him by having him ejected from the house? Such a childish plot belied his reputation, but it fit well with a man who admitted beating his wife and who threw out a servant over so trifling a transgression. So the original rumors were probably true.

She walked slowly back to the rout. The footman should not have been expected to carry out such a plan. But it gave her the ammunition she would need to counter her mother's fury when she accepted Philip. Not that she could do so tonight. He was undoubtedly gone, and Atwater was no longer receiving guests. She spotted him in the drawing room, apparently looking for her.

She hastily retreated, too furious to risk meeting him face to face. Instead, she sent word to Andrew that she was unwell, then refused to bid farewell to Atwater before Andrew escorted her home.

\* \* \*

"How dared you leave a party at which you were the hostess?" stormed Lady Forley the next morning.

"I was not the hostess," she declared angrily.

"Nonsense. Atwater considered you his hostess, and it was your duty to assist him. How dared you leave?"

"I had a headache."

"A lady does not have headaches under such circumstances, Angela. You insulted him. You are fortunate that he did not take you in disgust."

"It would be better if he had."

"Imbecile!" Lady Forley pulled herself up to her full height. "I have put up with enough of your megrims. You will dismiss Garwood today. He will not be admitted to this house again. It is not your place to question someone older and wiser than yourself. Your betrothal will be announced as soon as Atwater and Andrew agree to the settlements."

"No."

Lady Forley collapsed into a chair, frantically waving a vinaigrette. "Ungrateful child. What have I done to deserve such spite?"

"There is no spite, Mother, but you overstep your own position. This is Andrew's house. He alone can bar callers. You must accept that I do not share your interests. Yes, you are older and have more experience of the world, but you never consider that others might not enjoy the life you favor. I will not marry where I cannot love. Of my two suitors, I am more likely to achieve that state with Garwood. And I want a partnership with my husband. Atwater is a tyrant, something I will not tolerate. As we are discussing my marriage, my feelings will prevail. And you will discover that Andrew agrees with me." She paused in the doorway. Lady Forley's mouth worked frantically, but no sound emerged. "I will send Wilson to attend you."

She reached the breakfast room before reaction set in. She hated scenes. Despite its necessity, the confrontation had left her shaking. But peace soon settled over her. Finishing her meal, she called for her horse and headed for the park.

# Chapter Nine

Angela drew her horse up near the Serpentine. Riding in the morning when few people were about was far nicer than at the fashionable hour. She did not admit that she also enjoyed mornings because she so often ran into Blackthorn. Nor did she acknowledge the warmth that filled her breast as the marquess trotted out to meet her.

"You look more relaxed this morning," he said by way of greeting.

"An argument with my mother cleared the air," she admitted. "Perhaps now I can enjoy the rest of the Season."

"Argument?" His brows rose in question.

"She cannot understand that I dislike London and wish to live my life in the country."

"Some of us are like that," he agreed. "Though Lady Forley is not."

"You, too, prefer the country?"

He nodded.

"What is your estate like?"

"Wyndhaven?" He looked beyond her as if he could see it in the distance. "It is the most beautiful spot on earth. It sits on the south coast, so it offers everything I love—cliffs that drop away to beaches that can change in an instant from a quiet place for thought to an exhilarating spot of crashing waves; forested hills that protect the house from storms; a pair of lakes; a marvelous fishing stream; even some authentic ruins."

"It sounds like a combination of Forley Court and Carrisford Grange." The Grange was Hart's estate. "Are your ruins the remains of an abbey?"

"Actually, the site was a fortified Plantagenet-era manor that replaced an ancient walled keep. When it burned two centuries ago, my ancestor rebuilt in a new location."

"Better?"

"I think so. It gave my great-grandfather room to expand." He went on to describe the house—currently with a Palladian facade—and the grounds that Repton had recently revised. His love for the land sang in every word, giving her more insight into his character than any of their former exchanges and providing new evidence against his reputation. No man who cared for his estate as Blackthorn did could be the evil villain society claimed.

"But enough about me," he said at last. "Why are you in town if you dislike it so much?"

"Stupid question." She shrugged. "I must find a husband, and there is a dearth of unattached males near Forley Court."

"So you'll accept Atwater rather than return home unwed?"

"Hardly. We would never be comfortable together. Fortunately, he is not the only choice."

"Garwood?"

She nodded.

"But will you be given a choice?" His tone was now serious. "Unless she has changed greatly, your mother is not a woman who willingly admits mistakes or accepts defeat."

"You know her from before, I suppose." She paused long enough to note his confirmation. "I hardly knew her at all until Father died, for she rarely visited the Court. Papa came more often, to relax and study in his library. He hated town, but he loved Mother and couldn't stay apart from her for long. She made his life hell."

"I've long suspected that. Don't let her do the same to you."

"She's tried. She encouraged Atwater shamelessly despite my protests. She cannot see that I take after Papa rather than her. Her delusions were the subject of our argument this morning."

She described Atwater's rout and the reason for her early departure.

"So he dismissed the footman?"

She nodded. "I wish I could do something for the man. Without a reference he will be hard-pressed to find a new position."

"I will find one for him," he promised absently, a frown adding intimidating lines to his face.

His offer came as no surprise. In fact, her own comment had deliberately sought it. Some instinct had suspected that he would help—because of Mickey, perhaps, or maybe she truly saw beyond his facade. "Why do you continue courting censure when your character is so benign?"

His eyes narrowed. "Don't mistake me for an angel," he warned. "I am well named. But your mother's behavior concerns me. This insistence on throwing you and Atwater together goes beyond the usual quest for titled wealth." He must have caught her frown, for he smiled. "Believe me, I've plenty of experience with fortune hunters and matchmaking mamas. They may ignore me now, but I faced my share some years ago. Lady Forley's behavior doesn't fit."

"She is annoying, but only because she is selfish and assumes everyone shares her values. Now that she knows differently—for even she cannot misunderstand plain English, and I kept my objections short and simple this time—we will manage better."

"I hope so, but be careful. I have a feeling that there is more going on than you realize."

Without another word, he left her, but she understood his abruptness. The hour was too advanced to risk staying together. He was as conscious of maintaining her reputation as she was.

His parting comment stayed in Devall's mind all the way home. No lady who cared for her daughter would ignore that daughter's wishes as Lady Forley was doing. Why was she so determined to tie Angela to Atwater? Even if she had initially been ignorant of Atwater's faults, recent stories should have raised grave questions about the man.

He had never liked Lady Forley, though she had quitted town when he was still a callow youth, so he didn't know her well. He cast his mind back to the days before his disastrous betrothal.

She had much in common with encroaching mushrooms despite her better breeding. Determined to push her way into higher social circles, she had flattered and fawned while ignoring any hint of censure. And there had been plenty. Her greed had made many people roll their eyes behind her back. As had her entertainments, which had been lavish to the point of vulgarity. Since her return, the ostentatious opulence was absent—a victim of limited finances, or possibly of Angela's better taste. But Angela was too inexperienced to counter the machinations of a determined social climber. The fact that Lady Forley was her mother would make it even harder to stand up to her. So she needed help.

He vowed to keep a close eye on Lady Forley.

"Mr. Garwood has called to see Miss Warren," announced Paynes, standing stiffly erect in the drawing room doorway.

"She is shop—" began Lady Forley, abruptly closing her mouth. "Show him in, Paynes."

She smoothed the skirt of her morning gown and slipped her needlework into its basket. One of a mother's responsibilities was seeing that her children married well. Never would she ascribe to the notion that inexperienced, innocent girls were capable of choosing proper mates. And Angela was one of the worst. Thanks to Lord Forley's idiocy in forcing her to share her brother's tutors, she had acquired unladylike ideas and an unbecoming independence. It was long past time that she assume her proper place in society as the wife of a peer of wealth and consequence. If the girl was too stupid to plan her own future, she would have to do it for her.

"Lady Forley," murmured Garwood politely. "I had hoped to speak with Miss Warren. Will she be down soon?"

"She is out at the moment."

His face fell, but manners forbade leaving. "I am putting together an outing to Richmond next week and would be delighted if you would join the party. Miss Warren and Lady Sylvia will enjoy escaping the city for a few hours."

"I do not think that would be wise, sir," said Lady Forley with a smile. "The Season is far enough advanced that Angela must turn her thoughts to her future. There will be no more time to dally with acquaintances if she is to set everything in train before Lord Forley's own wedding. I am sure you understand."

Shock suffused Garwood's face. "I assure you that my intentions are honorable. In fact, I had intended to speak with Lord Forley soon."

"I am sure they are, but you cannot understand our situation. Angela has no dowry so cannot afford an alliance with one whose own financial position is precarious."

He drew himself up in cold hauteur. "You have been misinformed, my lady. My situation is comfortable. Miss Warren is familiar with it and has expressed no reservations."

The determination glaring from Garwood's eyes sent shudders down her back. Even her lie about the dowry had not affected him. Casting all scruples aside, she assumed the open expression that had always bent gentlemen to her will. "It is you who have been misinformed, sir. It never occurred to me that Angela would not have told you. London must have turned her head, the silly girl. She has never received so much attention before. I know she has enjoyed your friendship, but that can hardly excuse such callous disregard for your feelings. The truth is that she was promised to Atwater before we came to town, though they delayed the announcement in deference to his recent bereavement. You may curse me as an indulgent parent for agreeing to such secrecy, but I never thought she might use the time to practice her wiles on innocent parties."

His brain in turmoil, Garwood could hardly take in the words. "But she had not met him until her come-out ball," he objected, yet he could not stop the pictures unrolling through his mind—Atwater leading Angela into the first set following her obligation dances with her brother and host; Atwater's proprietary stance at nearly every ball; her demeanor with the earl, making no attempt to flirt or otherwise attract his attention. And now he knew why. Contrary to his own impressions, she was relaxed because no effort was necessary. Pain stabbed his heart that he immediately converted to anger over her deliberate deceit.

"That is true," said Lady Forley. His thoughts had winged ahead so rapidly that he had nearly forgotten the words to which she responded. "But the arrangements had been made before we came to town. He met all her requirements for a husband—wealth, estates, high title. He needed an heir as soon as possible, but had little heart for a lengthy courtship. It was a pleasant surprise to find him so congenial, but they agreed to leave the official announcement until later."

"Why did she not tell me this herself?"

"She is enjoying your attentions too much. It is always gratifying to have a court. And attracting multiple offers increases a girl's credit in some circles. Had you pressed a suit, she must have revealed the truth, of course. But waiting that long is unfair to you."

He took his leave, anger and pain still boiling in his mind. By the time he reached his curricle, anger had overwhelmed all else. She had deceived him from the beginning, and not just about her betrothal. Her character was sadly lacking. To court a gentleman's affections solely to feed her own conceit was the height of dishonesty. He had hinted at a future together often enough that she could hardly claim ignorance of his intentions.

He would cut her from now on, of course, but that offered little comfort. She deserved ostracism. His expression darkened. She would get it. Even Atwater's cachet would not protect her once the truth was known.

Unaware of Garwood's reaction to her lies, Lady Forley smiled in satisfaction and returned to her needlework. The future looked brighter. Angela would have the husband she deserved and would reward her mother by assuring her a permanent place in society. Atwater would set her up with her own town house so that she need never set foot in the country again. She must remind Andrew to include that in the settlements. Humming a gay little tune, she exchanged blue thread for red.

Angela's first inkling of Lady Forley's interference came in the park that afternoon when she received several odd looks from passing carriages. No one stopped to exchange gossip, instead giggling behind gloved hands and animatedly conversing with their escorts. She recognized the actions as the *ton*'s response to the subject of the latest gossip, not that she could guess the cause. Blackthorn was the only person who knew anything derogatory about her, and he would never blacken her name.

Even Sylvia knew nothing. "Are you the target?" she asked in surprise. "I thought it was me."

"What do you mean?"

"There was a sudden silence at Lady Beatrice's when I entered. You know the one—everyone abruptly stops talking when the object of their discussion arrives, then immediately begins a new topic."

She nodded. "Or someone close to the subject if the story is truly reprehensible." But what could it be? And about whom?

Andrew described a similar experience at his club. Whatever the rumor, society seemed to blame the entire household.

But when she arrived at Lady Chartley's ball, Angela knew that she was the primary target. More than one high-stickler deliberately turned away as she approached. The cut direct. The signal to society that she was an undesirable *parti*, a pariah, beneath contempt. Even Atwater looked at her strangely, though he hovered as usual and signed her card for two waltzes, having charmed Lady Jersey into approving her a week earlier. Three young bucks had also signed for early sets, but the evening steadily worsened.

It was her third partner who revealed the tale. "You needn't try to attach my affections," he drawled, leading her down the set. "I've no intention of settling down for years."

"What are you talking about?" she demanded, bewildered at his words.

"What you did to Garwood was cruel, my fancy lady, but now that we know your game, it will not happen again. I would wish you joy in your marriage, but the heartless don't deserve it."

"Mr. Huggens, I have no idea what you are talking about. I can only surmise that some tale is making the rounds, though I cannot imagine what it could be. Would you be so kind as to enlighten me?"

He stared as though he suddenly found himself dancing with a worm. "Very well, I will play the game." He shrugged. "Society knows about your betrothal to Atwater and is justifiably incensed at how you have been leading poor Garwood around by the nose simply to feed your own vanity."

"I assure you, there is no betrothal," she snapped. "Who has been spreading such lies?"

"Garwood himself. He learned the truth this morning and is angry over being deceived."

"He learned no truths. I have not spoken with him today. Excuse me, sir, for I must discover who is going to such lengths to blacken my name." Garwood had just arrived.

"Very well. A confrontation will be more entertaining than dancing." He threaded the other couples, heading for the stairs.

Angela was opening her mouth to speak when Garwood spotted her approach. Glaring at her for several seconds, he deliberately turned away and requested another young lady to honor him with the next set. His affable voice and warm glance made it clear that she was worthy of his attention while Angela was not.

In shock, she belatedly noted that Atwater and her mother were slipping from the room.

"Thank you for the dance, Mr. Huggens," she managed to say. "I fear the heat has affected me overmuch. If you will excuse me, I must seek the retiring room for a moment's rest."

His smile was tinged with understanding as he released her arm and allowed her to exit.

A voice rose in an antechamber as she hurried down the hallway. Recognizing her mother, she reached for the door handle, then froze as Atwater angrily replied.

"What is the meaning of these stories, Lady Forley? Are you trying to force my hand?"

"How can you think such a thing?" Her tone hinted that she was on the verge of tears, though Angela knew her too well to believe it. "I cannot understand them myself—unless Mr. Garwood has become deranged. It would seem that the story started with him. All I can think is that he is seeking revenge. Angela turned him down this morning. How he could have expected otherwise is beyond my understanding. Marrying him would be a step down for the poor girl. He is naught but the younger son of a baron."

"She did not start these rumors herself?"

"How dare you impugn her honor? She was astonished at his offer, for she had made it clear early on that she was not interested in a serious relationship with him. When he persisted, she asked my advice. I thought him merely amusing himself so allowed him to continue. But he must have decided that he loved her, conceiving this campaign in spiteful retaliation when reality intruded. You know what I mean—if he cannot have her, then he will make sure no one else does. If I had thought for a moment that he was unstable, I would have forbidden him the house."

"I too never suspected that he was capable of deluding himself," agreed Atwater, sounding much calmer. "And I was sure his tale was a hum, for he also claims that she is a bluestocking reformer, which I know to be false. I will do what I can to counter the rumors, of course. This is but a tempest in a teapot. If you can bear it for a few days, it will blow over."

"Thank you, my lord. We are grateful for your support."

Angela slipped down the hall as he took his leave, so that she was approaching when he opened the door. How ironical that he disbelieved the one true fact in this whole fabrication.

"I will escort you back to the ballroom," he said, extending his arm.

"I am looking for my mother."

"She is inside."

"Thank you." She dismissed him curtly, not caring what he thought. Even his offer to help her weather the storm was of no consequence.

As soon as he retreated, she shut the door and glared at her mother. "How could you lie to Atwater? I turned down no proposals, as you well know."

"He needs to understand that Mr. Garwood is spreading lies," she replied calmly.

"And why would Philip do so, Mother?" The ice in her voice made Lady Forley step back a pace.

"I cannot imagine."

"I can. He is repeating exactly what you told him, is he not? You knew that I would welcome his suit, so you poisoned his mind against me." Her voice shook. This betrayal went beyond anything she had ever imagined. Blackthorn's warning had been prescient. Why hadn't she taken his fears seriously?

"It had to be done, Angela," insisted Lady Forley. "You are too young to understand the world. I cannot stand aside and watch you throw yourself away on an ineligible suitor. And he has proven himself ineligible. A gentleman would never wage a spiteful campaign to hurt you just because his own shortcomings were exposed. Despite your fantasies, he would never be able to offer you your rightful place in society." A self-satisfied smirk twisted her lips.

Angela stared, engulfed in cold fury. Lady Forley was determined to force her daughter into her own mold.

"You lying, manipulative harpy!" The words exploded from her throat. "Never have you understood me. Never have you made the slightest attempt to understand me. Do you think you are God? Why else would you try to bend people to your own will? Well, it won't work. I would die before patterning myself after you. The shallow stupidity and acid condemnation that masquerade as conversation in this town make me sick. As does the whole giddy pretense of society. I want no part of it. Which is just as well. It is too late for that now. You are well served, are you not? Your scheming lies have made me an outcast. I hope you are satisfied!"

In tears, she fled the room, not waiting for a response. Where could she go? A laughing cluster of young ladies blocked the retiring room. A larger congregation of gentlemen barred both the ballroom and the stairs leading to the street. Neither group had yet noticed her. An anteroom across the hall was empty so she ducked inside, locking the door behind her.

*Control, control*, she repeated desperately, sinking onto a couch and pressing her palms to her eyes as though she could force the tears back inside. The last thing she needed was to return to the ballroom with red eyes and a blotchy face. There were enough rumors already.

It took only a moment to concede that Lady Forley had driven Garwood away for good. He hated deceit so would continue assaulting her reputation, for he would not readily admit his mistake.

She shook her head. When she had approved his high moral stance, it had not occurred to her to question whether his judgment was sound. He should at least have spoken to her before deciding her guilt. Did his affection count for nothing? He knew she disapproved her mother's manipulation. He knew she judged people on their own worth, not their social position. He knew everything important about her, yet he had accepted her mother's statements as gospel.

In that sense, Lady Forley had actually done her a service. As had Atwater. If he had not interfered, she would have been betrothed last night. Would she have discovered Garwood's intolerance in time to call off the wedding? At best, life would have been uneasy with such a husband. Had the others against whom he held grudges been similarly innocent?

It mattered not. Drawing a shaky breath, she fished an inadequate handkerchief from her reticule and mopped her face.

Her pain was rooted in betrayal and anger. And grief, though she shouldn't grieve over being spared a marriage that she would not have liked. But now that the initial shock was subsiding, she had to face a very real fear of the future.

Atwater was now her sole suitor, but her feelings about him remained unchanged. So how was she to find a husband? A lifetime spent playing aunt to Sylvia's children was untenable.

New tears sprang to her eyes, tears her sodden handkerchief could not absorb.

"The stories can hardly be so bad that you must fall apart, Miss Warren," drawled a deep voice. Blackthorn stood in the shadows of a window alcove.

"What are you doing here?"

"I believe that is my question. I was here first."

"Forgive me for intruding." Still sniffing, she pushed the handkerchief back into her reticule and rose. Tears stained both cheeks.

"Devil take it, you can't leave looking like that." He pressed his own handkerchief into her hand, then pulled her head against his shoulder when his rough kindness triggered renewed sobbing. "How did this tale arise?" he asked at last. "Having been the target of so many stories, I am curious."

His detached tone steadied her. "You should be able to guess, for you obviously suspected her. Mother decided to discourage Garwood with a series of lies, all of which she attributed to me. He despises deceit, so retaliated by pillorying me in public."

"Good God!"

"Precisely." She exhaled in a long sigh of despair. "But I am not quite falling apart, my lord. I only needed a moment to collect myself before again facing the cuts." More than a moment, she conceded. Her eyes must be swollen. She had never been able to cry prettily.

"Facing them is essential, of course." He wandered over to examine a vase on the mantel. "If you run now, the stories will take root and grow until you can never return."

"Is that what happened to you?"

"Not quite. I care nothing for what society's denizens think. If anything, my ouster set me free, for I need no longer consider their absurd sensibilities. My friends know the truth, and that is all that matters. You might consider life in that light. There must be something about this situation that you can turn to your advantage. And I will do what I can to counter Garwood's lies—not that the gossips would believe a word I say, but I still have friends who are received."

"I knew you were not as black as your reputation suggests. But if you have the power to counter gossip, why have you not used it to help yourself?"

"I like my reputation just the way it is," he drawled blandly, though a hint of pain crept into his words that made her wonder what he was hiding—and from whom. "It suits me to hold society at bay—and the tales do contain grains of truth."

Which portions were factual? She couldn't face the ballroom just yet, instead sinking onto the couch. "So you are not the gamester and rake gossip assumes?"

He shook his head, turning back to face her. "I am no saint, but neither have I ever debauched an innocent or taken advantage of inexperience. Gaming is a way to fill the time on those occasions when I must be in town, but though I lose frequently, I also win and have never continued play beyond what I had allotted for an evening's entertainment."

"And what of Lady Atwater?"

"That is one tale that contains no truth whatsoever."

"I had already deduced that. All else aside, she died more than nine months after her supposed conception. So why does everyone from Atwater to the most exacting dowagers claim she suffered a miscarriage?"

He chuckled, starting a treacherous glow in her stomach. "You must be the only person in London who can count. She was only four months with child when he beat her senseless." He paced the room. "Poor Lydia. She was one of the few relatives I had who was worth knowing. Frankly, I would not wish my family on my worst enemy."

He paused a moment, and she had the odd impression that he was trying to control a sudden urge to tears.

"Lydia was lovely in both form and spirit. If I'd had any hint of how things would end, I would have stayed in town the entire Season, or would at least have checked into his background, but her parents had things well in hand, and she was ecstatic over attracting Atwater's attention. They made a handsome couple—two blue-eyed golden-haired angels capable of lighting any room they entered. Her only problem was shyness. In all her life she had never been able to assert herself with strangers, though once she became acquainted, her natural charm invariably surfaced, so I had not considered it a liability. I loved her dearly, but like the sister I never had. Never would I have harmed her. In fact, I was not even in town when she accepted Atwater's hand, and I avoided her wedding lest my presence spoil her day. The other guests would have objected."

"I see."

"I hope you do, for though I ignore exaggerations, I despise deliberate falsehoods." He pulled her briskly to her feet, taking a moment to examine her face. "You'll do. You must return to the ballroom if you've any hope of carrying off the evening. Whatever happens, do not let either pain or anger show in your face. Let the world see that *your* behavior is unexceptionable. In the end, truth will prevail."

He watched her go, then sought out Jack. This was not a night he could spend on his own campaign, though it would be long before he wangled another invitation from society's reluctant hostesses. But Angela's problems were more urgent than forcing retribution on Atwater for Lydia's death.

Damnation! He should have anticipated this move—an objective analysis would have revealed that Lady Forley was capable of such deceit. She never allowed scruples to interfere with achieving her goals. His failure to prevent this attack made him responsible for repairing the damage. And perhaps he could devise a fitting punishment for Lady Forley.

"I need your help to defeat Garwood's unwarranted persecution," he declared when he had run Jack to ground.

"How?"

"Garwood's tale is false from start to finish." He sighed. "Lady Forley concocted the lies, though you needn't delve into her motives. Much as I despise him, the only counter I can devise is to use Atwater's continued devotion as proof that Miss Warren is innocent. He believes the tale to be false. Remind people of that. The gossips swallowed all his lies about Lydia's death, proving they still dote on the bastard, so they should follow his lead. Garwood can't hope to compete with his credit."

"What is your interest in the girl?" Jack asked.

"I despise slander." His glare squelched further questions. "Get acquainted with her. She needs friends."

His stomach turned at where this might lead, but he could think of nothing else. If her protestations were true, she would turn Atwater down. Or try. Did she have the fortitude to withstand pressure from both her mother and her brother, who seemed equally anxious to marry her off? But her future was none of his concern.

He repeated that several times as he made his way to White's, but deep down he didn't believe it. His hand shook whenever he recalled cradling her head against his shoulder. That reaction frankly terrified him.

Jack went to work immediately, seeking an introduction to Miss Warren and leading her into the next waltz. He had watched Devall embroil himself in many scandals over the years, but he'd never seen him as grim as he'd appeared tonight. Was it only because this approach risked throwing Miss Warren onto Atwater's not-so-tender mercies, or did Devall have stronger feelings for her than he was willing to admit?

Miss Warren's appearance was striking enough. Her blazing auburn hair was arranged in waves, setting off moss-green eyes whose slight puffiness hinted at an earlier bout of tears. Devall's shoulder had been damp, he realized, his spirits plummeting. There was definitely more to this case than altruism, damn Blackthorn all to hell.

How deeply were they involved? Nothing but pain could come of it. If the relationship became public, it would ruin her far more than Garwood's charges.

He grimaced. After brutally jilting his fiancée, Devall had sworn that he would never harm another girl. It wasn't like him to renege on an oath.

So what was he doing with Miss Warren?

But he pushed the question aside for the moment. He had promised to help. A closer look into her eyes detected a core of steel that would see her through the present crisis.

"You are doing very well," he commented as he twirled her onto the floor. "It should blow over soon."

"You believe me innocent?" she exclaimed, and immediately blushed. "Forgive me, sir—"

"Relax. I have it on the best authority that you are honest, and I have agreed to turn what little influence I possess to redeeming your credit."

New tears glistened in her eyes, but she blinked them away. "Thank you. Would it be too forward to ask who is championing my cause?"

"Blackthorn. He is a good friend, one whose word I trust implicitly," he added as she raised her brows. Devall must not have mentioned his plans. Typical. The man was the most reticent person he had ever known—especially when it came to anything that showed him to advantage. How much of Devall's true character did she know? If she cared for him even as a casual acquaintance, she must see well beyond his reputation. In that case, he could not condemn Devall for getting involved. The man had so few friends. But he must face the truth about where even friendship would lead.

Again Jack pushed consideration of Devall's relationship with Miss Warren into the future, but it could not hurt to reveal some of Devall's better traits—and it might give her hope for her own situation. Suppressing the shudder that always wracked him at the memory, he smiled. "He rescued me from just this sort of campaign several years ago."

"Are you going to explain or not?" she asked as his pause stretched. "It can't be too painful, or you would not have mentioned it. And I admit to curiosity. I've not yet managed to reconcile my impressions with his reputation."

Her eyes promised that his words would go no further if that was his wish. But beyond that, he read her unwilling attraction to Devall. It was worse than he'd feared. Friendship was bad enough. A *tendre* would destroy them. What was Devall about, to encourage the chit, knowing that his reputation could only harm her? Championing victims of injustice was one thing, but she was likely to wind up as *his* victim. Damn them! Unless . . .

His breath caught as he twirled her through a complicated turn, automatically, sidestepping a couple with shorter legs. Could this at long last be his chance to repay Devall for salvaging his name, his career, and probably his life? It would be tricky, but just maybe . . .

That question also got shelved for later. This was not the time or the place for deep thinking. The immediate problem was too urgent and Miss Warren was getting impatient.

"I had won a considerable amount at the tables," he began, mentioning neither the unsavory hell he had played in nor his four-figure prize. "Unfortunately, one of my opponents was far into his cups and cried cheat. Despite other players' efforts to deflect the sot by pointing out his condition, he repeated the charge the next morning."

"Oh, no!"

"Afraid so. By noon it was all over town, and I faced the ruin of my career. That's when Devall stepped in. I never questioned how"—Devall's penchant for unconventional behavior made knowledge of his methods deuced uncomfortable—"but two days later, the lad made a public statement conceding that no cheating had occurred and admitting that he had been so terrified of facing his father with his staggering losses that he had succumbed to temptation. He'd squandered half a year's allowance that night, though not all to me."

"He is a good friend."

"I would never argue that." She didn't seem surprised at the tale. Had Devall mentioned it? Or did she understand his character that well? *Later*, he reminded himself. Right now they needed to counter Garwood's lies. "Can either Garwood or your mother be talked into revealing the truth?"

"No. He never admits a fault and she has already compounded the problem by spinning new lies to Atwater."

He sighed. "We will have to follow Blackthorn's suggestion, then. Much as he hates the idea, he thinks Atwater's continued good will must soon defeat the rumors."

"More likely support them," she grumbled. "It will confirm the notion that a secret betrothal exists."

"Shall we put it about that Garwood made that up to explain the failure of his own suit?"

"That is one of the lies Mama told Atwater."

"Which makes it useful."

"Dear Lord, I hate this town! Is no one allowed to be honest?"

"A reasonable question," he agreed, trying to soothe her obvious distress. "Normally I would say yes, but this situation is too complicated."

Angela's fears grew as the days passed, though Atwater's allegiance had quickly defeated the rumors, allowing her to maintain her social schedule and again be received in drawing rooms. Sylvia also helped deflect the gossip. Often she accompanied her friend Lady Ashton, leaving Angela and Lady Forley to make their own rounds. By splitting their forces, they could cover more territory, and Lady Ashton was one of the highest sticklers in town.

Garwood's claims were hastened toward their grave by the discovery of Miss Sommerton in the indecent embrace of Mr. Throckmorton, and were buried entirely the day eighteen-year-old Lawrence Delaney lost control of his team in St. James's Street, killing Marchgate's heir and injuring two others. Angela's reputation emerged intact. Garwood's was slightly tarnished. Within a week, a newcomer would not have known anything had happened.

Angela tried to remain optimistic, though Atwater was now her only suitor and time was inexorably ticking away. And she had derived one large benefit from the experience—Major Caldwell's friendship. He was not a suitor by any stretch of the imagination, nor did she want him to be. Instead, he treated her like a revered sister, replacing the warmth that had been missing in her life since Andrew fell in love with Sylvia. Only now did she recognize that lack—and it made her situation even more urgent. She must marry. Jack would soon leave. Forley Court could no longer offer her a congenial home. Life as the Court's resident spinster would be unbearably lonely and barren.

Jack also confirmed her suspicions about Blackthorn—not that they ever discussed him. But the Black Marquess of rumor could never earn the respect and loyalty of Major Caldwell. More than ever, she wanted to learn the truth. She tried to believe that the urge was mere curiosity, though deep down she suspected that it was stronger than that. But concentrating on Blackthorn kept her own problems at bay, problems that appeared grimmer each day.

She could not accept Atwater. That decision was bad enough, for it condemned her to life as a spinster. But even spinsterhood was preferable to outright ostracism. Was that what would happen when she sent him packing? She feared it might be. No mater how she did it, society would hardly forgive her. Jilting him—for that was how the gossips would see it—would almost certainly revive Garwood's tales, and worse. If anyone had a legitimate complaint about having his hopes falsely raised, it was Atwater. Never mind that it was Lady Forley who had encouraged him.

# Chapter Ten

Devall urged his horse forward the moment Angela appeared out of the morning fog. It had been several days since he had joined her on her morning ride, so she seemed surprised to see him. But he hadn't dared risk being spotted when her reputation was already suspect. Yet time had stretched interminably since the ball.

Thrusting the thought aside, he smiled. "Truth has prevailed at last."

"Yes, and good has come of it, as you suggested. I thought I could be comfortable with Garwood, but who can live with a man so quick to judge and so loathe to forgive once he has done so? Thank you for your efforts on my behalf."

"I did nothing." He was oddly uncomfortable, having had little experience with praise.

"Not according to Major Caldwell."

"Jack has a way of exaggerating."

They trotted in silence for several minutes.

"Why haven't you tried to improve your own reputation?" she asked at last, repeating a question she had uttered before.

He shrugged, supplying his usual answer. "I care nothing for society's opinion."

"I find that hard to believe—unless you hate people. Your life must be quite lonely."

He glared at her.

"Think about it," she persisted. "Society shuns you, yet the lower classes can only stand in awe of your title. Major Caldwell is a wonderful friend, but he is out of the country much of the time. Doesn't that leave you isolated?"

"I have other friends." But a wave of loneliness washed through him. He rarely saw any of his friends, and Jack was the only one he could really count on to support him. He pulled himself together. "I have more freedom than society would ever allow."

"Freedom to do what? Flout convention? Pursue personal feuds regardless of morality or law and with little regard for the innocent bystanders you might harm? I cannot believe you enjoy hurting people. So why have you often done just that?"

"I have my reasons, which I need not explain to you," he snapped, not wanting to admit that her words cut deeply into his heart. He was suddenly choking, as though a giant bellows had sucked half the air from the park. A lifetime of self-preservation instincts rose, igniting his temper.

"As I suspected," she said smugly. "You are hiding behind your reputation. If your actions are noble, why not admit it? If they are not, then you cannot claim that rumor exaggerates. Or are you afraid to face society as an equal?"

"I fear nothing."

"Then try it. Tell people who you really are. Only truth can set you truly free," she declared, paraphrasing the Bible. Without another word, she cantered away, leaving him shaking.

What did she expect him to do? He had no wish to participate in the shallow inanities that passed for entertainment in London. And his position as an outcast gave him the freedom to address wrongs that could be righted in no other way.

He galloped in the opposite direction. Why was he listening to her anyway? She would move out of his life as quickly as she had moved in. He would doubtless never see her again, and that was best for both of them. She disturbed him in ways he did not want to think about. She deserved marriage, a home, and a family. He could offer her nothing. Six years ago he had accepted the lonely road fate had placed before him. He had never regretted it, and wasn't about to do so now.

*Only truth can set you truly free.* Damn her! Why did she linger in his mind? But he could not ignore the fact that even Jack did not know the full truth. Nor could he escape the heartbreaking, soul-crushing loneliness . . .

Angela was still furious when she left for the daily round of morning calls. Blackthorn was stubborn as a mule, but she knew she was right. Somewhere buried under all that stubbornness was a wish to belong, a need to be like other men. She must help him, and not just out of gratitude for her restored reputation. She cared what happened to the very unhappy marquess—deeply. And she suspected that it was a blackness of spirit rather than deeds that made his sobriquet so fitting.

Just how bad were his deeds? He had admitted that most of the stories contained seeds of truth. But she needed to know details before she could decide how to help him.

Their arrival at Mrs. Bassington's house on Davies Street interrupted these thoughts. The drawing room was decorated in a sparse Greek style with white stuccatori garlands and bas-relief vignettes against light blue walls. Red and blue upholstery provided the only real color. Several marble busts reminded visitors of the late Mr. Bassington's obsession with ancient Greece.

"I hear Garwood has turned his eyes to Miss Cunningham," said Lady Beatrice slyly when Angela appeared in the doorway.

"Really?" twittered the elderly Lady Barton. "Dear Sally Jersey noted only last night how devoted he was to Miss Derrick."

"Well, I saw for myself the look on his face when he and Lady Barbara returned from the terrace," declared Mrs. Collinsworth stoutly. "If they had not been kissing, then you can lock me in Bedlam."

Angela smiled indulgently. She almost felt sorry for Garwood. Her own redemption had tarnished his image, and the town tabbies were joyfully watching his every move.

"Lady Horseley," announced the butler.

"You won't believe whom I just spoke with," said her ladyship, sending a look of such triumph at Lady Beatrice that Angela wondered what was coming.

Lady Horseley paused to collect all eyes. "Miss Styles has just accepted Mr. Harley's offer of marriage. The announcement will appear in tomorrow's paper with the wedding scheduled in three weeks." Her glee at stealing a march on Lady Beatrice injected excitement into an event that everyone had expected for some time.

"Hardly earth-shattering news, Emily," drawled Lady Beatrice. "He's been hanging on her sleeve for weeks."

But the buzz of a dozen voices drowned out the comment. This would be the first wedding of the Season and thus was worthy of attention.

"You wished to see me, Andrew?" asked Angela from the study doorway. His message had awaited her when she returned from calls.

"Yes. Shut the door." His light-hearted expression stood in sharp contract to the tension of the past week.

She settled into a wing chair, noting again how different this room was from the library at Forley Court. Few books filled the small cabinet, and most of those were collections of sermons, their pages still uncut. One could expect no more when renting a house, but she badly missed the Court's library.

"Lord Atwater called on me this morning," Andrew began, ignoring her gasp. "He has offered for your hand. I gave him permission to pay his addresses tomorrow morning."

*Not yet!* She wasn't ready for this. "Why?"

He looked at her oddly. "Do you not wish to accept him? Mother was adamant that you would welcome him, but I will never force you into a distasteful union."

She felt torn in two. Now that the decision point had arrived, every pressure to wed rose up to flail her. How could she face her lifelong neighbors after failing to snare a husband? Yet how could she tie herself to Atwater? The mental struggle sent tremors clear to her toes.

"I know I must accept someone, and he is the only suitor left, but I cannot like him, Andrew. He is not the paragon that society declares, for I heard him myself cruelly dismiss a servant for a trifle. I don't know the truth behind the death of his first wife, but I suspect he is capable of brutality. Never have I been comfortable in his presence. Yet how can I go home unwed? I am already nearly on the shelf and will be a confirmed spinster by the time we can afford to revisit London. Besides, it would be unfair to Sylvia if I were to remain at home."

"Angie." He sighed in frustration. "I had no idea that you were torturing yourself like this. I will never approve giving you to a man you do not love. You would be miserable in such a union, and I would be miserable for you. I know too well what love is like to ever countenance a marriage without it. So you must refuse him."

"I'm sorry," she sobbed. "You sacrificed so much to give me this Season, and now I've wasted it."

"There was no sacrifice, Angie. The estate is back on its feet, and finances are better than you suppose. This Season was as much for my benefit as yours. I had been away from London too long and will bring Sylvia back every two or three years—more often if Hart has his way and embroils me in politics. You are under no obligation to me, nor will it matter if you remain at home for a time after I wed. Sylvia will not mind."

"She cannot help but mind. I am five years her senior and have been running the Court since Father died. She will feel an interloper if I remain."

"Fustian! You and Sylvia are both intelligent, rational people who know right from wrong. Your place at the Court is not the issue. Choose the course that is right for you. And quit listening to Mother. I just realized that not once have you accompanied Sylvia and me to events Mother finds boring. She must have brow-beat you into denying your interests. Have you done anything but gossip, sip tea, and dance since we came to town?"

"Not much."

He frowned. "I'd best talk to her."

"Not today," she begged, rising to leave. "I cannot listen to another of her tirades right now. If she learns that I am determined to turn Atwater down, she will throw hysterics. It will be bad enough afterward, but at least she must then accept my decision. In the meantime, I believe a headache will keep me home this evening. I cannot abide another ball with the pair of them hovering over me."

"Why is she pushing so hard?" he asked as she reached the door.

She shrugged. "You know her views. Social position, title, and wealth are all that matter." Lady Forley accepted society's opinion on every subject. But society was only as correct as the fashionables who were leading it, and they were not infallible. Perhaps she would have made fewer mistakes if she had realized that earlier.

"I wish I had paid more attention to your come-out." He sighed.

"Forget it, Andrew. Sylvia is more important to your future than I am. And I'm old enough to look after my own interests."

If only she had found the backbone to be herself. She might still have failed, but at least the failure would have been based on honesty, she admitted as she headed for her room. For a supposedly intelligent woman, she had been remarkably stupid to believe her mother's claims without checking them. If she had asserted herself more forcefully, she would not now be facing the distasteful task of turning down a gentleman of questionable temper.

Two hours later she was engrossed in a novel—and more relaxed than she had been since arriving in town—when a footman delivered a thick letter. She didn't recognize the dramatic hand, but the signature was Blackthorn's.

*Dear Miss Warren,*

*Forgive me for angering you this morning. I have little experience with well-bred ladies.*

*In contemplating your situation, I realize that I owe you the full truth of my quarrel with Atwater. At one time you planned to turn him down, but I am informed that he has now formally offered for you. You will undoubtedly be under pressure to accept and should not face so important a decision without having all the facts.*

*As you know, his first wife was my cousin. In the beginning, she loved him and sought to please him. From all reports, I believe that he loved her as well. But there is that in his makeup that cannot tolerate opposition to his will. If his orders are not instantly obeyed, he resorts to violence.*

She sighed at this confirmation of her suspicions. Poor Lady Atwater. What had she suffered? Between suffocating possessiveness and violence, her life must have been miserable.

*My evidence derives from three sources—Lydia's maid, whom Atwater tried to force into involuntary emigration to Canada shortly after Lydia's death; the footman you heard him turn off*

*during his rout, who also served at his estate; and Ned Parker,*
*the son of one of his tenants. He is the soldier who accosted*
*you at the theater that night.*

*At first, Atwater merely fell into a rage when he was dis-*
*pleased. Lydia never knew what would anger him. That un-*
*certainty made her avoid his company and cringe when in his*
*presence, but that too made him angry. Soon the tirades esca-*
*lated into slapping, the slapping to hitting, until that last day*
*when he beat, kicked, and slashed her. Her maid described*
*her injuries, and frankly they made me sick.*

*The final argument arose because Lydia wanted to visit her*
*family. Her pregnancy had been difficult from the beginning,*
*and his growing violence terrified her. She hoped that the*
*safety of her father's home and the care of her old nurse*
*would protect the child from harm. Her maid encouraged her,*
*finally convincing her to leave without his permission. Poor*
*Smith now believes herself guilty of Lydia's death, but she is*
*not at fault. Once Lydia placed herself in Atwater's power, no*
*one could have saved her.*

*Ned Parker witnessed Atwater's last beating. He had just*
*arrived home from the Peninsula to discover that Atwater had*
*debauched and beaten his youngest sister. He was heading for*
*the house to confront him when the earl caught up with Lydia*
*near the estate gates. Appalled at his savagery, Ned attacked*
*Atwater, turning the earl's wrath on himself. Atwater smashed*
*his leg, beat him insensible, then dumped the body along a*
*little-used lane where exposure to the winter elements was*
*certain to kill him. But a shepherd found him and nursed him*
*back to health. As soon as he could walk, he followed Atwater*
*to town, bent on revenge. It was he who started the rumors.*

*Think well before you follow in Lydia's footsteps. You may*
*hate me for this warning, but at least my conscience is now*
*clear.*

*Blackthorn*

She quietly folded the letter and laid it on her escritoire. Poor
Lydia. Poor Ned Parker. And his sister. How many others had Atwater brutalized? And how could society remain so blind? Could
no one else see beyond that angelic exterior to the black rot
within?

Sighing, she returned to her book. If he was this prone to violence, she must couch her refusal very carefully.

"My dearest Angela," Atwater began the next morning. "I trust you know why I am here. You are the most perfect lady ever created, a light that must defeat every shadow. My heart has been in your keeping since first we met, my love. I want nothing more than to find you always at my side . . ."

She listened silently as Atwater's absurdities filled the drawing room. The words were too flowery for belief, and she could now see beyond them to his need to possess her, body and soul. That intensity was what had made her nervous.

". . . I know you well, my love, for though you find it difficult to speak openly of that which lies in your heart, your dear mother has often described her loving daughter. Marry me, my love, and I will dedicate my life to making you happy."

"Forgive me, my lord," she said gently. "I cannot accept your kind offer, for we should never suit. I am not the biddable miss you think me. My apologies if my mother led you astray, but though she has long championed your courtship, I have never been warm to it."

Atwater looked as if someone had just shot him. "Are you daft? Where else can you acquire the social cachet held by Lady Atwater? Where else will you attach such wealth to your name?"

"I care for neither," she said coldly. "As you would know had you made any attempt to converse with me. I prefer to judge people on their character. It is for that reason that we should not suit, for you desire a meek wife and I would demand recognition as an equal."

"An equal? A more stupid chit I have never seen. Turning down the Earl of Atwater!"

"What arrogance!" She forgot to school her tongue. "Go flummox someone else, my lord You need an awe-struck seventeen-year-old with more hair than wit."

"You actually believe the lies, don't you?" He slapped her face hard enough to raise a red welt on her cheek.

"With justification, it would seem," she snapped, rising to ring for Paynes. "You will leave this house, sir. After such an insult, you will not be welcomed here again."

"You have not heard the last of this," he rasped, nostrils flaring. His eyes narrowed until his brows formed a continuous slash across his face. "Think you to cast off the Earl of Atwater? Garwood was right. You are little better than a harlot with your teasing ways. You will rue this decision for the rest of your life." Turning on his heel, he stalked from the room.

"Angela!" Lady Forley slammed the drawing room door hard enough to rattle the paintings on the wall. "Why is Lord Atwater so angry?"

"I informed him that we should not suit," she stated calmly, though her hands were trembling with reaction.

"How dare you?" screamed her mother, slapping her other cheek even harder. "How dare you turn down the most eligible earl in town? You ungrateful chit. What am I to do now? You will be forever a spinster, beholden to your miserly brother, who is even stricter with me than with you. How can you be so cruel? I cannot stand being buried in the country! I will die if I cannot live in town!"

*"Enough!"* Angela sidestepped another assault, appalled at her mother's selfishness. "You care nothing for me. Your every action had just one purpose, didn't it—to create a cozy home for yourself where you could foist your outrageous extravagances on someone else's purse. Well, forget it. You have harmed me more than your empty head could possibly understand, first by driving off the man I had chosen, then by encouraging one whose pretty face hides a fiend the likes of which you have never imagined. God only knows what he will do to repay this insult."

"But why did you insult him? Surely you can return him to your side. Simply apologize for your unthinking words."

"I will never wed the man," she swore, staring at Lady Forley until the woman blanched. "And you can forget your odious plots. Never will I countenance you hanging on my sleeve. If I do marry, I guarantee that you will be welcome only for occasional brief country visits, and never in London. Nor will I allow a husband to expend so much as a shilling on your behalf."

"Oh, that I would live to see my daughter treat me so foully!" she cried, grasping her vinaigrette.

"You can blame no one but yourself, madam."

"Hartshorn!"

"Ring for your maid." Too angry to care, she stumbled from the room, running into Andrew and bursting into tears.

"What happened?" he demanded. "How did your face get so bruised?" He pulled her into the study and forced brandy down her throat until her hysteria subsided.

She poured out the tale.

"I'll kill him."

"No, Andrew. Leave him alone. It was Mother's fault more than anything. She convinced him that I would welcome his suit—just as she convinced you. Any confrontation can only worsen the rumors that some still believe. He already has too much reason to hate us."

"Something has to be done about Mother." He sighed.

"Yes. You cannot have her poisoning Sylvia with her spite. It was hard enough living with it before. Now it will be worse."

"The dower house won't satisfy her, and I hate to think of the slander she will pour onto the tenants and villagers."

"To say nothing of the neighbors."

"I can't expose Sylvia to her filth. And God knows what she'll do to you while we are on our wedding journey."

But try as they might, they could think of no way to deal with her.

Angela retired to her room. She managed to put the events of the morning out of her mind, but only by concentrating on Blackthorn. He had been right about the dangers Atwater posed. And his desire to avenge his cousin's death was noble—though she did not agree with his methods. But it increased her questions about his other deeds. Was there a noble purpose underlying all the stories?

She reviewed the tales. Jilting his fiancée? Even if the action were justified, choosing so public an arena was not. Too many witnesses recalled that night, making it impossible to believe that memories of the scene were exaggerated. But the Graceford story was different. At least half of it had already been debunked—by Garwood, of all people. Perhaps the rest was fiction as well. Eloping with Lady Cloverdale? He had never denied the charges, not even during the crim-con trial. But the deaths of Cloverdale and Coldstream were more nebulous. No hints of his responsibility had arisen at the time. He had been genuinely surprised when she had mentioned them. Did that mean he was innocent, or was he merely shocked that others knew of his involvement? And what nefarious service had he been purchasing from those soldiers? Were they the same three who had known Mickey? Perhaps providing for the lad was part of their price.

He had become angry the last time she'd asked for details, but she would keep trying. She needed to know. He needed to talk. It was something she instinctively understood, though he would deny it. But this was one time she could not question her impressions.

# Chapter Eleven

Angela felt better after a nap than at any time since coming to town. Turning down Atwater had set her mind at peace. She would not find a husband this Season, but accepting that fact set her free. The words echoed Blackthorn's, and she began to understand him a little better.

The rules expounded by the polite world were confining. No longer having to adhere to every expectation was like removing a particularly tight corset. She could breathe again. The occasional ball might be fun, but she need not wear herself out with a social schedule she neither wanted nor enjoyed. And now she could attend other events—musicales, literary soirees, lectures, even one of the concerts presented by the newly founded Philharmonic Society of London.

In retrospect, the failure of her Season was at least half her own fault. Six years of Lady Forley's praise for London society coupled with criticism of her daughter's training, her activities, and her interests had stripped away her confidence. Instead of using the brain she was so proud of, she had meekly crawled into the mold her mother demanded. But conforming to that image had added a fear of revealing her true self that placed the last straw on her mountain of pressures.

What an ass she had been. Her bluestocking education would not have harmed her chances on the Marriage Mart. It would have deterred Atwater and his ilk, of course, but where was the harm in that? Cassie had been out for five years before wedding Hart, but her overt intelligence and independence had nothing to do with such longevity. She had waited for love, turning down several offers each Season. Sylvia had numerous friends among the intelligentsia, some of them high-ranking members of society.

Disgusted with herself, she ran down the list of respected gentlemen who had knowingly chosen bluestocking wives—Hartleigh and Andrew, of course, Hartford, Bridgeport, Carrington, and several others. None of them flaunted their learning in society ballrooms, but neither did they hide it. Only in the rigid drawing rooms favored by Lady Forley was education derided.

She should have studied others instead of blindly accepting Lady Forley's claims. Knowing that she was not as out of place as she felt would have reduced the pressure, allowing her to converse with the ladies and relax with the gentlemen. Instinct, pleasure, and her own interests would not have lost the battle to fear, nerves, and stress. She might even have detected her mother's secret goals in time to thwart them.

She deserved whatever censure society would confer for jilting Atwater, for by projecting a false image, she had perpetrated a fraud upon the *ton*. Blackthorn's initial charge that she was acting a role to attract Atwater's attention was true, though hardly deliberate. She should have understood that hiding her most basic character was dishonest and could never lead to a compatible marriage. But she had trusted her mother's experience. After all, the woman had spent much of her life in London society. Who would expect a parent to so callously use her own child?

Sylvia was delighted when Angela decided to accompany her and Andrew to a literary soiree. Lady Forley stayed home, to no one's regret.

The evening passed quickly. Those attending included the authoress Mrs. Baillie, two playwrights, and several aspiring poets. Conversation was animated and intelligent, in sharp contrast to the shallow posturing that was the mainstay of Marriage Mart events. Humorous discussion continued in the carriage, ceasing only when an angry Lady Forley confronted them in the hall.

"I hope you are satisfied," she stormed at Angela.

Paynes's demeanor slipped at this unconscionable lack of breeding, shock clearly showing in his eyes.

"What now, Mother?" She wanted only to sleep.

Lady Forley threw two missives in her face. "I warned you

what would happen if you turned down the most eligible lord in the *ton*, but would you listen? And now you reap the rewards. You are ruined. You will never be able to show your face in town again. Oh, that I would be plagued by so unnatural a daughter!" Sobs punctuated the words.

"You are absurd," snapped Andrew. "Refusing someone's hand is not cause for censure."

"Then how do you explain that?"

Angela silently handed the notes to her brother. They came from two of the starchier matrons, repealing her invitations to upcoming balls.

"This makes no sense." Andrew shook his head. "Even Garwood's lies did not lead to anything like this. Have you been spreading more of your spite, Mother?"

"How can you accuse me of such infamy?" she wailed, ignoring the source of Garwood's stories. "Your father must be turning in his grave to witness his son's perfidy."

Angela shuddered. It was as she had feared. Atwater did not like being crossed. *You will rue this decision . . .* "I'll bet Atwater revived Garwood's tales," she said in resignation.

Andrew's eyes widened.

"Nonsense," scoffed Lady Forley. "Atwater is a gentleman."

"No, he is not. He not only killed his first wife, he brutally assaulted a tenant who tried to rescue her from that final beating, then forced her maid out of the country to silence her tongue. In this very room, he slapped me and vowed to punish me for daring to refuse him. And within hours we find that I am to be ostracized. There can be no other interpretation. The only question is whether he will be content with reviving the old stories or will invent new ones."

"How can anyone be so cruel?" sobbed Sylvia.

"I mean to get to the bottom of this," vowed Andrew. "You girls go up to bed while I visit my club."

"Yes, go to bed," urged Lady Forley. "And consider your mistakes. Atwater cannot be responsible. People are right to bar you from their homes after you callously disregarded his feelings by jilting him. If you are lucky, he will give you another chance. Take it."

"I would not marry him if he were the last man on earth,"

swore Angela angrily. "The one who misled him was you, Mother. If you had not forced me to assume a false facade, I would not have attracted his interest. If you had not encouraged his attentions despite knowing that I distrusted him, he would never have pressed his suit. If your despicable lies had not prompted Garwood's campaign, he would not have thought of his revenge. And the lie you told him to explain Garwood's misinformation outlined the tactic he is now turning on me. *If he cannot have her, he will make sure no one else does,*" she quoted bitterly. "Your meddling has ruined any chance I had of finding a husband this Season, and I hold you fully responsible for every cut I will receive in the future."

She headed for her room, a sobbing Sylvia close behind. This would not be a night for sleeping comfortably.

"It is worse than I feared," said Andrew at breakfast the next morning.

"How bad?" Angela pushed bits of ham around her plate, unable to eat. Nightmares had haunted her sleep, far worse than those precipitated by Garwood's betrayal.

"Atwater did not just revive the rumors. He added new ones, and they are not pretty."

"Get it out," she urged him as he pretended to drink his coffee. "I have to know."

"He never offered for you, but abandoned his courtship when he surprised you in the arms of your footman. This occurred two days after he found you in a disheveled condition in the mews, your groom looking flustered at his arrival. You have admitted that you are not an innocent and have lied about your dowry. He also hints that you may be with child."

Bile rose in Angela's throat. "Dear God. The man is evil beyond belief. Those are the same charges he leveled at his wife when excusing the beating that killed her."

"Yes. He is evil. But he is also cunning. His righteous indignation at being so deluded is a sight to behold. Fortunately, Ashton was at hand to restrain me, or I would have called him out. We had not yet entered the gaming room where Atwater held court, and I doubt anyone else knew I was there. But you were right, Angie. He is no gentleman. I am sorry to have placed you in such a position."

"You had nothing to do with that. And Mother is not wholly to blame, either. If I had been stronger, she could not have manipulated me. Instinct warned me that hiding my character would lead to trouble. But I was too unsure of myself to fight her."

"I blame myself for that. I should have known that her constant criticisms would destroy your confidence."

"Enough. We have all contributed to this debacle. But Atwater is most at fault. His wife haunted my dreams last night. He did horrible things to her, Andrew. It turns my stomach to think of it."

"How do you know? In fact, how do you know anything about Atwater? Half of your claims weren't even part of those absurd rumors last month."

*Idiot!* She had not guarded her tongue. Again. But if she was to take charge of her life, she could no longer be guided by her mother's prohibitions. "From Lord Blackthorn."

"My God, Angie! The man is a pariah, London's premier scoundrel. Do you have any idea how disreputable the fellow is? I was there the night he discarded his betrothed, mocking both her and all civilized behavior. I will never forget the ignominy of it."

"I'm sure it was awful," she agreed. "Though I suspect Father's death the next morning contributed to your impressions. Yes, the man is a scoundrel, but he is not evil. I find him an incomprehensible mixture of angel and devil. By his own admission, truth underlies most rumors, but that truth is less black than society believes."

"You sound as though you like him." He shuddered.

"Surprisingly, I do. He is the closest friend I have in London, though he is arrogant and can be odiously rude. But he is also kind and generous. He helped me rescue an orphan who was in ill health. And it was he who directed Major Caldwell to champion my cause when Garwood's rumors began. They are close friends."

Andrew's brows raised. Major Caldwell was an honorable and very knowing gentleman. "How did you meet him?"

"At Hatchard's. Quite by accident, you understand." And she related all her contacts with the Black Marquess.

"I can see why you believe him honorable," he said when she had finished. "He could have ruined you long ago."

"A better form of ruin. Unlike my suitors', his tales would at least have been true."

"What do you know of his quarrel with Atwater?"

She repeated what Blackthorn's letter had said.

"Dear Lord," Andrew's face was ashen. "That surpasses the worst tales of Blackthorn's deeds."

"It does. I had decided to turn Atwater down long before I learned the details, but knowing Lady Atwater's fate made facing his anger easier. I doubt we can counter his revenge. I may as well return to Forley Court."

"No." Andrew paced restlessly around the table. "You are innocent. I will not allow one arrogant, brutal nobleman to bar you from society. If you run now, you will never be able to return. And leaving would add credence to the tale that you are increasing."

"I have already concluded that I have no future in this town," she said sadly. "I have little in common with the ladies and do not meet the expectations of the gentlemen. There is nothing to do but resign myself to life in the country. And three weeks will hardly dispel the myth of my supposed condition." They had to return to Forley Court then.

"But what will you do?" he demanded. "Much as I love you, I have to agree that you cannot stay permanently at the Court. And you cannot set up an establishment of your own without destroying the last vestige of your reputation. You will go mad in the dower house with Mother. I cannot see you in the guise of a poor relation, and we have few relatives in a position to take you in anyway. Your only chance of a meaningful future is to fight these stories, prove that you are innocent, and expose Atwater as the fiend that he is."

"Easy to say, but how am I to do that?" She went to the window, staring sightlessly at the minuscule garden behind the house. "My reputation was already besmirched by Garwood, so anything I say is suspect. Only Atwater's continued attentions rescued me the last time. Now that he has turned against me, I have no hope. One word of support from Blackthorn will ruin me beyond repair. Major Caldwell will be gone within the month. Ashton has much credit, but he can hardly buck the entire *ton*, and there is no guarantee that he will continue to believe me. I begin to think there is some flaw in my character beyond allowing Mother's manipulation. Why have I attracted only suitors who spitefully use me when their will is crossed? Are all gentlemen like that?" She angrily wiped away her tears. She had already cried too much over this debacle.

"You are not to blame," he said soothingly, handing her a handkerchief. Leading her back to the table, he poured fresh tea to replace the cold mess in her cup. "All men are not like that. You need think no further than Hart. Devil take it, I wish he were here."

"In all fairness, we must tell him what has happened. We cannot allow Sylvia to be hurt through association with me. I wish her sister, Lady Trotter, would arrive so she can move out. She will be better off anywhere but here."

"Damn!" He made another circuit of the room. "If only I had not been so involved with Sylvia. I might have kept a tighter rein on Mother."

"It is too late for regrets. Ashton was at White's last night. Does he still believe I am innocent?"

"Yes. He saw you often enough last summer to know that you would never behave as Atwater claims. He is also very high in the instep, giving his words more weight than Sir Alan's, who was also scoffing at the stories."

"Will he dare speak with me in public?"

"I believe so. His own position is so solid that he runs no risk."

"Good, for I would hate to see Lady Ashton suffer. She is a decent girl."

"What are you planning?"

She pondered her options for some minutes before answering. "I cannot run, for you are right about the effect that would have on my future. If, by some miracle, I ever wed, I must be able to bring out my daughters. Which means I have to fight for my honor. But it won't be easy. If I appear at Almack's, the patronesses will revoke my voucher in a trice. I can only hope they will make no hasty decisions if I don't push them. I will attend those events for which I have invitations, and comport myself as befits a lady. With luck I won't break down. There is too little time to truly change opinion, but perhaps I can raise a few doubts."

"I don't see any other choice," he agreed on a long sigh. "At least we will soon learn who our real friends are."

It was even worse than she'd expected. After only an hour at the Bradbury ball, Angela feared she would never survive the evening. Tears burned the backs of her eyes, but she kept a smile fixed on her face, ignoring the cuts. No one spoke to her. Lady Hervey and Grace Styles stalked to the farthest point of the room when she arrived. Miss Gumply, a chronic complainer who had not taken well, surprisingly found herself the center of an attentive audience when she fervently criticized Angela's temerity for exposing them to such immorality. Three starchy dowagers loudly condemned her. Lord Heatherton, who had a reputation as a cutting mimic, drew round after round of laughter as he parodied her supposed transgressions, employing the girlish tones of a pea-brained widgeon loudly proclaiming innocence even as she is discovered *en flagrante*.

She danced a set with Andrew and one with Ashton, then refused several libertines and a couple of lecherous old men who were looking for an illicit relationship.

Atwater put on a show of horrified outrage to find her there, tempered only by his duty to control himself in deference to his hostess. But his tongue was busy. New details were already making the rounds. She was little better than a harlot, leading a steady parade of gentlemen to her bed. In fact, she was now being compared to Lady Darnley, London's most notorious matron, who made no effort to hide her liaisons despite having been widowed only three weeks before. The woman was rapidly becoming a courtesan.

The next night was worse. Her mother refused to accompany her. Her hostess refused to speak to her in the receiving line. Society's tongues tripped over themselves in their eagerness to condemn her, though many voices sounded almost envious of her supposed daring.

What had she done to deserve such a fate? she cried into her pillow that night. Her name had been sullied by the very people who professed to love her—her mother, the man she had chosen to wed, and the man who claimed to adore her.

She was galloping through Hyde Park's early morning fog when Blackthorn joined her.

"You are out early today," he said.

"I couldn't sleep—which should surprise no one."

"You have my deepest sympathies." He sighed. "I had no idea Atwater would turn on you like this. Perhaps it would have been better had I not warned you off."

"You did nothing, my lord. You know I was determined to reject him. Your disclosures merely made it easier to withstand his anger and my mother's hysterics."

"I always knew you were intelligent. Any idea why she pushed so hard?"

She nodded. "It came out after I refused him. She planned to use his purse to support her permanent return to town, which explains why she refused to listen to me and kept him close at hand. He was impervious to my coolness, deciding that it denoted shyness. I should have just told him straight out that I would never consider his suit. Marriage must be a partnership if it is to succeed, and he is not a person to ever consider his wife as an equal."

"You have unusually clear sight."

"For a female," she finished for him.

"I did not say that. Nor did I mean it," he protested. "I might have tempered it with *for one of your experience*. It is difficult to read hidden character when one's life has been spent in the country."

"That is society's arrogance talking. Having cast aside my mother's blinders, I've discovered that human nature varies little from class to class. I have spent much time working with the people who live near our estate."

"What led you to turn him down, if I might be so bold? Surely it was not solely because of how he discharged that footman."

"His possessiveness, for one. It implied a poor opinion of my character, for he trusted me with no one else, even on a dance floor. And his eyes flashed in anger whenever someone contradicted him or argued his ideas. His treatment of Ned Parker at the theater was insupportable, of course. Then there were the rumors. Even before stories of Lady Atwater's death surfaced, I had heard of an incident in which he nearly came to blows with another gentleman in Lady Debenham's drawing room. It hinted at an ungovernable temper."

He nodded. "His character is there for all to see. But you are one of the few to actually do so. Too bad he is bent on revenge."

"It has been difficult," she agreed in vast understatement. "Andrew convinced me to stay in town and face the charges, but I have been wondering if my situation is too hopeless to warrant the pain. It must hurt both him and Lady Sylvia to associate with me."

"You must face society. You cannot allow this cloud to continue, for it is entirely false."

She nodded. "And not even original. The initial charges were a variation of those he leveled at you and his wife, which themselves were a twisted version of your reasons for ending your betrothal. Now he has lifted Lady Darnley's reputation and applied it to me. Surely someone will eventually notice his sources."

"They will, but since they are true in Lady Darnley's case, people can easily accept them." His brows had risen at the reference to his own past, but he said nothing. "The gossips are out of control for the moment, but if you persist, they will eventually begin to question the facts. I will do what I can to hasten that end."

"Thank you, but I can't think there is much to be done."

"We shall see. What will you do when this is over?"

She shrugged. "Not much. It will be years before we can return to town. Sylvia will take over the Court, so I'll practice biting my tongue and being invisible. Setting up my own establishment is out of the question—especially now." She pulled her horse to a halt, appalled at the self-pity that had entered her voice. "Forgive me. Fatigue has gotten the best of me. Normally I would never burden another with my problems."

"There is nothing to forgive. What of your mother?"

"She will move to the dower house, whether she will or no," she declared firmly. "But I will not go with her. I cannot live with her complaints and abuse."

He shook his head. "Try to keep up your spirits. The truth will emerge eventually. And when it does, Atwater's reputation will be in shreds."

"A comforting thought. I will try to believe it."

Blackthorn watched her leave. She couldn't hide her bitterness, though she had every right to it. His heart bled for her, but he thrust pity aside. Exiting the park, he headed for Jack's rooms.

The major had been out of town for several days and had not yet heard the news. They spent the morning compiling a list of friends and army officers who might counter the rumors. Then Jack headed for Clifford Street to assure Angela of his support.

Lady Forley stormed into the house, nearly in hysterics.

"You have ruined us!" she wailed at Angela. "Even the tradesmen smirk at me. One even refused me service. I will never be able to hold my head up in London again. And it is all your fault. I will die!"

"Do you begin to understand why I could not accept him?" she asked, trying one last time to reach her mother. "He is evil and would have made my life miserable."

"Fustian!" swore Lady Forley. "A man's character means nothing, for a knowing woman can always bend him to her will. You would have had rank and wealth. What more could you want?"

Shaking her head, Angela left her mother to her megrims.

Another evening of cuts made her question whether fighting for her reputation was worth it. And the blow she received on awakening did nothing to help. A note accompanied her chocolate.

> *Angela,*
>    *I cannot accept the life of an outcast that you have deliberately and maliciously forced upon this family. Your father would have been appalled, but as he is no longer here to whip you to your senses, I must plan my own future.*
>    *Henry has asked for my hand. We are leaving at once for Italy. I do not expect to see or hear from you again, as I am determined to cut all contacts that could lower my consequences. As Henry's wife, I will retain my credit and once*

*again be able to hold my head up in town. It is time he takes*
*his seat in Parliament.*

*now Lady Styles*

It was too much. She burst into tears, but anger was even stronger than the pain of yet another betrayal. How dared the woman leave at such a time? It could only make her own position worse.

Throwing on a gown, she joined Andrew at the breakfast table.

"I see you've heard," he commented dryly, motioning to his own missive.

"She decided to leave lest she be tarred with my misdeeds. It seems I have deliberately heaped dishonor and disgrace on her head, maliciously preventing her from enjoying the society she should be running," said Angela. "I am informed that she is severing all contact with a family that can only be considered a millstone around her neck."

Anger suffused his face. "Of all the gall . . ."

But her own anger died as the ramifications of her mother's elopement became clear. "She has made her bed. Let her lie in it. I hope she enjoys Italy, for it is all the society she will ever know."

Interest lit Andrew's eyes. "What tale is this?"

"I have often been forced into Lord Styles's company, for he hovered around Mother almost as much as Atwater did. One of our more agreeable conversations—which did not include her—compared the merits of country versus city living. He despises towns, forcing himself away from his beloved hunting grounds only to bring out one of his daughters—usually in York. Grace is the last. Her marriage now forces him to look for someone to run his house and care for his tenants so he can continue the sporting life unencumbered. Why did it never occur to her that she has not seen him in thirty years even though she spent every Season in town before Father's death?"

"Good God! He lives in Northumberland!" Andrew's eyes widened as he burst into laughter.

"Yes, and his estate is even more isolated than Forley Court."

"Nor is he weak-willed like Papa was, much though I loved him."

"As did I. But Lord Styles will never bow to the wiles of a mere woman. He is firmly set in his ways and cares for nothing beyond his own interests. He is also a confirmed miser." She joined in his mirth, though reality soon intruded. "There are problems that we must immediately address. Her defection will trigger new rumors."

"We can handle that."

"Sylvia cannot remain here without a chaperon. Even were I pristine, it would not do. The last thing I want is to tarnish her reputation."

He paled. "Dear Lord. Does that mean we must run for home after all?"

"When is Lady Trotter due?"

"Yesterday, unless her doctor forbade travel. I'd better call at Trotter House and find out if she has arrived."

"If so, Sylvia can join her immediately. If not, then she must return home to the Grange. We can still remain in town."

Barbara, Lady Trotter, was appalled at Andrew's story.

"Nonsense," she scoffed when he announced that Sylvia would join her that afternoon. "Your sister is innocent. I will move to Clifford Street immediately."

"What about Lord Trotter?"

"He will not arrive for at least a fortnight as James is suffering another bout of fever," she explained, mentioning her oldest son. Had she not promised to assist Sylvia, she would have stayed at home herself, for she was barely six weeks out of childbed.

She ordered her trunks sent to Lord Forley's residence and accompanied him home.

"You may have performed the good deed of the century," said Sylvia that night, laughing.

"What?" Angela met her eyes in the mirror—Sylvia's maid was still readying her for bed. They had attended different events that evening.

"Miss Gumply. You know what a harridan she has become."

"Don't we all!" Miss Gumply's acidic criticisms had driven away scores of potential suitors. For all she was an antidote, her extravagant dowry should at least have attracted the fortune hunters, but few could abide her tongue. The more her popularity waned, the more she found to criticize. "She has been on a downward spiral for weeks."

"Not any more. Given the current fashion, her willingness to pillory you has attracted an admiring audience, begging your pardon."

"I am immune to reminders."

"And you've doubtless noticed Lord Heatherton's impersonations."

"Were I not personally involved, I could laugh myself silly at some of them. Who can blame people for being so entertained?"

"Well, he has recently noticed Miss Gumply's antics. All the approval has encouraged her to inject humor into her tales, making them an admirable complement to his pantomimes. They have begun working together."

"My God!"

"They may well make a match of it. They slipped into the garden for quite half a set tonight. You know, she's not really an antidote when she smiles."

She laughed. "Will wonders never cease?"

"There is another story making the rounds," Sylvia continued. "It seems Garwood has need of a new secretary."

"Was he abandoned for an employer of higher consequence?"

"No, the fellow apparently made a fortune and can now pursue life as a gentleman. His own breeding is good."

Angela remained silent. So Garwood had unjustly accused Lord Renford as well. It was his own secretary who had absconded with his papers.

But that was of no consequence. The rumors were even worse now that Lady Forley had eloped. No one believed that a mother would abandon an innocent daughter.

# Chapter Twelve

"We need more support if we are to rescue your reputation," said Barbara at breakfast. A round of calls the previous afternoon had demonstrated the extent of the problem. Society was in a feeding frenzy, with Angela as the main course. "Who believes you so far?"

"Lord Ashton," said Andrew.

"And Lady Ashton," put in Sylvia.

"Major Caldwell has recruited several of his friends," reported Angela.

"I had not heard that he was in town," Barbara said in delight. "He is a strong champion."

"For the moment. He will return to Spain any day now. And some people interpret my sudden attraction to so many officers as proof of immorality."

Everyone sighed.

"Hart is writing letters," said Sylvia. "And Lord Shelford has taken Hart's support to heart."

"If Hart came to town, it would be even better."

"He can't leave Cassie alone," said Andrew.

"If he didn't hover, she would feel better," declared Barbara firmly.

"Only his insistence is keeping her from a full schedule in town," Angela reminded her.

Barbara frowned, but accepted it. "I can't ask him to lend a hand then. My own friends will help, of course. And Trotter's. We must go on the attack and make people question these stories. Most are too ridiculous to be credible."

"Credibility is not the issue. It is fashionable to vilify me," said Angela gloomily.

"Then we must make if fashionable to vilify Atwater. His estate is only a few miles from ours. Unsavory rumors have abounded for years. I cannot understand why they never reach town."

"Atwater has the most powerful gossips in his pocket, and they will never admit that they misjudged him."

The truth of that was revealed again and again over the following days. Even Barbara's friends taunted her for believing Angela, most attributing her credulity to her recent childbed. Lady Debenham was one of those.

"Do not let the sensibility arising from your confinement lead you into exaggeration," she chided her. "Lord Atwater is the most gentle and caring man of my acquaintance. I can understand his horror. He loved that girl with all his heart. Discovering that she is a grasping harpy with the morals of an alley cat was crushing."

"I am not exaggerating," swore Lady Trotter. "His stories are blatant lies uttered in retaliation because she refused his suit. I know her well, for we grew up on neighboring estates. And I know Atwater, for his land runs with my husband's. This campaign is typical of his behavior at home. A groundskeeper who informed him that tulips do not bloom in August was discharged with no reference, and a neighbor fell victim to this same sort of character assassination when he refused to redirect a stream onto Atwater's estate."

"I'm sure you are misinformed about the cause of both incidents," said Lady Debenham firmly. "And I can understand your loyalty. After all, your sister will soon wed Lord Forley. But you needn't fear that the connection will harm you. Every family has its black sheep. As soon as she admits that society is closed to her, all will be well."

Major Caldwell was likewise stymied. "I have never seen the tabbies this ferocious," he admitted during supper at that evening's ball.

"Nor I," agreed Ashton. "I was sure that reason would have prevailed by now."

"No one wishes to admit making a mistake," said Angela with a sigh. "Not the mistake of misjudging me," she added as Lady Ashton raised a brow. "I am too little known to matter. But they have long assigned every virtue to Atwater. Accepting that his tales are lies concedes that his charm has blinded them for years. Do you honestly believe that puffed-up dowagers like Lady Beatrice and Lady Horseley can admit to poor judgment? They may believe the worst of others, but not when it calls their own intelligence into question."

"You sound as though you have given up." Jack sounded troubled.

"In part. Even those who might believe me cannot speak out without jeopardizing their own reputations. You've no idea how much I admire your courage on that score," she added. "I have no intention of quitting the fight, but my hope of success is fading fast."

"Things may yet change," said Jack. "A friend is interviewing Atwater's neighbors and should find evidence that society cannot ignore."

"Thank him," Angela murmured, knowing he referred to Blackthorn. But she doubted that anything would help. The efforts of the dozen people fighting for her were merely a drop in the bucket of public opinion. A well-worded question might raise doubts about the details of the latest story, but the central lie was too firmly entrenched.

She sought a moment's reprieve from the cuts and snide remarks three sets later. There was no point visiting the retiring room, for in that isolated place, society's matrons abandoned all manners and attacked without mercy. Her last appearance had earned her two slaps. So she waited until attention shifted to Lord Heatherton, then slipped into the garden for a breath of fresh air.

The night was warm, filled with the perfume of roses. For the first time in days, she managed to empty her mind as she moved away from the terrace. Peace descended. Music drifted from the ballroom, muted by distance. Wandering among the roses relieved some of her stress. But no matter how restful it was, she knew she must return. She was heading back when a hand suddenly grabbed her arm and spun her around.

"Let go of me," she demanded coldly, glaring at a paunchy, middle-aged gentleman.

"I need a little kiss," he slurred, wine strong on his breath. He pulled her closer.

*"No!"* Shoving against his chest, she twisted her face away. "Leave me alone."

"What's the matter?" he demanded. "You've entertained every other gentleman in town. Why not me?" Steely arms imprisoned her. Kicking him made no difference.

"Help!" she screamed. "Will no one help me?" His wet mouth smothered her cries, his teeth cutting cruelly into her lip. Had she really been reduced to this? Blackness threatened even as she clawed ineffectively at her attacker.

Suddenly she was free, falling helplessly to the ground. The landing knifed pain through one hip, snapping her mind out of its fog. The crack of skin on bone exploded into the night. A flurry of blows ended with a dull thud.

"He won't bother you again," murmured Blackthorn, helping her gently to her feet. His breathing was slightly faster than usual, but he was otherwise unscathed.

She pressed her face against his shoulder, fighting back tears. One hand softly stroked her hair while he murmured into her ear. His spicy scent offered comfort, recalling that other time he had soothed her pain. Terror drained away.

"Where did you come from?" she asked, pulling away at last.

"I arrived just as you slipped out the door. That was a foolish thing to do."

"So it would seem, but I could not stand it another minute and needed time to pull myself together. The retiring room is worse than the ballroom, so I came out here to be alone for a moment. I thought no one had seen me."

"Didn't you consider that others might have already been outside?"

"My mistake. Thank you for a timely intervention."

"It was nothing. I wish I could do more, but any direct support would ruin you."

"Yet another reason you should redeem your reputation." She hadn't brought the subject up in days, being too immersed in her own problems.

"And how am I to do that? You've seen how difficult it is to debunk even blatant lies. How does one surmount tales that are at least partially true?"

She started to respond, but he placed a finger over her lips.

"No arguing tonight," he said softly. Waltz music floated from the ballroom. She hadn't realized that he still supported her until he swung her into a gentle dance in the corner of the garden. Everything was proper, even the distance he maintained between them, but the movement wove a spell that affected her as never before. Her heart pounded in time with the music, and light-headedness weakened her knees as magic filled the air.

Devall was stunned. He had not intended to waltz with her. He had not even intended to speak with her. His sole reason for slipping in without an invitation was to pass along information that Jack could disseminate to the gossips. Or so he had thought. He was unwilling to admit how often he sought Angela out just to talk. Even in the earliest days when he had followed her about merely to glare at her for being like every other greedy miss, his underlying motive had been to see her—unadmitted at the time. He rapidly suppressed the image.

They could never be friends. Given his lurid reputation, he had no right to pursue an acquaintance with an innocent lady. And he certainly should not be keeping her here in the dark or leading her into a provocative dance that fed temptation. How long had it been since he had danced with a lady? How long since he had touched even the fingertips of a respectable female?

Without volition, his arms tightened. Stepping further off the path, he caressed her lips with his own. Shock at the contact shot through him—and her. Her mouth opened as she leaned into him, sliding her arms around his neck and pressing against his body.

Sweet. God, she was sweet. Soft; warm; comforting. The kiss deepened, shooting heat and desire along every nerve. Her fingers glided into his hair, sending new shocks tumbling through his mind. Closer. He needed more. He needed . . .

His desperate hands tried to merge two bodies into one, seeking the intimacy that had eluded him all his life. Had he ever known anyone with whom he could share his thoughts? He groaned.

*What are you doing? Do you want to ruin her in truth?* Even as his loins tightened, threatening to explode, he eased away from her, tasting the blood from her cut lip.

*Damn!* Shame washed over him. He was little better than her attacker, forcing himself on her when she was in too much shock to think clearly. How could he risk destroying the only good thing in his life? She could hardly have missed his reaction. He had probably confirmed every rumor she had heard about him.

"Forgive me. That was an impertinence you did not need," he said huskily.

She reached up to stroke his cheek. "There is nothing to forgive." But confusion filled her face.

"You had better return to the house," he urged, leading her to a door around the corner, anxious to escape before he kissed her again. "This is the library. Once you are recovered, you can slip down the hall and enter the ballroom as though you had been in the retiring room."

"Thank you again. For everything."

Her look sent new heat into his loins, but he ignored it. This was hardly the time to consider the evening's events.

"You are a true friend," she added.

"In that case, you may as well call me Devall."

She raised her brows.

"Appropriate, isn't it? My father must have been prescient."

"I doubt it, Devall." She smiled. "I am Angela."

"Very appropriate, which society will soon acknowledge. After all, they haven't ostracized you."

"No." Her smile faded into a frown. "I almost wish they had. If I disappeared, the tale would soon die. But they are not ready to drop so delectable a scandal, so they still invite me. My presence assures a squeeze, for everyone gathers round to display disdain. It is this week's fashion."

"Dear Lord! I've been out of town and had no idea it was that bad. The worst I ever experienced was being a nonentity attached to a title. For years the only invitations I received were from those on society's fringe who wished to bag a marquess for their guest list, but who would have died of apoplexy had I dared speak to their daughters."

"Poor Devall. But I will not have to endure this much longer.

As soon as they grow bored of being shocked, the furor will wane. Then I will be dropped as a social liability."

"Don't despair, Angela," he said, placing a gentle kiss on the palm of her hand. "Truth will win in the end."

He left her in the library and returned to the garden. What the devil had gotten into him? He shuddered at the remembered feel of her in his arms. Never had he known a woman who felt so good—or who inflamed him so easily. She was yet another cross he would have to bear, for he could never pursue her.

Shaking his head, he went in search of Jack.

Devall threaded the traffic in Kensington, but his mind was not on his driving. What else might help Angela? It was infuriating the way society refused to even listen to Atwater's crimes. The man had mesmerized them with his charismatic charm, deafening them to any hint of the truth.

He was headed for the cottage where he housed disabled veterans until they regained their health. Many stayed on until he found them jobs. Some he had established in business; others worked on his estates or in the convalescent hospital he had founded where those with the most crippling injuries lived. A few he staked to a new life in America, though since the stupidity of two governments had resulted in war with the United States, he was restricted to sending them to Canada. He had been seeing off two of his protégés when he'd stumbled across Lydia's maid. Rescuing her from the brute who was forcing her on board had required the combined efforts of all three of them.

So how could he help Angela? She had been right to accuse him of hiding behind his reputation. It gave him the freedom to pursue activities that society disapproved. But it also prevented him from countering people like Atwater.

He sighed.

He really ought to set the record straight, not that he would ever be fully accepted. But only a little effort should clear the air of the most serious charges. Yet this particular moment was bad. Society would hardly accept two black sheep into the fold at once, and restoring Angela's good name was more important. He had already demonstrated his ability to live outside accepted circles. She had not.

Atwater's phaeton was drawn up in front of Devereaux's love nest. Former love nest. Devereaux had recently sold the cottage, but the name of the buyer had remained secret.

Atwater could not have cared much for Angela if he was already setting up a ladybird. Or did he need someone on whom he could vent his frustrations now that he had no wife? It was an uncomfortable thought, and one that demanded action. He would have to delegate someone to keep an eye on the house and report any abuse. It was one more entry to the growing account he must settle with the earl.

If only he had investigated Atwater when the man had first turned his eyes toward Lydia. But he had not. She had been wildly excited about attracting his attention. Her mother approved his title and charm, her father admired his fortune and estates. Assuming all was well, he had left town early in her courtship. But a serious investigation would have revealed Atwater's deficiencies. Lady Trotter wasn't the only neighbor who knew damaging tales.

Atwater must pay for his cruelty, though Devall no longer knew how. His original plan was fatally flawed. The earl would never challenge him, no matter what the provocation. But while he had collected much evidence of abuse, he had nothing that could be taken before the House of Lords. Unfortunately, beating one's wife was not a crime. Nor was mistreating tenants and servants. Actions that would get the lower classes transported—or even hung—were accepted in the aristocracy. It was an inequity he had long decried.

So he must redress the wrong by himself. But not with violence. Angela would never approve, even against a beast like the earl. Perhaps depriving Atwater of something he prized would be sufficient punishment.

He frowned.

What did Atwater love? There was his reputation, of course. The man had always been the darling of the *ton*, for his angelic features and natural charm had the gossips eating out of his hand. There was also his wealth. And his looks.

Debunking the charges against Angela would badly damage his reputation, but that was not enough. The looks could only be destroyed in a fight, but he had just forsworn violence. That left money. But how?

He mulled the question until he reached the house, then pushed it aside. He had found the perfect situation for Ned Parker, a place where his missing arm and weak hip would not hinder him.

Angela's morning visits to the park were the only time of day she could truly relax. Even at home, tension mounted. Everyone was so determinedly optimistic that she wanted to scream. But for this half hour, she was free to be herself.

Devall joined her two days after rescuing her in the garden. That kiss had kept her awake ever since, but she was determined to forget it. The man was an admitted rogue. So though she would never complain of something she had enjoyed, the kiss meant nothing to him beyond a moment's pleasure. Yet she blushed as he greeted her. And she was very surprised to see him. Sylvia was riding with her.

"You seem to be holding up well," he said once the introductions were complete.

"I must be a better actress than I thought." She sighed. "I expected to fall apart by now, but we will be gone in another two weeks. I suppose I can survive that long."

"Running away?"

"Never. Sylvia and Andrew will wed a fortnight later. I must be there to make the final arrangements and welcome the guests."

"So we have only two weeks to expose Atwater." He frowned.

"I doubt it can be done. My only hope is to plant enough seeds of doubt that people will eventually realize the truth. Then I can someday return to town."

"You are resigned to becoming a social outcast, Miss Warren?" His voice was cold, his address formal in deference to Sylvia's presence, though the girl had dropped back to ride with the groom. "It has its advantages."

"For you, perhaps," she snapped, her spirits revived by his change of tone. Sparring with him was always exhilarating. "A man can use a wretched reputation as an invitation to flout convention. A lady can never do so. Without respectability, I am treated like a courtesan, as you well know. Reputation is a lady's only protection. We have not the physical strength to ward off assaults. We have not the financial security to live on our own. Perhaps if I commanded the wealth of Lady Hester Stanhope, I could attract enough respect to overcome my perceived foibles, though even she chose to leave the country rather than endure society's censure. If only I could follow her example. There must be some place in the world where people would accept me for myself."

"You cannot believe that I flout convention."

"You claim to be conventional?" She stared, shocked. "You elope with another man's wife and abandon her overseas. You fleece a man of his fortune without regret."

"You, of all people, should know that rumor often lies."

"So why not tell me the truth? I've asked for it often enough. You know I prefer to judge facts."

"And you know that I prefer to live in the shadows." But he lowered his voice, moving his horse nearer hers. "I did not elope with Constance, though I did escort her out of the country." Glancing back at Sylvia, he inched even closer. "We are of an age and grew up on neighboring estates. I remember her from childhood escapades as a vivacious hoyden who was invariably kind. She treated everyone from marquess's heir to tenant's son exactly alike. Not that she had much choice, for there were few children our age in the area. Anyone who shunned the lower classes had no playmates."

She nodded. Her own childhood had been similar.

"Once I left for school, I saw less of her. She staged her come-out shortly after I started at Oxford, married Cloverdale two months later, and settled on his estate. The affair held no interest for a student." He shrugged. "I had not seen her in several years when she sent an urgent message begging me to meet her in Green Park. I was appalled at her appearance."

"What?" The word escaped without thought.

His face twisted at the memory, his voice dropping to a whisper. "She had been badly beaten. Both eyes were swollen nearly shut, her nose was broken, and bruises covered her arms."

"Dear Lord!" The choking exclamation came from Sylvia. Even his softest voice carried on the quiet morning air.

"My feelings exactly," he agreed, abandoning secrecy by resuming his normal tone. "She didn't need to explain that the beating was far from her first. Older, fading bruises were still visible. She begged my help, claiming that she had been under assault for seven years, starting immediately after her marriage. But the attacks were growing harsher. After several miscarriages, Cloverdale believed that she would never produce an heir. Fearing for her life, she wished to leave him."

"Could no one stop him?"

He shook his head. "A wife is chattel under English law, subject to whatever treatment her husband metes out. It is one of the inequities that must change, but for now there is no legal redress against men like him."

Sylvia paled at his words.

"Forgive my plain speaking, Lady Sylvia," he begged. "And do not fear for your own future. Lord Forley is nothing like the brute we are discussing."

"I know."

Angela nodded. "What did you do?"

"A distant branch of her family lives in Ireland. I escorted her there, and they agreed to take her in. She had no intention of remarrying—and who can blame her—so the fact that she was legally bound bothered none of them. All she wanted was to build a new life where she could be safe. She changed her name and now lives in a remote cottage. I wrote to her after the divorce to let her know she was free in case she ever changes her mind."

"So you let your own name be dragged through the mud to protect her." This was the inner Devall she had glimpsed before; the caring man she had long suspected he was. And he was right. Truth underlay the lurid tale, but oh, how badly it had been twisted.

He shrugged. "My reputation was already so black, it made no difference. I could only have countered his claims by producing Constance, but that was out of the question."

She did not ask about Cloverdale's death. Sylvia was too young for a tale that might not be so clearly altruistic. "What about Lord Graceford? I do not believe you cheated, but was it necessary to strip him of everything?"

"Yes." His eyes dared her to contradict him. "He was another whom the law couldn't touch. He supported himself by fleecing green youths. Though many suspected him of cheating, no one had ever caught him at it."

"Couldn't you have exposed him? Society would have taken care of the rest."

"Exposing a cheat is difficult. Even a hint of your suspicions is grounds for a duel, with the winner considered truthful. He fought one such match early in his career, proving to be such an accurate shot that few dared challenge him. And he had always been a very good card player."

"So was he a cheat?" she asked, catching an odd look in his eyes.

He grinned. "He was indeed. It took me weeks to figure out how he marked his cards. It was very subtle—he must have had eyes like a hawk to see the marks in the dim light found in most gaming rooms."

"Yet you didn't expose him."

"Society would have been satisfied to run him out of town. But that would have been cold comfort to his victims. Many were starving. Two killed themselves when intoxication waned and reality intruded. They had been the sole support of families who were subsequently turned out of homes lost at the gaming tables."

"Dear God!"

"Exactly. Having satisfied myself that he was cheating—and probably had done so for years—I arranged a game and surreptitiously replaced his deck with an identical one of unmarked cards. He immediately recognized the exchange, of course, but he could scarcely remark upon it without admitting his sins. He was under no constraint to continue playing past the single game we had agreed upon, but he had faith in his abilities. Believing himself to be a master at piquet, he failed to consider that he had relied on marking for so long that he had forgotten how to concentrate. When he had to rely on skill, it was no longer there."

"So you stole his fortune."

"I prefer *recovered*," he chided her softly. "He could have quit, but anger distorted his reason. Then he fell into the gamester's trap of trying to reverse his luck when it was obvious the night was not his. When the last card fell, he could only flee the country in disgrace. And much as it goes against my reputation to admit it, I did not keep any of the fortune I won from him that night, instead dividing it among the hardest-hit of his victims."

"Anonymously, I suppose. That's what you meant by preferring shadows."

"Of course. It is not difficult to arrange an unexpected inheritance or return on investment. I have a reputation to protect."

"You sound just like Hart," said Sylvia in disgust. "Why do men find it so difficult to admit that they care about others?"

Blackthorn raised his brows.

"Hart has long helped abused servants and orphans, yet he refuses to lend his name to public efforts aimed at those same groups."

"So that is the orphanage you consigned Mickey to." He stared at Angela.

"Yes, and Jimmy before him. He really does wish to keep his activities secret," she reminded Sylvia.

"As do I," murmured Blackthorn, but Angela heard the words.

"So you also run secret charities."

He nodded. "I won't have a shred of reputation left after this."

"Tell me about them."

Sylvia seconded the request.

"There is little to tell." He shrugged. "One is aiding injured former soldiers who have no families they can turn to. It is criminal the way the government uses them, then abandons them the moment they are unfit to fight."

"I have often thought so," agreed Angela.

His eyes softened. "There are many things they can do with only a little training or financial assistance. But too many people cannot abide deformity, and many of them have lost a limb. I do what I can, starting with reversing the starvation of the streets."

"That is how you stumbled across Mickey, I suppose." The boy had been living with three former soldiers. And that explained that overheard conversation on Piccadilly. He had been directing them to a place to stay. Or perhaps to a job.

"He had been caring for the men, all of whom suffered illness atop crippling injuries. Then he was kicked by a horse. I suspect he was ducking across a street after lifting someone's purse, but the wound festered until he could not rise. All were in desperate straits. I hope he is improving."

"I have heard nothing since Hart picked him up," admitted Angela. "But I will let you know when I do. You said one of your concerns was soldiers. What is the other?"

"Tenants turned out by enclosures. Many cannot find work, so their children wind up either thieving or slaving in manufactories for pennies. I have a cousin who moved to Georgia some years ago. He has often helped immigrants find land. I provide passage money and a small grant to meet expenses until they can produce their own income."

"You are a fraud, my lord rogue." She shook her head. "You cannot be happy at how people revile you. Isn't it time to cease hiding and show society what you really are?"

"Truly a reformer." He tried to sneer, but couldn't make it credible. "Worry about your own reputation. I can take care of mine."

Sylvia pestered her all the way home for an explanation of how she had met Blackthorn, but Angela refused to discuss him. She had long suspected that his core was not black, and now she had proved it. The knowledge built a treacherous glow that she did not want to contemplate. The last thing she needed was an attraction to so ineligible a man.

And he *was* ineligible. He was not a suitor. Nor would he ever be. His concern for others would prevent him from endangering her standing.

# Chapter Thirteen

That afternoon Angela again ran into Devall, this time at Hatchard's. He was in the back corner with no one else nearby.

"Why aren't you making calls?" he asked when she joined him. "Small groups would give you a chance to state your case."

"Hardly. Few are willing to stray from fashion even in private, and they are on their best behavior in mixed company. I have to be careful how hard I push. If the patronesses revoke my voucher, I will have no hope for the future. You know they have never restored one that they've repealed. That leaves me tiptoeing along a very fine line. Ballrooms I can tolerate, for the antagonism is expressed in rituals. Drawing rooms are little better than retiring rooms. If I was admitted at all—which is doubtful—I would face unrestrained scorn, hatred, and even physical assault."

"Good God! But the facts are out in the open, so they must come to their senses soon."

"And pigs may fly." She snorted. "The tabbies are too puffed with their own consequence to admit poor judgment."

"I'll ram the truth down their throats if that's what it takes!"

His frown stopped her from asking what he had in mind. She could only hope that he would limit himself to the intimidation that must have routed Major Caldwell's accuser instead of the violence he had employed more recently.

He made sure she didn't probe his intentions by changing the subject. "I saw a question trembling on your lips in the park this morning. Why not ask it?"

"Very well. Having already rescued Lady Cloverdale from her husband's brutality, why was it necessary to kill him?"

"I didn't, at least not the way you mean. His death was an accident."

"It was not done to get out of paying the judgment he won against you?"

He relaxed against a shelf. "That is what people believe. And in a way they are right. I told him that he would never see a penny-piece of the money and explained why I had spirited Constance away. He could have left it there. He was free to remarry and get himself an heir. His brutality remained private. His best course was to ignore me and get on with his life. Instead, he attacked. It was either kill or be killed." He shrugged.

"Are you sure you didn't goad him into an attack so he wouldn't marry some other innocent girl?"

His eyes blazed, but his voice remained calm. "Not at all. I had no intention of paying for an act that was morally right, no matter what the law claimed. But I had no interest in him beyond helping a friend."

She frowned. "So what about Coldstream?"

He checked the area for possible listeners before answering. "I hadn't realized anyone connected me with that until you mentioned it. What does rumor report?"

"Only that you had had a disagreement with him the day before he died. If not for Cloverdale, I doubt anyone would have suspected you."

He shook his head. "Pure coincidence. It's true that I killed him, but our argument had nothing to do with it. And again, I never intended him physical harm. Coldstream was an evil man. Normally I would not dream of discussing him with a lady, but you are pressing."

She nodded.

"He had been engaged in questionable activities for years," he said with a sigh. "And they were growing increasingly degenerate. Stories of his sadistic use of women were common, though never in society—you must remember that I move in different circles than you do. I hear many things that aren't discussed in drawing rooms—or even in the clubs."

Again she nodded.

"He was a nasty one. Other tales involved the torture of animals, occasionally hinting at ritualistic practices."

"I have heard of satanic cults," she said, understanding where his careful wording was heading.

His brows raised, but he relaxed and continued in a more natural voice. "Then you will know what he was involved in. Unfortunately, it did not stop there. Even the denizens of Seven Dials and Haymarket, who yawn at most vices, blanched at mention of his name. I discovered his worst crimes by accident—in part because my own reputation is so bad. A lad I barely knew asked if I would accompany him to a secret meeting. The group was a revival of the old Hellfire Club."

She gasped. The Hellfire Club had been formed sixty years before by a jaded set of high-ranking libertines as an excuse for drinking, debauchery, and blasphemy. The founder, Sir Francis Dashwood, had previously installed a large globe atop the steeple of his parish church, inside which he and his friends could get blissfully drunk while admiring the countryside through its portholes. They also used it for orgies, its position atop a sacred site adding to the impropriety. Club meetings were held in a ruined abbey, and later in a network of caves carved into a chalk hill on Sir Francis's estate. Over time, mockery of religion evolved into satanic worship, and orgies grew more brutal and perverted, until thirty years after its founding, an outraged society closed it down.

"It had only just been revived and as yet had only four members," he continued in a hard, flat voice. "They were looking for new recruits, as their more reprehensible activities required crowds. Coldstream was the force behind it. The other three were young sprigs who had not yet discovered how corrupt it was, and who were blinded by gaining the attention of so fashionable a gentleman—Coldstream was a pink of the *ton*, high in the instep, and absolutely fastidious, at least in public. I declined the invitation, but fear of what such a group might do forced me to investigate. Under his respectable facade, Coldstream was more depraved than even the inner circle of the original club, delighting in torture and blood. Evidence pointed to the murder of at least four girls after early club meetings, and I have no doubt he had dispatched others before deciding he needed an audience.

"But surely the law could have taken care of him," she protested.

"That was what I intended, but I was still gathering evidence when he learned of my interest. One thing led to another, and I lost my temper, allowing him to see my disgust. His own temper broke, and he challenged me." He shrugged.

"You did not have to accept."

"No gentleman could refuse."

She shook her head. "You use your reputation often enough to justify ungentlemanly behavior. You can't have it both ways, Devall. Either you are a social outcast who cares nothing for the dictates of society, or you are a gentleman, bound by the code that defines that label. Do not use standards you deliberately discarded to excuse your conduct."

"I have never claimed to be less than a gentleman." He straightened, seeming to tower over her. "Society finds it convenient to label me so, but I cannot control their minds."

"You must think me a flat. Does a gentleman interfere in a man's marriage?" The whisper that prevented their voices from carrying added intensity to her words. "Does a gentleman conduct duels without regard to the rules governing affairs of honor so that he can execute men without paying the price? Does a gentleman force others into issuing the desired challenges so that the choice of weapons is his, thus insuring that the execution proceeds as planned? Does a gentleman throw over his intended bride, staging a public show to guarantee maximum pain for all concerned? You, sir, are no gentleman."

Anger burst across his face as he grabbed her arm. "Must a gentleman sit idly by and watch innocent girls be beaten into submission?" he hissed. "Must a gentleman follow society's dictates when doing so allows evil men to deal death to helpless victims? Must a gentleman ignore injustice and approve depredations because the victims are from the lower classes? The world is not a black and white place, Angela. There are few absolutes. Before you sit in judgment, at least do me the courtesy of examining the facts."

"And what are the facts in Atwater's case? I accept that he beat his first wife. And no one knows better than I how unscrupulous he can be. But nothing can alter Lydia's fate, and killing him will not alter mine. You are not trying to rescue a Lady Cloverdale from death or retrieve ill-gotten gains for starving victims. There is no future disaster looming over anyone's head, Devall. You are seeking revenge, pure and simple. But vengeance is for God, not for man. You endanger your own soul by continuing this course."

"What do you care for my soul?"

"I care for everyone, as do you when you are not in thrall to your passions. You cannot eliminate every person who is less than perfect. There would be no one left, including yourself. Nor can you save every person who chooses a path that might lead to pain. Misdeeds must be punished. I have no quarrel with that. But there has to be a line somewhere. When you draw that line so that an individual can take a life, you are playing God. Expose the truth, but let the law decide who deserves death. If the law is faulty, use the power of your position to change it. By refusing to assume your seat in Parliament, you've abdicated your responsibilities, hiding in the shadows to assist a handful of individuals instead stepping into the sunlight to help thousands."

"I have never set out to deliberately trap someone into dying," he protested, ignoring the rest of her charges.

"Fustian! How else can you describe your campaign against Atwater? What possible motive can you have for forcing a duel on the man if you do not intend to kill him? You keep urging me to examine the facts. Why don't you follow your own advice? Look into your heart, Devall. There can be no other explanation for your behavior. You are as manipulative as my mother and just as loathe to admit it. It is not your place to act as prosecution, judge, and executioner."

He sighed, running his fingers through his hair. "You are right, and I had already decided to abandon that particular quest. I will find some other way to deal with Atwater."

"Why not bring Ned Parker to town and allow him to speak for himself. Granted, his words might not carry weight with some as he is only a tenant. But at the moment, no one believes the tales because they are attributed to you—a man everyone knows is trying to force a duel on Atwater."

"Damnation!" he muttered. "Have I really become so blind?"

"That is the danger of taking the law into your own hands." She held his eyes with her own. "The power over life and death is corrupting. Sooner or later you see all problems in absolute terms with absolute consequences. Only God can make godlike choices without harming his core. Reconsider your deeds before it is too late, then stick to what is humanly acceptable. Perhaps it won't be socially acceptable, but that distinction has never bothered you. Just leave the life-and-death decisions to others."

He nodded. "I should have brought both Ned and Smith out sooner," he admitted. "Thank you. As for your own problems, I suspect the feeding frenzy is nearly over. People are growing bored and will become receptive to new ideas. All it will take now is a new scandal. Just don't expect any apologies."

"I would be satisfied to be ignored," she claimed with a shaky laugh.

"Take care. I had better leave. Someone is bound to come back here before long. It won't help you to be seen with me."

"Use the power of your title to change bad laws, Devall. If you redeem your reputation, it would be possible."

"I will think about it." Placing a quick kiss on her forehead, he collected his books and left.

She watched until he rounded a corner. He could do so much if he decided to work within the system. And it would require little effort to take his rightful place. The men involved in government affairs were less prone to quick judgment than the tabbies and fribbles of society. He could become a powerful voice for reform.

Devall was the most complex man she had ever known. What had started him down this path? Breaking off his betrothal had pushed him into the shadows, but his concerns must have arisen earlier. Most of the evil he battled involved abuse of some sort. Had his mother suffered in such a way? Or was he an abuse victim himself? She knew little of his background, but she had a burning desire to learn more.

Devall cursed himself all the way home. Why had he not thought of something so obvious as having Ned and Smith tell their tale in public? How could he have grown so single-minded? Angela was right to call him arrogant. Every problem he tackled had many potential solutions. Meting out death should have been a last resort.

And it *had* been before Atwater, he assured himself as he turned toward Kensington. Perhaps he could have been more diplomatic with Cloverdale, but fighting had never crossed his mind before the earl attacked. Coldstream had been pure bad luck. The man had caught him questioning the Seven Dials abbess who had lost two girls to Coldstream's depravity. Hiding his intentions at that point had been useless.

He sighed. Angela's harping had nearly convinced him to make a push toward redeeming himself. Baring the details to her had been a test of sorts. She had readily accepted the truth—not that he had expected otherwise. His real surprise was that Lady Sylvia had likewise believed him. Now he had to decide whether these two were indicative of society as a whole. It was a question he could not yet answer.

Shelving his thoughts, he pulled up before the veterans' house. Ned should be in. The man had not yet moved to his own lodgings. It took only a moment to collect him and head for Jack's rooms.

Jack and Ned called on Brummell that afternoon.

"Lady Atwater's maid will corroborate the story," Jack told an astonished Beau when he had concluded his explanation. "As will several other servants and the shepherd who revived Mr. Parker." He gestured toward the former infantryman.

Brummell nodded. "It fits. Hartleigh claimed in his last letter that Miss Warren was being unjustly persecuted. Why?"

"I wish I knew," said Jack with a sigh. "This goes beyond all reason. All she did was refuse his offer."

"Which would indicate that she has some intelligence—despite her idiot mother." He idly swung his quizzing glass while he considered the situation. "I believe you, Major. This should be an interesting evening."

"I am so sorry," said Barbara when Angela joined her in the drawing room before dinner.

"What now?" Had Atwater contrived some new charge that would get her kicked out of society for good?

"Sylvia did not tell you?" she asked in surprise.

"She had already left for the Seatons' when I returned from Hatchard's."

"Just after you went out, Andrew received a message from

Forley Court. A fire broke out in the stables last night. They were able to save the horses, but the building is a total loss."

Angela shuddered. "Was anyone injured?"

"A few minor burns. But much equipage was lost, and everything is in turmoil. He left immediately."

"Dear God. Troubles never come alone, do they?"

Barbara shook her head. "He does not know if he will be able to return to town. Lord and Lady Ashton will accompany us tonight, but we must make other arrangements for tomorrow."

What could have happened? A careless stable boy tipping over a lantern? A horse gone berserk? But either possibility seemed out of character for both the staff and the animals. Perhaps this was the excuse she needed to leave town. In light of the fire, no one could accuse her of running away.

Yet Devall had been right, she admitted two hours later. The cuts and stares continued, but those not actively shunning her seemed less judgmental. Perhaps it was because no one could identify even one of her supposed paramours—the two libertines Atwater had named had each denied any contact—or maybe Devall's friends were finally winning converts, but occasional whispers now questioned the tales. And nearly half her sets were spoken for.

Brummell delighted the hostess by appearing unexpectedly after supper, then shocked the *ton* by immediately seeking out Angela for a brief conversation that ended in mutual smiles and a courtly kiss on her gloved hand. He followed up this performance by disdainfully quizzing a matron who had cut her and a sprig who was miming one of the parodies, then gave Atwater the cut direct before retiring to the card room. The crowd buzzed for the rest of the evening. Brummell's actions drove the first real wedge into Atwater's armor.

The following night, her entire card was filled, and she actually enjoyed the ball. Her supporters were rapidly discrediting Atwater now that several of his former servants had publicly recounted their experiences with the earl. Jack's voice carried more and more weight as people recalled that Wellington's staff officers were both honorable and intelligent.

By the time the shocking affair between Lady Driscoll and Lord Hunt exploded into Mayfair drawing rooms, she was accepted by all but the highest sticklers. With only a week left before she returned home, she turned her thoughts to the future. Would Andrew allow her to remove to the dower house—properly chaperoned, of course? Their mother would no longer be needing it.

# Chapter Fourteen

Atwater sprawled despondently behind his desk, staring at the portrait above the mantel. The picture lied. He had never been so carefree. The artist had painted him as he would have appeared had life been fair. But it was not.

Why was the world so vicious? No matter how hard he tried, people inevitably turned against him. And he *had* tried, adhering to every stricture of polite society, conscientiously carrying out his duties, judiciously chastising the lawless who came before his magistrate's bench, protecting those in his care. All he asked in return was love, honor, and respect.

But fate had cursed him. Everyone he had ever loved had rejected him, abandoning him without warning.

The first had been his mother. His fingers clenched, driving a penknife painfully into his palm. Eleanor, Lady Atwater, daughter of the Duke of Rainsbrough. He could hardly remember her face, though many claimed he strongly resembled her. She had spent much of her time in the nurseries—playing games, sharing the wonders of the world, supporting him through injury and illness. *I will always be here to comfort you*, she had sworn after a riding accident. It was a promise she had repeated often, a promise he had foolishly believed. But she had not. The day after his sixth birthday, she had left without a word, leaving him behind as if he were a trifle no longer in fashion. His father admitted that she had gone away for a while, proving that her protestations of love had been a sham. He had waited years for her to return. Not until he left for school did he give up hope, repudiating her and consigning her memory to the dust bin. She had proven herself unworthy of his love. Only after his cold, brutal father died did he learn the full truth. She was buried in the churchyard, having died six months after her disappearance, and a two-month-old brother with her. No one had thought to inform him. But it changed nothing. She was false, promising what she could not deliver. And they had lied, every one—his father, his nurses, his aunts and uncles and cousins. In a wave of revulsion, he had repudiated the lot, barring them from his doors forever. How could they have been so cruel? Again his fist closed around the penknife, adding a new cut to a palm scarred with scores of others. Furious, he cast it at the portrait and raised a glass to his lips.

Then there was his sister. Amelia. So full of life. Her laughing blue eyes and silky blond curls danced before his eyes. After their mother disappeared, he had clung to her, ignoring all other efforts to comfort him. Only a year older than himself, she knew no more than he about the fate of the lady who had been the center of their universe, but Amelia's solace touched him. He needed her gaiety to counter his devastation, needed her love to plug the rending hole in his soul. When he repudiated their mother, Amelia became even more vital, for she remained alone in her love for him. Their father had grown even colder since their mother had run away, withdrawing into his study and rarely showing his face to his children. But Amelia too had run. Literally. She had angrily lashed out at him, striking him and calling him hateful names before taking flight. Vengeance had been swift and merciless. A moment's careless inattention, a shifting stone, and she had hurtled over a cliff, her cruel words still echoing on the breeze. Amelia. Her bright eyes forever dimmed, her golden curls drenched in blood.

Everyone blamed him. His teasing had caused her death, they sobbed. None of them understood, but the accusations hurt. And there was no Amelia to offer comfort. If only she had accepted her role. But at fourteen she had grown indifferent to his wishes, allowing the flirtations of the squire's son to turn her head and bragging about the beaux she would attract in London. In shock, he had reminded her that she would not join society until he had no more need of her, but she had scoffed and taunted him, running from his love and turning her back on his need so that God was forced to strike her down. Her death had left him alone with their father, who unfairly blamed him for the tragedy, turning a cold shoulder to the heir who had snuffed the last ray of sunshine from their lives.

He had resigned himself to a life of loneliness and grief—until he met Lydia. A sob tore from his throat. Lydia. Dearest Lydia. He had loved her most of all, more than life itself—her sweet shy ways; the light that appeared in her eyes whenever he approached; her beauty; her grace. She was his joy, his most precious possession. Fate had finally relented. He showered her with gifts, worshipping at her feet. His love knew no bounds. Yet she too had run. Why? The question still tormented him. He had corrected the mistakes of the past, protecting her from the corrupting influence of unworthy men, keeping her away from dangerous parts of the estate, personally escorting her whenever she left the house lest some harm befall her when he was not at hand to help. All he asked in return was that she care for him as his mother had cared for her family.

She had vowed to love him for all eternity. Just like his mother. He should have suspected then, but he had not. In the end, she too had betrayed him. Despite his love, despite his gifts, despite the care and attention he devoted to her, she had run. She had not even done it defiantly as had Amelia. She did it surreptitiously, without even leaving him a message. He had discovered her sneaking away to rejoin her parents. In a burst of spite, she threw his love in his face and cursed him even as he fought to quiet her fears and return her to the bed her condition required she occupy. Fate had punished her for her betrayal, but he suffered as well. She had died that night, and his son with her. What had he done to deserve such pain?

Then there was Angela. An appropriate name, he had decided the moment he saw her. Perhaps fate would relent if he chose someone who did not resemble his faithless mother. Angela. Shy and demure. Her soft green eyes had glowed when he first danced with her. Her auburn hair had burned like a new dawn, offering him a last chance at happiness. He wanted nothing more than to love her, care for her, and revel in fate's reprieve. Yet after basking in his adoration for much of the Season, she too had run, publicly repudiating him in a way even Lydia had not dared, making him a laughingstock among his friends. Such cruelty could not be borne. He had tried to teach her a lesson by letting her feel rejection for herself. He had prayed she would repent and return to his arms, but she had remained defiant, flaunting her disdain as she danced and laughed with lesser men.

His fingers dug holes into the leather arms of his chair. The pain was unbearable. He had paid enough. Fate had sent Angela to relieve his agony. It was time she accepted her destiny.

"Andrew will return the day after tomorrow." Angela announced, glancing up from his letter as Sylvia entered the drawing room.

"Has he finished at the Court already?" Her eyes lit with excitement.

"Work is underway to replace the stables. The steward has everything in hand, so Andrew need not remain."

"Two days. I can hardly wait. It has been so very dull since he left."

"Are you implying that London cannot amuse you for even one week during the height of the Season?" she said teasingly. "Society's hostesses will be devastated. The fops and fribbles will rend their peacock feathers in despair. The gossips must cast all their stories aside since they hold so little interest."

They laughed.

"Goodness! How long has it been since you've laughed?" asked Sylvia when she had caught her breath. "It is good to see you so relaxed."

"Life has settled into such a pleasant routine, I am almost sorry to be leaving."

"Forgive me. I never meant to belittle how your affairs have recovered." Distress dimmed her eyes.

"Don't apologize. You know I was teasing."

"Did he learn what happened?"

Angela's light mood evaporated. "The fire was deliberately set, though no one knows why or by whom. It began in the disused end of the stable."

"Dear God!"

"Precisely. There are too many deranged people loose in the world."

Barbara joined them, followed by Paynes with a tea tray. She was as incensed as they over the news. "And he has no idea why someone would do such a thing?"

"None that he committed to paper," said Angela. "He did not even say whether this was a random incident or an act aimed at him."

"He may not know," said Sylvia with a sigh.

"I merely wondered in light of everything else that has happened to you of late."

"But that was pique that I turned down Atwater's offer," explained Angela. "The man is overwhelmingly conceited and could not stomach the thought that someone as unprepossessing as myself would not fall at his feet in worshipful adoration."

"A perfect description. Has Andrew any enemies?"

"None that I know of." Angela shrugged. "He is a proper and conventional gentleman who has worked hard to rescue the estate from our mother's profligacy. His treatment of the tenants is exemplary, and none of the staff has been so much as reprimanded, so I doubt anyone harbors a secret grudge. In fact, under his care, both tenants and staff have improved their living and working conditions beyond what they can possibly remember. My grandfather was as blind to country affairs as my father."

"It was likely a wanderer of unbalanced temperament then, or perhaps a vagrant whose cooking fire got out of hand," decided Barbara. "Such fools care nothing for the suffering they cause. Let us hope that he is not still in the area, or Hart may suffer similar problems."

They all sighed.

"What are your plans for the day?"

"I am paying calls with Lady Ashton," said Sylvia, glancing at the mantel clock. "Heavens, I had best get ready or I will keep her waiting." She hurried from the room.

"I will take a turn around Green Park," said Angela. "Major Caldwell is driving me in Hyde Park later, so I won't be gone long." She rarely accompanied Sylvia on calls these days, having no interest in gossip. Since she had given up all hope of marriage, she no longer needed to turn the tabbies up sweet. Or so she claimed aloud. The truth was that she could not feel comfortable with women who had been pillorying her only a few days ago. Her reputation might have recovered, but it would be long before the pain lessened.

"Good. I need to finish opening Trotter House. Geoffrey will arrive soon. But I will be back for dinner."

Two days of rain had washed everything clean. Sunlight enveloped the park, accompanied by a gentle breeze that ruffled Angela's hair. Green Park was one of her favorite afternoon rides, for it was less crowded than Hyde Park and better suited to reflection. Society was engaged in paying calls. People clustered only near the dairy herd, where maids dispensed fresh milk. She could relax, rebuilding her energy so she could face the evening's ball.

Leaves rustled overhead, playing a spring song that reminded her longingly of home. She looked forward to returning to the country, away from soot and grime and noise, away from cruel gossip and the rules that were so much stricter than seemed reasonable.

She must talk to Andrew about the dower house immediately. It had already been refurbished for Lady Forley, so he should not object to her using it. Her needs were simple enough to require only a tiny staff. If Andrew invested her dowry, she could probably live on the income. Her only problem would be finding a congenial chaperon.

She turned down a new path. What about Mrs. Giddings? The daughter of a baronet, Edna Giddings had married beneath her, eloping with the youngest son of a country vicar. Mr. Giddings had been a writer, though never earning enough to provide more than the bare necessities. He had died the previous winter, leaving his wife only a tiny income. Her nephew now held her father's title, but the lad was an arrogant fool who refused to recognize the connection. Perhaps Edna would consider joining her. An educated mind was the most important trait for a companion. She couldn't tolerate a simpering fool.

Closing her eyes, she turned her face up to catch the sun's warmth. An image of the dower house shimmered against her lids, a modest Elizabethan manor with leaded windows and ivied walls that lent it charm. The head footman at the Court had his eye on the parlormaid. Would they like to come to her as butler and housekeeper? She would also need a cook, two maids . . .

A thump distracted her thoughts, and she glanced over her shoulder. Her groom lay unconscious on the path, his horse galloping wildly away.

"No!" she screamed as a hand grabbed her bridle to drag her mount into a canter. "Let go!"

Atwater merely laughed. "You've had your fun, my love. It is time to come home."

She fought swirling black spots, determined not to swoon. Fanaticism gleamed in Atwater's eyes. Why had she never detected it before? She shivered.

"You are mine," he vowed. "Payment from the gods for the pain I have endured. You worship me. I've seen it in your face, so you need no longer hide the truth. I will make you happy, my love. Happier than you ever dreamed possible. Nothing is too good for you. Nothing will harm you ever again. I will protect you from all evil."

Terror nearly choked her. "The only way you can make me happy is to leave. Now." Rage shook her voice. "Release the bridle and depart."

"There is no need to continue the game, Angela," he said, his voice now revealing dangerous undertones. "You will come with me. I have a special license, so we can be married immediately. You must not be left to the mercies of an evil world."

"Absolutely not!" She sliced her crop across the hand that held her bridle. "The only evil I see is in you."

A snarl bared his teeth. "Do not strike me again, my love, or you will force me to punish you. Punishment is painful; so very painful. Don't put me through that again. You have caused me enough agony."

Dear God! What could she do? His obsession had clearly crossed into madness. How did one reason with a madman? Panic darkened her mind. Unwanted images rose of Lydia and Ned Parker.

The moment he pulled up next to his coach, she leaped off her horse, running wildly. The street was deserted. His arm wrapped around her waist and lifted her from the ground. A hard hand slapped her face, stopping her voice in mid-scream.

"The game is over, my love," he repeated softly. "You will come home now, I will take care of you forever."

He deposited her in the coach, his face twisting in pain when she broke into sobs.

"Don't cry, my love," he crooned, cradling her and stroking her head as if she were a child.

Hysteria threatened, but she fought it back as the realization hit. For some reason, he needed to care for her. When she appeared vulnerable, he became soft and gentle. When she countered him, he turned vicious. Her only hope lay in humoring him until she could escape. But she must be patient. Her next attempt had to succeed. God only knew what he would do if he caught her.

"Wh-where are we going?" she sobbed, trying to force her body to relax. Her skin crawled at his touch, and it took all her determination not to scream.

"A special place where we can be alone," he whispered, the sensual voice eliciting new shudders. "The world won't intrude on us. We will be married tonight."

Panic inched closer. Surely he couldn't get away with forcing her into wedlock! But he was the beautiful and beloved Earl of Atwater, who could undoubtedly convince a vicar to ignore her protests. And she was of age, so she did not need permission from Andrew. Only by postponing the ceremony could she hope to escape.

"You cannot expect me to wed in this old riding habit." Her voice shook, but she could do nothing to control it. And she didn't dare look directly at him lest he see her hatred. "Are you not worthy of a splendid gown?"

A frown puckered his forehead even as he jerked her arm, leaving a bruise. She bit back a protest. "Why have you put me through such pain?" he demanded.

She forced her hand to rest soothingly atop his. "I thought you understood," she whispered at last. "I had to get rid of my mother. She would have hung on you and squandered your fortune."

"You never meant to hurt me? Your love is true?" His eyes blazed with increasing ferocity.

"Of course." Bile rose higher with each new lie. "Will you allow me to dress properly?"

"That primrose gown you wore last night will be suitable." He resumed his quiet stroking. She shuddered, praying he would interpret the movement as pleasure. "We will marry tomorrow. I can retrieve your wardrobe by then."

"Would it not be better to collect it now?" she dared.

"No!" He shook her violently several times, snapping her neck. "You will not leave me. Not like the others. I can never allow that again."

Dear God! How was she to escape such a madman? She choked back words and forced relaxation on battered muscles still taut with horror. Her tongue was bleeding by the time her tears finally calmed him. He resumed his crooning. Barely able to control the revulsion sweeping through her, she pressed close against him, allowing her rending sobs to continue. It was the only sound that didn't incite attack.

The carriage stopped on a street of small houses that gave no clue to their location. How much time had elapsed? It could have been minutes or hours. Her terror mounted as he carried her inside. How could she return home? She had few coins in her reticule and no idea how far they were from Clifford Street—or even in which direction it lay.

How was she to escape? Even if he left to fetch her wardrobe, he would undoubtedly post a guard. His cunning still functioned. He was not mad enough to leave her alone. Somehow she must get word to her family.

"If we are to marry tomorrow, I must invite my brother to the wedding," she tried softly. "Perhaps you can talk to him when you fetch my gown."

"Impossible," he declared calmly. "He is still at the Court. How can you tolerate his disinterest? That country squire mentality will always place his estate above his sister. But you are first in my heart. Nothing is more important than protecting you from harm."

She stiffened, then forced herself to relax, not daring to mention her sudden suspicion. Was Atwater responsible for the fire that had taken Andrew from town? If so, then this was something he had plotted for some time."

That last fear was confirmed when he carried her up to a back bedroom and laid her on the bed. A sturdy lock gleamed in the door—a brand-new lock. One glance took in the Spartan furnishings—bed, stand, chest, chair, heavy draperies pulled tightly across the single window.

"Will you get me something to wear?" she asked softly. "This wrinkled habit seems so dowdy next to your splendor."

"Later, my love," he said absently, locking the door and sliding the key into his pocket.

Her breath caught, her body turning rigid with fright.

"You are mine now," he repeated. His coat dropped to the floor. "I will show you how much I love you."

She rolled off the far side of the bed and bounded to her feet. "We are not married, my lord." Somehow she kept both fear and accusation out of her voice. "If you truly loved me, you would never debauch me in so vile a fashion."

"Fustian." No force underlay the exclamation. His voice remained calm—almost dead—more frightening than his earlier violence. His waistcoat and cravat joined his jacket. "We are already married in spirit. The ceremony is but hours away. You know that I will care for you. Yet I sense fear. We must banish that. Prove your love. Now."

"This has nothing to do with love. I will not be used in such a fashion outside of marriage." Anger crept into her voice despite her efforts. Her eyes darted around the room, desperately seeking a weapon. Sidling to the night stand, she idly fingered the candlestick.

His eyes turned blank. A bulge strained at his breeches. The gaping neck of his shirt bared half his chest, exposing a mat of dark blond hair.

"This is what you were born for, my darling Angela, my divine angel," he crooned. "You will serve me always, running my home, satisfying my needs, bearing my children. I must get an heir, you know. My cousin is deranged. We will start one now." With a sudden lunge, he sprang across the bed.

She swung the candlestick, smashing the base into his face even as she whipped around the bed and across the room. Frantically, she tried to recall everything she had read about the art of fighting. It wasn't much. Unusual though her education had been, she had never expected to need such information.

Contrary to her expectations, he did not fly into fury, but his restraint increased her terror. None of his previous actions had so clearly demonstrated his madness.

"I cannot accept that," he stated calmly, smiling as he walked slowly around the bed. Blood dripped from his nose and from a cut on one cheek, landing unheeded on his shirt. Despite the wounds, he looked angelically handsome, the answer to every maiden's prayers. Gentle. Caring. Excitingly sensual. But his eyes—dear God, his eyes. They held no trace of warmth. Or of intelligence. Reason had fled, leaving a hulking shell bent on a single purpose.

"Now be a good girl and come to bed." His hand stretched out in command.

Hampered by her habit skirt, she was not sure she could elude him again. One hand gathered its bulk out of the way, even as fresh terror engulfed her.

He was unfastening the buttons on his breeches.

One . . .

Two . . .

Three . . .

One side of the panel fell open, the bulge growing larger as its shackles loosened. He stepped closer.

Four . . .

Her eyes stared at his fingers, terror making her own reason waver. Another step.

Five . . .

She launched a vicious kick at his manhood even as her free hand crashed the candlestick into his head.

Furious bellows reverberated around the room. Gone was the handsome, immaculate gentleman. Gone was the gentle, crooning lover. What faced her now was a savage beast with the strength of Atlas and the ferocity of a wounded bear. She had failed to knock him senseless, and now she paid in full.

She swung again, rapidly backpedaling as she tried to place the bed between them. Her next swing caught his chest, but he tore the candlestick from her hand and hurled it away. Blows rained over her body. Pain exploded through her midsection, her shoulders, her arms. Desperate, she landed a second kick to his groin, raking her nails deeply down his face and chest, biting savagely at the hand he held over her mouth.

But his superior strength made defeat inevitable. Too close to kick, she tried to use her knee, but her skirt hampered its motion and it glanced harmlessly off his thigh. He picked her up, shaking her mercilessly, snapping her neck until she feared her head might fall off. She clawed at his face, trying desperately to dig into his eyes. With a feral roar, he hurled her against the wall.

Stars burst through her skull, followed by darkness.

# Chapter Fifteen

Sylvia returned from afternoon calls, still smiling at the latest tales. She was handing her parasol to Paynes when a footman clad in Atwater's livery arrived. The butler accepted a letter, slipped a coin to the man, then closed the door with a frown.

"Is that for Miss Warren?" she asked.

"For Lord Forley."

From Atwater? What did the earl want with Andrew—unless he was starting new rumors against Angela. He could not like the way her reputation had recovered.

"I will take it to the study," she offered, unsure what to do about this latest twist. With Andrew out of town, it would be days before they knew what it contained.

Paynes handed her the note.

"Is Lady Trotter here?"

"No, my lady."

"How about Miss Warren?"

"She has not yet returned from her ride."

She frowned, heading not to the study but to the room she shared with Angela. The brief outing to Green Park should have concluded. Angela would need to change before Major Caldwell arrived. Had she met friends and lost time talking? But despite her improved image, she had few friends in town.

Atwater's note burned through her glove. If he was launching a new campaign, they needed to know the details immediately. She paced as she wrestled with her conscience. Awaiting Andrew was impossible. That much delay could only play into Atwater's hands. Barbara would not return until dinner, but she should at least wait for Angela.

Within five minutes, curiosity overcame manners. She broke the seal only to gasp and sink into a chair.

> *Forley,*
>   *Miss Warren has reconsidered her hasty decision and accepted my hand in marriage. Due to the distressing situation in London, we will wed privately and retire immediately to the country.*
>
>                                    *Atwater*

Could it be true? Could Angela really have eloped? She had certainly chosen the ideal time to slip away. Everyone else was occupied. Directing the note to Andrew allowed ample time to make an escape. Under normal circumstances, no one would dare open a letter addressed to another.

But reason quickly returned. Angela had been too enthusiastic about returning to the country to have planned such an escapade. Hart's groom had accompanied her—not someone she would take on an elopement. Nor was she the sort to hide behind secrecy. She hated Atwater. Her intense bitterness could never have been feigned. And girls who eloped usually left their own notes behind—or did nothing. She had never heard of a case where the groom sent round a note after the fact.

So Atwater must have abducted her. Hands shaking, she reread the message. Dear Lord! What could she do? He had been very clever about it. No outside markings identified the author. The footman had not indicated any urgency. If she had not noticed his livery, the note would have remained unopened until Andrew returned. Paynes would not have mentioned it.

Poor Angela. She would be ruined if this came out. Either she would spend the rest of her life shackled to a man she despised, or society would shun her for confirming all the rumors. She was hopelessly compromised.

In tears, she paced the floor, devising and discarding one plan after another. The abduction could not be made public, so she could not summon help. She must act immediately. But she could think of nothing she could do.

Biting her lip, she considered the few men who had been helping them. Ashton was out of town. She did not know the major well, and had no idea where he was staying. He would arrive in an hour—which gave her a back-up plan—but she hated to wait that long. Every minute Angela remained in Atwater's clutches increased her danger.

Her eyes suddenly lit on a letter atop Angela's escritoire. It was in a masculine hand, but neither Andrew's nor Atwater's. Abandoning all scruples, she unfolded it and gasped. It was from Blackthorn. But her horror at his description of Atwater's venality died under her growing elation. She had forgotten that he and Angela were friends. If anyone could help, it would be the Black Marquess, a man who never allowed convention to curb his behavior, a man whose antipathy to Atwater was well-known. Jotting a brief summons, she sent their footman running.

*Please let him be at home!*

Devall paced the Forley drawing room as Lady Sylvia explained her fears.

"What?" he demanded when she thrust Atwater's note into his hand.

"It cannot be true," she sobbed, her nerves giving way now that she could share the burden. "Angela hates him. She would never consider wedding him."

"It does not seem like her," he agreed, thrusting down terror. Was Atwater trying to destroy her? He could not like the way she had recovered from his slander.

"Excuse me, my lady," said Paynes from the doorway.

"Yes?"

"It's Frank, my lady. He just returned with a tale you should hear."

"Send him in," she ordered.

"Who is Frank?"

"The groom who accompanied Angela on her ride."

"Dear God!"

Frank's disheveled condition and the huge bruise on the side of his head warned them that his story would be ugly.

"You accompanied Miss Warren today?" asked Sylvia.

"Yes, milady. We was ridin' in Green Park, as she likes to do, when a 'orseman pulled up beside me. Fancy cove, but I 'ardly got a look afore 'e off and conked me. When I waked up, both she an' me 'orse was gone."

"When was this?"

"I don't rightly know," he confessed. " 'bout a hour after we left. I 'spect she was 'eadin' for 'ome."

"That would be about an hour ago," guessed Sylvia.

"Did you recognize the gentleman?" asked Devall.

"No, milord. I never saw 'im afore. You's the only one she ever talked to on 'er rides."

"Describe him, please."

"It 'appened fast. A 'at was pulled down over 'is 'air an' 'e was wearin' a cloak. But 'e 'ad a look I'll never ferget. 'is face was like a child's, almost purty, but the devil 'isself peeped outta 'is eyes. Mad."

Sylvia broke into sobs.

Devall felt the cold wash over him. *Mad, mad, mad . . .* The word echoed in his mind. He had no doubt that it was Atwater. And that explained so much. *Mad . . . mad . . . mad . . .*

"Dear God, where can he have taken her?" asked Sylvia. "The poor girl." Fresh sobs choked her voice.

"Thank you, Frank," he said gravely, trying to inject some sanity into the room so he could think. "You had best see to that head. I will send word the moment we discover anything."

Frank's eyes widened at this courtesy, but he nodded and bowed himself out. The knocker sounded.

"What—" Sylvia's question died when Devall dashed away. "Paynes!" he called down the stairs. "Who is at the door?"

"Major Caldwell, my lord."

"Send him up."

Jack's brows nearly reached his hair when he discovered Devall alone with Lady Sylvia. A few crisp words filled him in.

"That bastard!" he exclaimed in shock. "Beg pardon, my lady."

"Think nothing of it. But what are we to do?"

"Perhaps I know where he took her," Devall said slowly. At least he hoped so. If he was wrong, Angela might not survive. She wasn't the sort to tamely submit. "I believe he is the anonymous purchaser of that Kensington cottage that Devereaux unloaded."

Jack bit off a comment. "It's worth a try."

"Send regrets to whatever event you were scheduled to attend this evening," he ordered Sylvia. "Even if we find her, she will be in no mood to do the pretty in public."

"Try not to worry," added Jack as they headed for the door.

Sylvia nodded.

"What are you going to do?" Jack asked as he joined Devall in the hall.

"Check out that cottage. The rest depends on what we find."

Jack shivered at the grim voice. Devall was out for blood, but this time he felt no urge to deflect his hand. He admired Miss Warren. She was one of the few women he had ever considered a friend.


Angela slowly regained consciousness, unsure where she was or what had happened. Every inch of her body ached. Sharper pains stabbed her head, her arm, and her side. Moisture trickled down her face. Memory seeped back, sending new fears raging through her breast. What had happened after she hit the wall? Had he finished the job of ravishing her?

She tried to move, but dizziness and nausea forced her to remain still. One eye opened a slit. Blackness. It took a moment to realize that something blocked her view. Slowly sliding her arm up, she pulled the bottom of the curtain aside. She was still lying on the floor where he had thrown her.

Relief surged. He surely would not have ravished her in this position. So her resistance had bought her some time. Carefully she scanned the room. He was gone.

Weakness overwhelmed her, and it was long before she could again move. Silence reigned. Had he left the house?

It took several minutes to pull herself into a sitting position and several more before she could attempt to stand. Every movement brought a surge of nausea. She fought it down as she had earlier fought the terror, refusing to give in, forcing her mind to catalog her injuries instead of dwelling on the swirling sickness. She must be as healthy as possible when he returned.

Nothing seemed to be broken, though the bruises were deep and painful. It was possible that her ribs were cracked, and she doubtless suffered from concussion. The cut on her scalp had finally stopped bleeding, though considerable blood pooled on the floor. Using a bedpost for support, she managed to gain her feet. The dizziness increased, and she gasped for some time.

Her first hope was the window. If she could escape, she could get help at a neighboring house. But one glance dashed that idea. The draperies had been dragged open. New iron bars blocked her exit. He had prepared her prison well. Still grasping the bedpost, she concentrated on the next option.

It was four steps to the door. She counted them in her mind over and over before she tried to walk them. One . . . two . . . three . . . Her leg gave way on the fourth, but she avoided collapse by grasping the handle with both hands.

Locked.

As she had feared. Atwater would not have left if she could escape.

Despair threatened to overwhelm her, and she tottered to the chair, sinking into its soft depths. *What did I do to deserve this?* A barred window. A locked door. In her present weakened state, she had no chance of fighting him off a second time.

But she refused to capitulate. *I will not cry . . . I will not cry . . .* Taking a deep breath, she rose and set about the task of finding a weapon. Too bad he had removed her reticule. Her penknife was inside.

Devall sat in menacing silence all the way to Kensington. They had delayed long enough to collect a closed carriage, hoping that Angela would be able to use it. Neither Jack's phaeton nor Devall's stallion could have returned her to Clifford Street unnoticed. The coach was one he often used in London, sporting no crest or other identifying mark that might advertise his presence.

No plans formed as his grays sped through the streets. Nor did he respond to any of Jack's comments. His mind was trapped in a new hell, one he had never expected but that had closed about him the moment Lady Sylvia had explained her summons. He still could not believe it, though all his senses screamed the truth. How could he have been so incredibly stupid?

He was in love with Angela Warren.

It was so unexpected that he could hardly breathe. He had banished all tender feelings as part of his adjustment to ostracism. Marriage was out of the question. His reputation loomed between him and the world. Having just restored her own, he could do nothing to tarnish it—which meant avoiding her completely. Even if he corrected every rumor and every exaggeration, he would never be socially acceptable. The hard, cold facts condemned him on their own. He *had* jilted Penelope. He *was* responsible for two deaths, neither of which had occurred in battle or on a field of honor.

He brutally thrust emotion aside. His immediate concern was to rescue her. And this time he would not allow Atwater to escape. Abduction with violence put the man beyond all civilized responses. Even madness could not protect him from a well-deserved end.

His blood ran cold at the thought of what Angela might already have suffered. Jerking his mind from Smith's description of Lydia's condition after that last beating, he tried to devise a plan of attack.

What if she was not being held in Kensington? His watcher had reported little activity at the house. It was certainly not being used as a love nest—yet. And the man had promised to send immediate word if Atwater brought a female there. He shuddered. Had Lady Sylvia's summons arrived first? *Please, please, please . . .*

He clung to hope, for it meant that he might be in time, and firmly suppressed all thought that she was being held elsewhere.

"We can't just ram the door in," said Jack as they turned the final corner. "This neighborhood is not that decadent." Most of the cottages belonged to merchants. Only a few were used for immoral activities.

"I have no idea what servants might be present," he admitted, thankfully setting his fears aside. "If Atwater is near the door, he would never open it to me. Suppose we start by having you knock as though paying a routine call."

"Good. If that does not work, we had best go around to the back before forcing an entry. It is less conspicuous."

They pulled up before the cottage. Devall slipped into the yard, concealing himself behind a rosebush to one side of the entrance.

But the precautions proved unnecessary. Jack quietly turned the handle, pushed the door open, and walked into the hall. Devall followed swiftly on his heels, his stare locking onto the reticule carelessly tossed onto a table. It was the one Angela carried when she rode in the park.

Jack had stopped in the drawing room doorway, his rigid back announcing better than words that disaster awaited.

Thrusting his friend aside, Devall halted in turn.

Atwater lay curled on the floor, wearing only a shirt, boots, and partially fastened breeches. A crumpled, blood-stained coat was near the fireplace. Arms, covered with blood and bruises, wrapped around his shoulders as he rocked back and forth.

"My angel," he crooned softly. "My gift from the gods. Mine. All mine. For always."

Furious, Devall jerked the earl to his feet and slammed him against the wall. "Where is she?" he demanded.

More blood decorated Atwater's shirt. Jagged scratches furrowed his face and chest, intersecting two deep cuts. But no fear appeared in those blue eyes. Not even anger. "My own true love, my angel," he intoned.

The calm response froze Devall's hand in mid-swing. Cold seeped into his soul.

"My little love," continued Atwater as though he were alone. "I will protect you always. Keep you safe. You will never leave me. Never. Not like the others. My darling angel. So sweet. So beautiful. You adore me . . ." One hand lifted to push the hair from his brow, revealing a deep bite around the base of his thumb.

"No!" choked Jack, staring in horrified fascination at the blank, unfocused eyes that seemed oblivious to the hands tightening around his neck. "Don't do it, Devall. He is gone."

And it was true. Atwater was in another world, blind to everything, only his voice remaining behind. Devall stared at that childish face. Bile rose chokingly into his throat at the crooning words.

"Don't run! Why does everyone run away? Amelia. Lydia. Angela. Why won't you move? Nobody moves. So much blood and nobody moves. Let me protect you, my love. See? We'll wipe away the blood and you will be fine. Please love me. You must love me. Why won't you move?"

Cold seeped into Devall's soul. And pity. His anger drained away, replaced by fear. What had Atwater done?

"Look after him, Jack," he ordered, his fingers now turning out the earl's pockets. A knife, thankfully unbloodied; several keys; a cardcase; a handkerchief, also clean; a special license; a lady's ring. "Escort him to Bethlehem hospital. Perhaps they can do something with him."

Jack wrapped a cloak around the earl and led him to the mews.

Devall gingerly climbed the stairs, terrified of what he might find at the top. Whatever had happened, she had fought hard.

Angela surveyed her arsenal and tried to keep despair at bay. Even the eyes of hope could hardly call it intimidating. The candlestick, which Atwater had unaccountably left in the room. A heavy crockery pitcher and basin from the washstand. In her weakened state, she doubted she could swing them hard enough to inflict any damage. A piece of whalebone that had been stuck in the back of a drawer, too flexible to puncture and too dull to cut.

Footsteps on the stairs pushed her heart into her throat. Was this to be the last battle? A key scraped in the lock. Grasping the candlestick and again clutching her heavy skirts with her free hand, she drew in a deep breath and waited, her back pressed against the far wall.

The door swung open to reveal Devall staring at her in horror. The candlestick dropped from suddenly numbed fingers as tears sprang to her eyes.

Devall froze at the sight. Her face was a welter of bruises, her hands stained with blood. An enormous lump just above her right temple would have killed her had it been even an inch lower. Yet she stood defiantly ready to do battle yet again. Boadicea herself.

"Are you all right?" He stepped slowly into the room, unsure what her reaction would be.

"Devall?" Tears raced down her cheeks as she stumbled forward. He caught her before she had gone two steps, pulling her tightly into his arms.

"Angela," he murmured, tears clouding his own vision. "Angela." Lifting her, he settled into the chair, holding her close as she sobbed out her terror. "Everything will be all right now." He gently stroked her hair.

"It's really you," she said in wonder some time later, lifting a tear-streaked face to his own damp gaze.

"You are safe," he repeated for at least the fortieth time, lowering his head to hers. If the kiss he had stolen in the garden had been sweet, this was heaven itself. He tried to keep it light and gentle, but she met his lips, parting her own and allowing his tongue to plunder at will. Her hand smoothed a wayward lock of hair off his brow, pulling him closer. Her breath quickened in rhythm with his own. He groaned as his body responded, then forced himself to withdraw. This was the last thing she needed.

"How badly are you hurt?" he asked instead, fighting to steady his breathing.

"Bruises," she admitted. "But nothing seems broken."

"Did he—" He stopped.

"No."

Shivers convulsed her, and he again pulled her close, soothing and caressing, letting his strength flow into her until she was again calm.

"We had best get you home," he said at last. "Lady Sylvia is frantic, and Lady Trotter should be as bad by now."

"How am I ever going to explain this?" She swayed when she stood.

"I will explain." He supported her with his arms, resting her head against his shoulder. "You need not fear Atwater ever again. His mind is gone. Jack is taking him to the hospital. I expect he will end his days in a cozy asylum."

Wrapping his cloak around her, he carried her down the stairs.

Devall stared at the glass in his hand, morosely wondering what to do now. His neckcloth and jacket lay in an untidy heap on the floor, both ruined by blood from Angela's face and hands. Sprawled haphazardly across a chair, he dared not rise. Even if his legs somehow supported him, his stomach would rebel against all the wine it held. But his brain remained maddenly clear.

How could he have been so stupid? If only he really was the

heartless beast people thought him. But he wasn't. And now he had given that heart away. Living without it was going to be pure hell. And he wouldn't even have the satisfaction of knowing she wanted it. Her response to his kisses meant nothing. He had initiated both when she was in too much shock to think straight. He hadn't needed Jack's diatribe to know he was a fool.

Jack had called to tell him that Atwater was safely locked away. Already half drunk, he had not been capable of hiding either his satisfaction or his pain.

"You've gotten yourself in a real muddle this time, Devall," Jack had said, shaking his head. "What are you planning to do about Miss Warren?"

"Nothing." He'd emptied his glass and poured another. "She'll be home in another week, and I'll never see her again."

"What will she think of that?" demanded Jack sharply. "You've ruined her."

"Confound you—"

"Not publicly, perhaps," continued Jack, ignoring his anger. "Society will never know. But you pursued her, pressing for friendship and beyond. She's learned to rely on you. Your support is all that has kept her going these past weeks. Walking out of her life now can only hurt her."

He had changed the subject, but the words reverberated in his mind long after Jack was gone.

Was it possible that she cared for him? Friendship was all she'd offered—and even that had surprised him. He was not a man people liked. Even his own family hated and feared him, so he could hardly expect anyone else to be different. Thus Jack was wrong. Whatever Angela felt was rooted in gratitude. It would pass. And once she returned to her own milieu, she would need no one. If ever a woman could look after herself, it was Angela Warren. Having successfully beaten off Atwater, nothing could stop her.

Yet memories of their kisses teased his mind, raising unexpected guilt. God, he hoped Jack was wrong. How could he live with himself if he hurt her? And if she cared even a little, she couldn't help but be hurt. They could never be together.

*But why must you live without her?* asked an insidiously tempting voice. She preferred the country. If he worked hard enough, surely he could redeem himself—if not now, then over the next five or ten years. But brutal honesty admitted that it was a long shot. He couldn't chance ruining her life and the lives of any children.

And his reputation was the least of his faults. He was an unfit mate for so caring a woman—as she herself had seen. He might consider himself a gentleman, but he used the label mostly to hide his defects from his own scrutiny. He followed the code only when it suited his purpose. In truth, he was a predator who harbored a cruel streak every bit as foul as in the men he hunted.

He had enjoyed the fights with Cloverdale and Coldstream, and felt no sorrow at their deaths. If Atwater had shown even the tiniest spark of awareness, he would have throttled the man without remorse—and reveled in every second of it.

She saw him too clearly, even recognizing the way he had goaded Cloverdale into attack. It was a fact he had never before admitted, even in the darkest recesses of his mind. Growing up in a brutal world had left him hard, with no compassion for the perpetrators of violence. And whatever his excuses, he himself was just such a man. His father's legacy included more than his titles and estates.

Angela deserved better than life in limbo, suspended between a society that would ignore her and the lower classes who were forever separated by the gulf of his title. She deserved more than a husband who could not keep even sincere vows to live within the law, and who could bring her only misery as a result. She deserved someone she could love and respect.

He could offer her nothing. He was the antithesis of the husband she needed—satanic, violent, isolated, unlovable. It would never work. He must bury this unreasonable passion deep in his soul.

Sighing, he drained the last of the wine, finally sliding to the floor in a stupor.

# Chapter Sixteen

*Atwater slammed a fist into her abdomen while his fingers drilled holes into her shoulder. Blood flowed. A swift kick crushed her hip, collapsing the leg and tumbling her to the floor.*

*"You are mine! You must obey me!" he roared, dragging her up by the hair. Mad blue eyes stared sightlessly into her own.*

*"No!" She tried to push him away.*

*Fury exploded, and he shook her like a rag doll, kicking and punching all the while. His face swooped to meet hers. Braced against the nausea of a kiss, she nearly expired from shock when he bit off her nose.*

*Laughter taunted her ears. "Ungrateful wench!" cackled Lady Forley. "How dare you fight your husband? Do your duty like a good little girl. He'll give me gold and jewels and a house in London as soon as he beds you."*

*"No!" she protested again.*

*Atwater's shaking intensified, as did the force of his blows. "Open your eyes and look at me!" he demanded, chewing a chunk from her shoulder. Bones snapped under the onslaught.*

*"Well done, my lord," cheered Lady Forley. "Teach her obedience. Teach her humility. Teach her how a proper lady thinks and acts. So unnatural a daughter deserves to be punished."*

*Angela fought the groping hands, struggling to escape that predatory mouth, but it was hopeless. She watched in horrified fascination as her body disintegrated under his onslaught, an arm hitting the wall, a leg landing atop the bed, her head rolling across the floor, its bumping forming a counterpoint to Lady Forley's insane laughter . . .*

"Dear God, Angela, wake up! Open your eyes!"

The frantic shouting finally penetrated. Angela groaned.

Sylvia was shaking her shoulders, begging her to wake up. Every movement sent spasms of pain knifing through her injuries. "What . . . ?" she began fuzzily.

"You were dreaming," said Sylvia, dropping into a chair with a relieved sigh. "And screaming."

Nightmares. She burst into tears, allowing Sylvia to pull her into her arms as she convulsed in sobs that bordered on hysteria. *It was only a dream,* she reminded herself over and over, but it didn't help. The images were too real, and Sylvia's comfort too ephemeral. She needed . . . What did she need? The answer hovered tantalizingly just out of reach.

Severe stress had long triggered such dreams—her father's death, her first foray into society, Garwood's charges, Atwater's lies. She should have expected it. New shudders wracked her. That cackling laughter would not retreat. She never should have taken the laudanum. It prevented her from escaping from the dream world. She would endure any amount of pain to avoid being trapped there again.

"Here, drink this," urged Sylvia.

"No!" Spinning away, she buried her head in a pillow. "I must be able to wake up." Shivers wracked her as the nightmare again swept through her mind.

Sylvia frowned. Blackthorn's instructions had been explicit. *Don't ask questions. Don't annoy her. Keep her safe.* His eyes promised retribution if she failed.

The doctor's orders were slightly different. Angela had a concussion, cracked ribs, and numerous deep bruises. She was to remain abed for at least a week, taking laudanum to assure rest. But he offered a way out of her current dilemma. If Angela showed any aftereffects from the concussion, she was to cease the laudanum.

*Don't annoy her . . .*

"Very well. Would you like a headache powder instead? It won't work as well, but it might help."

Angela nodded. Sylvia was soon asleep, leaving her alone with her thoughts. Even if her pain receded enough to allow undrugged sleep, she was afraid to try. The nightmare hovered, waiting to pounce. And she now knew why Sylvia's ministraions were insufficient. The only place she felt truly safe was in Devall's arms.

Her eyes closed on a new wave of pain that had nothing to do with physical discomfort. She loved him. Foolishly, of course, or he could never return her love. At most, he considered her a friend. It was more likely that she was another of his charity cases. He hated abuse—especially of females—which explained why he had repeatedly jumped in to rescue her from emotional and physical attacks.

She shifted to a more comfortable position. As soon as she recovered, they would return to Forley Court. If she could not put his attachment behind her, she must abandon any thought of marriage. The lip service she had previously given the possibility had been a way to hide hope. But embarking on a marriage of convenience would never work now. Not with her heart engaged elsewhere. How could she play so dastardly a trick on an honorable man?

Again the nightmare pressed close. Only by recalling Devall's strong arms and soothing hands could she hold it at bay. Later she would forget her feelings, but for now she needed the memories too badly—their dance in the garden . . . his muscular body shaking with anger, yet weak with relief . . . his kisses . . .

As his lips moved sensuously down her throat, she slept.

Angela remained abed for a week. At first, she rarely slept more than an hour without experiencing a nightmare. Atwater was always there, undergoing that terrifying transformation from gentle lover to vicious madman. The details varied. Sometimes she relived the beating in Kensington. Occasionally she suffered Lydia's fate. Or Ned Parker's. Usually, it was a grotesque mixture of all three. Often her mother appeared, jeering her and applauding Atwater, her own mad laughter echoing long after Angela awoke.

Devall helped. And not just in memory. He sent flowers twice a day, accompanied by encouraging notes, instinctively knowing how to calm her fears. One informed her that Atwater had been judged irreversibly insane and packed off to a private asylum. Another mentioned that nightmares were inevitable, but that her good sense would soon prevail.

He was right. By week's end, she was able to sleep at least six hours before the horror intruded. Other irritations finally drove her from bed, despite her lingering pain.

Sylvia's hovering became annoying. And Andrew was nearly as bad. He had been delayed at the Court, not returning to town until four days after her abduction. Since they had expected him sooner, they had sent no word, so he was appalled to discover her injuries.

"I had no idea how corrupt the fellow was," he exclaimed after assuring himself that she suffered no permanent damage.

"Corrupt is not the right word," she countered. "He was mad. You have never come face to face with genuine madness, and I hope you never do. Not because of the beating he gave me—"

"How could even a madman have done that to a lady?" he interrupted to ask.

"You do not understand." She sighed, shifting until she found a comfortable position. "You accept that he is mad, yet *mad* is simply a word to you. Madmen lack reason. Their thinking—what little there is—follows logic unknown to you and me. The only reason in that room was mine. Escape was impossible. Help was unavailable. Eventually, I managed to deduce some of his reactions, which gave me a choice. I could remain docile to preserve the calm, gentle soul determined to ravish me, or I could fight back and unleash his vicious brutality. I chose to endure a possible fatal beating. If I had to go back, I would do the same. The real terror of that encounter was looking into eyes that had no soul, knowing that the body would continue its prescribed course without thought, until something more powerful halted its progress."

"I have seen madness," he declared. "I was on St. James's Street the day Delaney's horses went wild."

*Men!* The horses might have been terrified, but that was a long way from being mad. She refused to argue the point. "But madness in a human is worse," she said instead. "Especially when one is locked in a room with it, knowing there is no chance of overpowering it."

"Dear God, Angie! Thank heaven you survived."

"No, Drew. Thank Lord Blackthorn. If he had not found me . . ." Her voice trailed away as tears sprang into her eyes. "I could never have survived a second assault. But better that than rape by such a monster."

He pulled her into his arms as another bout of tears overwhelmed her. "If only I had not been away," he murmured when she was done.

"Oh!" Memory returned with a vengeance, replacing tears with a surge of anger. "Atwater set that fire to force you out of town. This was carefully planned, Andrew. He did not succumb to a moment's temptation when he found me with only Frank in attendance. Did Sylvia tell you nothing?"

"Only that Atwater had abducted and assaulted you and that Major Caldwell and Blackthorn rescued you." His brows rose in a question.

She realized that she had said nothing since her return. Even Devall knew nothing, though he had explained how he had found her. She had paid little attention, too grateful for the safety of his arms to question his presence.

"Atwater planned every detail," she declared now. "The ownership of the house was not generally known. He had altered one room, adding bars to the windows and a stout lock to the door. When everything was ready, he tricked you into leaving town by arranging the fire at the Court. Then he wrote a note claiming that I had changed my mind and eloped with him, addressing it to you and making it appear a routine communication with none of his own identification on the outside. He must have been stalking me, noting my habit of riding in Green Park in the early afternoons when few people were around. He had only to watch for the most propitious moment to spring his trap. Once he had successfully abducted me, he sent the note to Clifford Street, knowing that you were out of town and would not find it for some days. By that time, he would have forced me into marriage. If Sylvia had not seen his footman, it would have rested on your desk until your return. And if Lord Blackthorn had not known that Atwater owned that house, even Sylvia's interference would have done no good."

Andrew paced the room. "This should never have happened. We attach too much credit to title and wealth, assuming that all lords are honorable gentlemen. When I look back, there were plenty of hints that Atwater was not quite right in the head. Yet society ignored every one. As did I. Until you told me he made you nervous, I had considered him an admirable catch. Even after he struck you, I never thought him unbalanced. How could I have been so stupid?"

"It is not your fault, Andrew," she said, shaking her head.

"I cannot accept that. I have been derelict in my duty, Angie. I was so wrapped up in Sylvia that I never questioned Mother's plans for the Season. I hadn't even thought to ask your preferences until after Atwater offered for you. My negligence allowed her to manipulate you and led to two rounds of social disgrace and a beating. Can you ever forgive me?"

"There is nothing to forgive," she said, laying a hand on his arm when he resumed his chair by the bed. "Atwater decided he wanted me the first time he saw me. Nothing would have deflected him, even had Mother been against the match. Reason is irrelevant, for he was irrational. I suspect that his breakdown began when his wife died, though the instability was always there. There is no way to know why he chose me, but once that decision was made, nothing you or I or anyone else could have done would have deterred him."

He shook his head. "At least this puts paid to the last of the rumors. The tale of Atwater's madness has swept every club and drawing room in town."

She shivered. "I will never be able to hold my head up again."

"I should have phrased that better. Major Caldwell, probably at Blackthorn's instigation, has explained your injuries as a deliberate attempt by Atwater to run you down in retaliation for refusing his hand."

"Run me down?"

"Yes. He spotted you just inside Green Park and his mind snapped. He deliberately drove his coach over you and the footman that accompanied you, injuring both. When he realized that you still lived, he turned back to finish the job. Two passersby deduced his intent and restrained him. His ranting revealed both his purpose and his madness, so one gentleman escorted him to Bethlehem hospital while the other carried you home."

"Who rescued me?" she asked. "I must thank them."

"Major Caldwell and Lord Blackthorn, who were riding separately that afternoon."

"I see." Not that she did entirely. Why had Devall attached his name to the tale? Since there were no witnesses, he could easily have avoided all involvement and stayed in the shadows he loved. Or was Jack forcing him into the open? She hoped so. Society would never forgive all his misdeeds, especially the way he had jilted his betrothed. But if he reformed, his title and wealth would persuade most to ignore his past.

She hoped he would do so, for his own sake. No matter how worthwhile his goals, his methods were flirting with a boundary he could never recross. But he could accomplish so much more if he stayed on the right side of that line and solicited help to effect change.

She wanted desperately for him to do so, but not because of her love. Whichever course he followed would not affect her. Even if he offered, she must refuse. An offer would arise from his quixotic sense of chivalry. But she could never accept a man who did not need her.

Refusing to listen to Andrew's continuing apologies, she focused on regaining her strength. The sooner she left town, the sooner she could put Devall behind her.

Flowers poured into Clifford Street as society welcomed Angela back to its bosom. Opinion had reversed itself, all the gossips now ripping up Atwater with the same fervor they had previously employed in supporting him. Several even claimed to have suspected something odd in his behavior. They discounted every word of the slander that had circulated about Angela. She was held up as a pattern card of virtue, an innocent pilloried by an unscrupulous monster, a victim of her mother's greed—in accepting Atwater's guilt, many now charged that Lady Forley must have known the truth and ignored it in pursuit of his wealth and title. Like a flock of mindless sheep, the polite world followed this new course, equating Miss Warren's character to the angel her name implied.

Sylvia and Andrew were mobbed by well-wishers whenever they ventured out. Barbara and the Ashtons saw their own credit rise due to their long championship of the new heroine. Jack's standing likewise improved. Even Blackthorn's reputation began to crack as his rescue was trumpeted.

Jack pounced on the opportunity, judiciously leaking truths

about his friend. Finally, he could repay his debt. And perhaps he could do Angela a favor in the process.

"One can hardly be surprised that he rescued Miss Warren," he commented offhandedly at White's one night. "He understood Atwater's character better than any of us did. Atwater not only killed his cousin, but spread malicious lies blaming that death on Blackthorn."

"Quite right," Ashton agreed.

"But it is all of a piece," he continued casually. "I have it on the best authority that Miss Warren is not the only lady he has saved from a brutal lord."

"Really?"

"Cloverdale was very like Atwater, assaulting his wife at the least annoyance. She had known Blackthorn since childhood and appealed to him for help. He escorted her to relatives overseas, where she was able to recover from her injuries and build a new life."

"That cannot be right," protested Ashton. "I sat in the Lords during his trial. He never lifted a finger to counter the charges."

"How else could he have freed her?"

Jack left the matter there. Ashton was clearly pondering his words. And the story took root, sweeping Mayfair and returning Blackthorn's name to every lip in the unaccustomed role of hero.

Angela stared into the mirror. They were leaving for Forley Court in the morning, but Sylvia had convinced her to make one public appearance first. Too many people were anxious to see her.

The face that stared back was not one she wanted to show the world. Bruises still marked its cheeks, though they had faded from angry purple to sickly yellow. She had spent the afternoon altering her gown, for her cracked ribs disallowed a well-laced corset, and the flesh was still puffed around the deepest bruises. Multi-colored stains marred her neck and shoulders. But at least the identifiable pattern where Atwater's fingers had gained purchase to shake her had faded to a general mottling that could be passed off as the result of being run down by a carriage. Arranging a shawl unfashionably over her shoulders to hide the worst of it, she sighed and headed downstairs.

Which was worse? she wondered an hour later. Social censure or determined hero-worship? She could barely move for the people crowded around her—congratulating her on her escape and recovery, condemning Atwater and her mother, claiming to have known all along that the earl was missing something in his upper story. Her card was full before she reached the ballroom. By the supper dance she could stand the mindless fawning no more.

"I must get away for a bit," she said with a sigh. Jack partnered her for the set. "Would you mind terribly if I skipped this one. The retiring room should be empty."

He immediately headed for the hallway. "The accolades are overdone and you are still not nearly recovered." He stopped at the retiring room door. "Tonight will be farewell for both of us, Angela. I return to the Peninsula tomorrow. Take care of yourself."

"You, too. Thank you again for all you have done, Jack. If not for you, I would have been sunk without a trace weeks ago."

"Nonsense. Devall planned it. I just followed orders."

"Fustian. And you know it." She smiled. "You've a campaign of your own underway, haven't you? I hope it succeeds, for he deserves to be judged on the truth. Have a good journey. Stay safe."

He kissed her lightly on the cheek, then returned to the ballroom.

The retiring room was quiet and offered the refuge she needed for nearly ten minutes. Then three giggling girls entered, shattering the peace. She graciously accepted their best wishes before slipping out.

Devall was in the hall.

"You look much better," he said, saluting her fingers and sending shivers down her spine.

"Thank you. I doubt I adequately thanked you when last we met, and this will be no better, for words are insufficient. You saved my life, as you must know. Thank you, Devall. For that and for your other kindnesses. Your notes helped more than I can say."

"I'm glad—and relieved that your injuries were not worse. Are you enjoying your return to society?" he asked, leading her into an empty room.

She rolled her eyes. "They are like sheep. This adoration is ridiculous. They act as though I had single-handedly defeated Napoleon before breakfast, then swept away all misery by dinner. Why do I deserve accolades for being attacked and beaten by a madman?"

"Collective guilt." He shrugged. "They badly misjudged you both and must ease their consciences by trying to make it up to you."

"Idiocy," she snorted inelegantly. "Thank God I'm leaving. I prefer the honesty of the country. Real, down-to-earth people can never be replaced by the mass hysteria and forced frivolity of town."

"You return home tomorrow?"

She nodded. "Andrew's wedding is but a fortnight hence, and there is much yet to arrange. Our relatives will start arriving within the week. With Mother gone, I must act as hostess."

"Don't overtax yourself, Angela. You are not completely recovered."

"I won't. Cassie—Lady Hartleigh—is handling the wedding itself, though she tires so easily it cannot be comfortable for her. I must thank you again for all you have done for me, Devall."

"It was nothing."

"Hardly. But I am glad your own reputation is improving. Have you decided to work within the law?"

"Jack is responsible for that, though I had been considering setting the record straight."

"He sees clearly. If you are ever going to redeem yourself, now is the time," she reminded him. "Society is so abashed over Atwater's successful deception that they are willing to reevaluate anything. Of course, even that may not be enough to overcome that broken betrothal."

"Yes, I skewered myself quite thoroughly with that." He wandered to the fireplace, absently fingering a candlestick. "They may have listened to reason on the rest had I not already cut myself off."

"Would you have followed the same course had you not been ostracized?"

His brow furrowed in thought. "Perhaps not."

"I had wondered if there was not an element of living up to expectations in your actions."

"Devil take it!" He stared at her in shock. "I hope not. I have always considered their approval irrelevant."

"Is that why you jilted her so publicly? You are not cruel, Devall, despite allowing that perception to stand."

"It was the only way to free her." He shrugged.

"That's ridiculous. If she wanted out, she had only to jilt you. Both of you would have survived."

He laughed without mirth. "You want the whole sordid mess spelled out, I suppose."

She nodded.

"It was an arranged match." He wandered to the window to peer into the blackness. "My father was a rigid disciplinarian. Her father was worse—and greedy besides. Both believed that women were chattel, lacking intelligence and sense, and that sons were duty-bound to obey every command without question." His shoulders twitched as if remembering the touch of a switch, but his voice continued without pause. "They had been friends for years, though Quincy's station was lower and his finances were considerably worse than ours. But he saw his dutiful only child as the means to gain access to the Blackthorn wealth."

She shivered, understanding much of what he was not saying. Perhaps he was the devil's spawn after all. How else could she explain this unsettling ability to read his mind? But the truths she found there banished the question.

His father had been a brutal man who inflicted instant punishment on anyone resisting his orders. No wonder Devall abhorred abuse. So many of his traits had arisen in childhood. His remote self-containment had started as a defense against his father's brutality. His cynicism and belligerence hid a lifelong need for affection. What had he suffered? His mother had died while he was still in short pants. He had no siblings to ease the loneliness he must have endured.

"I learned of the match from the newspaper announcement," he continued flatly. "I had never met her, but there was no point in refusing. He had already signed the settlements. And I didn't really care. Girls had been throwing themselves at my prospects for years—the power and wealth of Blackthorn forgives any number of grievous faults. I liked none of them and could see little difference between them. If Father thought this one would do, it was fine with me."

He shifted his weight to his other foot. "When she arrived in London, I thought everything would be all right, for she was lovely and had considerable intelligence. But she seemed shy. At first I didn't think much of it. I've never been at ease in company, either, but the problem always disappeared with acquaintance. Yet she didn't improve. If anything, she grew more fearful, at times reacting as though I were her executioner. I finally cornered her and asked why."

He paused, and Angela waited silently for him to continue. Had he fallen in love with the girl? Maybe not, but whatever had happened still hurt. This was the pain she had long suspected lay at his core. It was even stronger than the agony inflicted by his father.

"She was in love with a neighbor," he continued. "Charles Gresham, the penniless younger son of a baronet, who had loved her for years. Her father had refused his consent to a match, barring him from the estate. If she objected to wedding me, he vowed to imprison her in a remote spot—assuming she survived the beating he would inflict."

She flinched.

"I could not marry her under those conditions, Angela. But allowing her to break it off would destroy her. The only solution I could devise was to jilt her in a way that would leave her unmarriageable, which would prevent her father from tracking her down when she disappeared. I arranged for her and Gresham to remove to America where my cousin helped them acquire land. Jilting her ruined me, of course, but I was so sick of society's toadying that I cared not. Yet I've wondered ever since if she used me to set her up with Gresham—I've only her word for her helplessness."

"Why would you think so?"

"Having talked me into jilting her, she used the occasion to taunt her father, adding to what we had agreed on, exaggerating and fabricating, and starting many of the lies that have followed me ever since."

More pain. She could hear it in his voice, harsher than before. "And your father?" What had so cruel a man done to the son who flouted his wishes so publicly?

"My one stroke of good fortune. He never heard. He had suffered several bouts of apoplexy that year, though few knew of it. While I was at Lady Jersey's that night, he was overcome by another, slipping into a coma. He died two days later without ever regaining consciousness." He turned back to the room. "How did we ever arrive at so maudlin a subject?"

"We were proving that you are not the blackguard people think. But I suspect you overreacted to her tirade. Do you really believe she set out to take advantage of you?"

"Why not? She played me for a fool. She had every opportunity to explain earlier, but she waited until just before the wedding to reveal how unhappy she was. Or maybe she planned to wed for power and keep her lover on the side, but discovered she couldn't tolerate me." His haunted eyes darted around the room, unable to meet hers.

"Stop this, Devall! You act like you were madly in love with the girl."

He frowned. "Perhaps I was a little. I had tried to fall in love with her."

"Which explains how she hurt you so badly. What did she say that haunts you?"

He shuddered, and for a moment she feared he would not reply. But he turned back to the window, resting his forehead against the cool glass. "I can still hear her," he whispered. "Lord Quincy accepted my prepared lies, turning on her and calling her names he would never have uttered in mixed company had his temper been even tenuously controlled. One listener swooned. But instead of cowering, Penelope flew at him, shocking him with her unprecedented fury. 'Selfish cad!' she screamed in his face. 'I am glad, do you hear me? Glad to be jilted! You would sell your own soul for a barrel of brandy. Why am I surprised that you sold me to a cold, heartless blackguard to pay your gaming debts? Did you care for even a moment that I would spend the rest of my days in thrall to one of Satan's own, a notorious libertine who thinks nothing of ruining society's daughters, a man whose father had to buy him a wife despite his prospects because

no one would dare wed him? Of course not! You would sell me
to the devil himself if it gained you the faintest hold over Blackthorn's fortune.' There was more—a lot more—but you get the
idea. Then she slapped his face and marched out, leaving me to
face society's wolves."

His voice cracked, breaking her heart. How many nights had
he passed reliving that scene? "Of course it was painful," she
said steadily. "Far more than anything I've faced. But you are
wrong about her motives."

"How?"

"Think, Devall. You know how difficult it is to withstand a
brutal and domineering parent." She met his eyes, letting him see
that she understood the pain of his childhood. "But she was
worse off than you. Girls have little control over their lives in
even the best of circumstances. With an abusive father, she
would have had none. How could she oppose his wishes? The
polite world would not have supported her. Society is too rigid.
No one dares counter a father's arrangements. Few believe girls
have the intelligence or the experience to decide how they wish
to live their lives. She was not of age, so she had no chance of
striking out on her own. And how could she have expected anything different from you? You were strangers. Did experience
convince her that anything would change? Your father was just
like hers."

"But we were past that. I *was* different. I proved it by agreeing to help her despite knowing what it would do to me. So why
did she lash out at me?"

"Unintentionally, I'm sure. That tirade sounds spontaneous.
Every grievance she had against her father rose up in that one
moment when she could finally turn on him with impunity.
Every assault. Every incarceration. Every threat that had commanded obedience. Blinded by rage and pain from a lifetime of
suffering, she would have flung any charge that had even a remote chance of hurting him. I doubt she knew half of what she
said. If she had realized how badly she'd injured you, she would
have tried to make amends."

"Have I been wrong about everything?" he whispered to himself.

Her eyes itched. "That was how it started, wasn't it? You sacrificed your reputation so she could be happy. Even when you believed she had betrayed you, you refused to waste the sacrifice—very like your lecture on turning bad events to good use. Instead of setting the record straight—which you could have done once she was safely gone—you decided to use your ostracism to protect society from its real predators. Tell the truth, Devall. You have more than paid for your sins. It is time to rejoin the world."

He nodded. "You were right, you know. I had allowed anger to corrupt my thinking. Perhaps Jack can perform one more miracle before he leaves."

"I must get back," she said, changing the subject before she betrayed herself by pulling him into her arms. Music announced that supper was over. "Thank you again for all you have done. You are the truest friend I have made in this town. One can never rely on them." She gestured toward the ballroom. "They bend with every breeze."

"Have you a set I could claim?" he asked as they moved toward the door. "I would like a real dance before you go."

"Andrew will give you his. Three sets from now. Why should I not publicly thank the man who rescued me from certain death. And what a Banbury story you made of that," she said, laughing.

"I'm glad you like it. But the truth would not have served."

"Agreed. Until then, Devall." The hall was empty, allowing her to slip unnoticed back to the ballroom.

She did not tell Andrew of her meeting. It was better to make it appear a spontaneous action. After all, she was not supposed to know the man. She could only pray that her instincts were right. Her current elevated status just might convince society to at least let him plead his case. She must see that Jack took advantage of the situation.

Their meeting did indeed appear spontaneous. Devall arrived as the second set was finishing and immediately moved to her side.

Andrew performed the introduction. She nearly giggled when she recalled her challenge that Devall find a respectable person to supply her name.

"Miss Warren," he said, the laughter sparkling in his eyes proving that he, too, recalled that meeting. "I am delighted to see you recovered from your ordeal."

Heads craned to watch. Ears strained to take in every word.

"I must thank you, my lord, for your timely intervention. I am told that you saved me from certain destruction."

"Would it be presumptuous to ask if you have a set free?"

She looked at Andrew, who nodded, his suspicions flaring as he caught that glint of shared mischief. "This one is open," he confirmed.

She smiled. "It will be a pleasure." Placing her gloved hand on his arm, she accompanied him onto the floor. The orchestra struck up a waltz.

"At least I know the steps," he murmured softly. "It is six years since I last danced at a society ball. If this had been something complicated, you would have been in trouble."

They spoke little as they twirled around the room. She was resigned to never knowing his love. He had bestowed his heart on Miss Quincy, her apparent betrayal scarring him deeply. Never again would he leave himself vulnerable. But with a little luck he could at least dispel some of the loneliness in his life. She would spend the rest of the ball urging society to accept him.

Devall savored her softness, stifling his fury at her lingering bruises. This was the last time he would hold her—or even see her. All he could do was enjoy it and store up the memories that must last a lifetime.

Several brows rose when he led her out, but these were quickly lowered. How could she not thank her savior? And Blackthorn was not as black as once thought. Was there a worthy person under the dramatic looks and lurid reputation? Jack fanned the suspicions with judicious observations and questions of his own. New rumors spread through the ballroom, quickly growing in intensity as more and more people hailed him as society's lord protector.

# Chapter Seventeen

Angela settled onto a low bench in the folly, her eyes drinking in the beloved view of lake and forested hill as she imposed peace on her mind. Calm. Order. Forgetfulness. Ten days of feverish activity had left her drained of all energy.

Andrew had agreed to her plans for the dower house. It gave the staff one more project to work on, for preparations had halted when Lady Forley eloped, but they were coping. She hoped to take possession the day after the wedding. Mrs. Giddings was excited at the prospect. She had already moved into the Court and was proving to be of invaluable assistance with the wedding preparations.

But it was not the incessant activity or even her impending change of status that weighed so heavily on Angela's mind. Guests had begun arriving three days before, and she had been inundated with questions, comments, and well-meaning solicitude ever since. Though none of the family had been in London for the Season, all had heard of recent events through correspondence.

"How could your mother leave you in the middle of such a muddle?" exclaimed Aunt Frances, Lady Forley's sister, hardly greeting her before posing the question. "But it is all of a piece. She always was a selfish one. Why I remember the time . . ." And she launched an involved monologue detailing a childhood slight, following it with a thorough examination of Angela's Season.

"I never would have believed Lord Atwater to be unstable!" protested Aunt Prudence, her father's sister. "Surely the tale I heard from poor Lady Cunningham cannot have been accurate. He has always been the most thoughtful, caring gentleman in society . . ." And she recited a litany of praise and support that had

Angela clenching both teeth and fists. The pointed interrogation that followed was even worse.

"How could you have allowed Blackthorn near you?" demanded Cousin Peregrine. "The man is a blackguard of the worst sort. Your reputation is bound to suffer."

So Angela was forced to recite the story again. As she had done with Uncle Bertrand, Cousin Michael, Cousin Patience, Peregrine's wife Phoebe, and so many more. Oh, to be back in town where society's sheep docilely followed a single lead, and no one judged anything for himself.

In retrospect, she should have kept to her rooms until everyone had arrived, then called a family meeting to enlighten them all at once. And Andrew was no help. A victim of endless jovial teasing over his rapidly approaching nuptials, and nervously excited on his own account, he had no time to consider the very different attentions his sister was receiving. Having agreed to give her the dower house, he forgot all about her.

But even worse was her restless dissatisfaction. She could not resume the routine she had lived with for so long. Memories beset her, intruding on every activity during the day and disturbing her sleep at night. But they were not the horror and lingering nightmares from her encounter with Atwater. Pushing Devall from her mind was proving to be far more difficult than she had expected.

She had never considered how often he had joined her on her morning rides. Nor had she understood how enjoyable those meetings had been. Their conversations, even their arguments, left her glowing for the rest of the day. Lone rides felt flat. His sympathy and encouragement had kept her from falling apart when all of society condemned her. His timely rescue had saved her from death.

But stimulating discussion and emotional support were not all he had provided, for any close friend could fill that function. It was the man himself that she missed. His physical presence never failed to affect her. Even that first encounter when neither had spoken a word had imprinted strongly on her soul.

Why had she fallen in love with him? Her treacherous mind recalled every word, every touch, every look. That last waltz had been the most exhilarating of her life. His glittering eyes had softened into tenderness as he gazed into her own. His touch had burned through her gown. The swooping whirl of the dance had affected her more than ever before.

Increasingly treacherous memories washed over her: the protective way he had comforted her that awful day in Kensington, stroking her hair, murmuring in her ear—very like Atwater, but with very different results—and gently kissing her to banish her fears. That kiss had been magical, even more so than the lustier one they had shared in Lady Lawton's garden, filling her with warmth and a desire for more—much more. The need was stronger than anything she had ever imagined. If this was what Andrew had been feeling for the past year, it was no wonder he was so frustrated at the long delay. How could anyone endure unfulfilled desire? The thought brought a blush to her cheeks, and she immediately thrust it aside.

None of this served any purpose. Devall was a friend. No more. His initial interest had been piqued by her confrontation with the street vendor. He had pursued the acquaintance as part of his campaign against Atwater. Beyond that, they had no future. She must put him behind her and embark on her new life. If he—

She cut her thoughts short, thankfully noting the arrival of yet another relative—Cousin Leonard and his French wife Francine, if her eyes could be trusted. Sighing, she headed for the house and another round of interrogation. Which aspect would they seize on first?

Devall twisted a wineglass between his fingers, his eyes focused on the fractured lamplight radiating from its cut planes. Garnet flashes sparkled across the papers on his desk. He tried to concentrate on the ever-changing patterns, but stray voices kept surfacing in his head.

*I must make a match this Season . . . unfair to my brother . . . can't waste his sacrifices . . .*

What had Angela's problems to do with him? She was too good to be saddled with so black a villain. It was true that Jack had succeeded in raising enough doubt about his past that men were actually asking him for the facts. And it was true that for the first time in his life he was willingly supplying those facts. Why?

He snorted. He had seen disapproval in a pair of moss-green eyes, had heard a wistful note in the musical voice that urged him to work within the law to change bad laws. She wanted him to take his rightful place in society. So he was violating his own reserve to do it. Would she think better of him?

He drank off half the wine, forcing himself to compare the new patterns with those of five minutes earlier. White dots interspersed with the garnet.

*Your kindness . . . you are not cruel . . .*

Her voice again broke through, dragging his mind back to what he did not want to consider. Had she repeated those words elsewhere? Both of those comments had tumbled off other lips in the past week. Even the tabbies were parroting his kindness, his lack of cruelty. Wrongly, of course.

Cruelty had long been part of his life. He had spent twenty years as its victim before deliberately employing it against those who enjoyed it. Neither Cloverdale nor Coldstream had died easily. Could he change? If he encountered another evil man, could he refrain from exacting retribution?

He doubted it. The law was impotent against so many who deserved punishment. He lacked the patience to endure the slow tedium required to effect reform. Sooner or later, something would happen that would demand action, and he would succumb to temptation.

Unless Angela was at his side. Courting renewed ostracism would hurt her. And that was something he could never do.

But there was no chance of her being at his side. Even his rehabilitated reputation was sordid. She deserved more, starting with a husband she loved. He could never qualify. Had anyone ever loved him? His mother had died when he was five. He had seen so little of her, he'd hardly noticed. His father had cared for no one. Penelope cared only for how she could use him. Constance? The same. Even Lydia had seen him as just another cousin. And an ugly one at that.

*Resign myself to life as a spinster . . . practice biting my tongue and being invisible . . . years before we can return to town . . .*

Damn the insidious memories! Downing the remainder of the wine, he refilled the glass and drained that as well. Why did she believe that she was condemned to live alone? She was beautiful, intelligent, passionate, caring . . .

Tears sprang to his eyes. His arms ached to hold her again. He could still feel her body trustingly curled in his lap as he carried her home from Kensington. The heat of her lips seared his brain, the memory of the moist softness behind them driving him to distraction. Angela! How could he live without her? But how could he condemn her to the hell he had built for himself?

He spent the remainder of the night emptying glass after glass of wine in a futile attempt to forget. *It is time to rejoin the world . . . the world . . . the world . . .*

"Lord Blackthorn begs a moment of your time, my lord, though he realizes how busy you are."

Hart sighed. "Show him into the study, Willowby."

Why would the Black Marquess turn up here? Though they had met on several occasions, their paths had not crossed in many years, and they had never been more than nodding acquaintances. Sylvia had explained the part he'd played in Angela's accident, but that would hardly have a bearing on this visit.

Devall followed a stiff butler along a twisting course that presumably led to a study. What was he doing here? And at such a time. Lady Sylvia's wedding was scheduled for the next morning. Preparations were noticeably frenzied, and the house was crawling with guests. Undoubtedly they were at sixes and sevens with last-minute crises and jangled nerves. His own business could have waited until it was over.

"Sorry to disturb you, Hartleigh," he said in apology when the door closed behind the butler.

"Blackthorn." Hart offered wine. "What can I do for you?"

"You have the question reversed. I hope that I can do something for you. Your sister mentioned that you run an orphanage."

Hart's eyes darkened, but he contented himself with nodding.

"The information slipped out when she overheard me ask Miss Warren how Mickey was doing. I was curious, though I had respected her refusal to describe the place."

Hart smiled. "Ah. You must be the one who directed Angie's attention to the rascal."

It was Devall's turn to nod.

"He has completely recovered from his injuries and has decided that civilized living has its merits. He is one of the brightest lads I have ever encountered. His thirst for knowledge is prodigious, and he should make a real success of life."

"Thank you. He has three friends who will be delighted with the news."

Hart raised a brow.

"I discovered Mickey while pursuing one of my own interests," he admitted. "He was caring for three ill and starving veterans when he was injured. They have been anxious about him."

"There appears to be more to you than rumor reports."

"Like you, I prefer to keep my charities out of the public eye. But that brings me to the reason for my call. One of my veterans has need of a job. His injuries prevent him from attempting anything strenuous, but he is gentle, loves children, and has a knack for building rapport with even the most withdrawn individuals. Could you use such a man at your orphanage?"

"Probably. What chores can he manage?"

Thus began a discussion of John Rushing that expanded into the broader topic of England's unfortunate and how to assist them. A rap on the window interrupted them. Hart grinned.

"For shame, Andrew. You are not supposed to be here today. You know it is bad luck to see your bride before the wedding."

"Why do you think I came around here instead of using the front door?"

"Wouldn't you be better off resting up for tomorrow's exertions," asked Hart with a leer.

"Not you, too! You don't know what you missed by skipping a big wedding!"

Hart laughed.

"Blackthorn." Surprise filled Andrew's voice as he noted Devall's presence.

"Forley. I must leave," he added to Hart.

"Not on my account," protested Andrew. "I will only be a moment." He stared speculatively before returning his gaze to Hart. "A small problem has arisen that I hope you can help with—at least until I get back. Mrs. Giddings will not be able to chaperon Angela after all. Her nephew suffered a near-fatal accident last week and now views the world in a new light. He is no longer bent on perpetuating his grandfather's heartless decrees and wishes to welcome his aunt back into the family and provide her a home."

"Permanently?"

"It looks that way."

"Not so small a problem," mused Hart. "Angie can stay here until your return, of course. But what will she do then?"

"I don't know." He surreptitiously turned his eyes to Blackthorn, lifting his mouth in a mischievous smile at what he read on the man's face. "She is adamant about not remaining at the Court, and you can hardly blame her. It must be tough to run the place for years and then have to sit back and watch someone else take over. But she cannot move to the dower house without a chaperon. Where will we find someone else who won't drive her to distraction with giddy chatter, or condemn her for being a bluestocking?"

Hart stared, surprised at this recital, for it contained nothing he didn't already know, and Andrew had never been one to waste words. But Forley's second covert glance at Blackthorn snapped his social mask back in place. His mind raced.

"I will ask around and see if I can discover anyone," he said. "Surely somewhere in England is a woman capable of being a comfortable companion."

"Thanks, Hart."

"Not at all. Now get out of here before you bring the wrath of God down on both our heads. Or the wrath of Cassie, which would be worse."

Andrew grinned and slipped away.

Blackthorn made final arrangements for John Rushing, then stood to leave, again apologizing for disturbing him at such a time.

"Things have been rather hectic," Hart admitted, still mulling the suspicions Andrew had raised. Blackthorn's eyes were quite revealing, and it would seem that Andrew both knew and approved. He dropped his own gaze to the letter opener in his hand. "But your visit has reminded me of my negligence. I have not informed Miss Warren of Mickey's progress. She has been too busy to ask, but I am sure she would be interested. Perhaps you could stop at the Court and ease her mind."

"That would be agreeable. I had wondered if I should inquire after her recovery while I was in the area."

"She would appreciate your concern. Her mother's defection left her with too much to do, and Mrs. Giddings's departure is sure to make it worse."

Angela had again taken refuge in the folly, hoping to snatch a moment of peace. Fate was not treating her fairly these days. All her plans were falling in ruins. Not that she wasn't thrilled for Edna, who deserved to take her place in genteel society rather than assuming a role as a paid companion. She had kept in touch with friends who would welcome her back. But now Angela faced finding a new companion, and she knew of no other candidates.

The sound of approaching footsteps interrupted her melancholy reflections. Glancing over her shoulder, she gasped.

"Whatever are you doing here, Devall?" she exclaimed, unaware of how her eyes had lit at the sight of him.

"I had some business with Lord Hartleigh and took the opportunity to see how you were faring. He mentioned that he had neglected to inform you of Mickey's progress."

"How is he?" She already knew the answer, for Cassie had given her a full report.

"Quite well. He's proving to be a feisty little devil. It sounds as though he will soon be running the place."

She laughed.

"And you, Angela?"

"Much better, thank you. I've been too busy to think about the attack."

"You look tired," he murmured, joining her on her bench. "Your brother must be too preoccupied to see that you get proper rest."

"He is so anxious to have it over and done with that he's not much good for anything." She shook her head in mock despair, then hurriedly changed the subject to distract her attention from his eyes. They were softer than she had ever seen them, closer to smoke than to ice. "I hear you are accepted without reservation by even the highest sticklers."

"Yes, and now I am expected to do the pretty with nauseating regularity. I am not sure you and Jack did me any favors by urging reform. Every matchmaking mama in town has me in her sights."

"It will give you a new challenge. Life would be unimaginably dull otherwise. Besides, the Season is nearly over. You can retire to Wyndhaven and remain as reclusive as you wish. Even matchmaking mamas can hardly follow you there."

"Don't count on it. The Earl of Wrexham had three very suspicious accidents on his doorstep before he married, but nary a one since."

She raised a brow, though now that he mentioned it, she had heard the tale before. Wrexham was Hart's closest friend.

"And what about next Season and the one after that?" he asked. "I'd best get shackled at once and save myself the trouble."

"What a ridiculous reason to settle down!" She glared at him. "I never thought you stupid, but I begin to wonder."

He ran long fingers through his black hair. "Damn, I'm making a mull of this, aren't I? And behaving with as much gaucherie as the greenest schoolboy. That is not at all what I meant to say. You have done more than force me back into the world, my dear. You have given me a glimpse of heaven. Now I can no longer tolerate living in hell. This last fortnight has been shatteringly lonely, for I cannot enjoy a day that offers no hope of seeing you. I love you, Angela. Somehow you have crept past all my defenses and taken possession of my heart."

"Devall?" Her hand crept across to brush back the lock of hair that had again fallen across his brow.

In one smooth motion he pulled her to her feet and into his arms, crushing her against his body as he desperately sought her mouth, parting her lips, his tongue eagerly ravishing her sweet depths.

Passion exploded, chasing away his darkness and strengthening the hope that had burgeoned from the moment she had welcomed him. Her hands slid into his hair, drawing him closer.

"Angela." He sighed, pressing kisses across her face and down her throat.

"Devall." She nibbled on his ear, shooting new heat deep into his groin. "May I please shorten that? If you are to cease living in hell, I cannot continue calling you after Satan."

"Anything, my love. You will marry me, then?"

"Have you truly forsworn visiting retribution on deserving villains?" She pulled back to scan his face, her own serious. "There can be no more duels, Dev. No more deaths. I cannot live with the fear of losing you, my dearest love."

He tightened his arms. "You can save me from myself. I could never expose you to contempt. From now on I will fight my battles in Parliament and the courts. It will be slow, but with your help, I can control my frustration."

"Good." She sighed in relief, pulling his lips down for another searing kiss, her palms sliding beneath his jacket to learn the muscular breadth of his shoulders. There was much to be said for loose-fitting coats. This one slid easily to the floor.

"Put me out of my misery, love," he pleaded hoarsely. "Will you marry me or not?" One of his hands still held her close, her body fitted snugly against his. The other teased one breast to a rigid peak, leaving her gasping in awe and need.

"Yes."

The smile that lit his face was like nothing she had seen before, as though heaven had parted, its holy light quenching the hellfire that had burned so long in his soul. Handsome? Undoubtedly. Few would have recognized the Black Marquess in that moment of revelation. He sealed their bargain with another passionate embrace, pulling away only when his control began to slip.

Settling onto the bench with Angela in his lap, he gently stroked her until her breathing slowed. His smile changed to one of mischief as he retrieved his coat.

"You once mentioned that you must marry before your brother, so that you will not be a burden on him," he reminded her, pulling a special license from his pocket.

"So I did."

"Tomorrow morning? Privately, before your brother leaves for his own?"

"Done. It might even distract him from his nerves."

He laughed, and for the first time, his voice carried no hint of pain or loneliness. He was free. "My angel." His lips again covered hers.

His waistcoat and cravat joined his jacket on the floor.